BATMAN: TEN NIGHTS OF THE BEAST

JIM STARLIN
WRITER

JIM APARO
PENCILLER

MIKE DeCARLO
INKER

ADRIENNE ROY
COLORIST

JOHN COSTANZA
AGUSTIN MAS
LETTERERS

BATMAN CREATED BY BOB KANE

DC COMICS

JENETTE KAHN
PRESIDENT & EDITOR-IN-CHIEF

PAUL LEVITZ
EXECUTIVE VICE PRESIDENT & PUBLISHER

DENNIS O'NEIL
GROUP EDITOR

BOB KAHAN
EDITOR, COLLECTED EDITION

ROBBIN BROSTERMAN
ART DIRECTOR

JOE ORLANDO
VP-CREATIVE DIRECTOR

BRUCE BRISTOW
VP-SALES & MARKETING

PATRICK CALDON
VP-FINANCE & OPERATIONS

TERRI CUNNINGHAM
MANAGING EDITOR

CHANTAL D'AULNIS
VP-BUSINESS AFFAIRS

LILLIAN LASERSON
VP & GENERAL COUNSEL

SEYMOUR MILES
VP-ASSOCIATE PUBLISHER

BOB ROZAKIS
EXECUTIVE DIRECTOR-PRODUCTION

BATMAN: TEN NIGHTS OF THE BEAST

PUBLISHED BY DC COMICS. COVER AND COMPILATION COPYRIGHT © 1994 DC COMICS. ALL RIGHTS RESERVED.

ORIGINALLY PUBLISHED IN SINGLE MAGAZINE FORM AS BATMAN 417-420. COPYRIGHT © 1988 DC COMICS. ALL RIGHTS RESERVED. ALL CHARACTERS, THEIR DISTINCTIVE LIKENESSES AND RELATED INDICIA FEATURED IN THIS PUBLICATION ARE TRADEMARKS OF DC COMICS.
THE STORIES, CHARACTERS, AND INCIDENTS FEATURED IN THIS PUBLICATION ARE ENTIRELY FICTIONAL.

DC COMICS, 1325 AVENUE OF THE AMERICAS, NEW YORK, NY 10019
A DIVISION OF WARNER BROS. - A TIME WARNER ENTERTAINMENT COMPANY
PRINTED IN CANADA.
FIRST PRINTING.
ISBN: 1-56389-155-7

COVER ILLUSTRATION BY MIKE ZECK
COVER COLOR ART BY PHIL ZIMMELMAN

AN EX-ASSISTANT EDITOR RECALLS SIMPLER TIMES

Once upon a time, long, long ago, before Knightfall, before Bane, in a magical place called the 1980s, a man had a dream. He surveyed his part of the world and determined that he could take a bold new course of action that would help make his dream come true.

The man was Dennis O'Neil, high zen master and editor of Batman.

The dream was to get more people to look at Batman comics.

The bold new course of action was changing the book's logo for four months and treating the familiar ongoing title as something grander, more serious, more important than it ever was before.

So he did it. Jim Starlin, the regular writer on the monthly Batman series, had a four-part story in mind that Denny knew was something special. So he worked with designers and marketing folks and created a formula for what was to become, at first, a remarkable sales phenomenon, and, eventually, an industry standard. At the time, the formula was called the "miniseries-within-a-series," and it buoyed sales across the comic-book industry for years. Today, we call it the "story arc."

This was the secret of his success:

#1) If you are editing a monthly title that isn't getting enough attention, select an upcoming multipart story that has a cool name. Important note: Make sure you know how long it is.

#2) Take your preexisting cover logo and, for as long as the story runs, modify it so it looks really serious. Either that or add a logo that's entirely new (but no less serious-looking).

#3) Right on the cover, tell the readers which part of the story they're

READING, AND WHEN THE STORY WILL END. (SEE THE IMPORTANT NOTE IN SECRET STEP #1.)

#4) SIT BACK AND WATCH THE REGULAR, UNDERAPPRECIATED CREATIVE TEAM PRODUCE AN EPIC.

WHILE THIS MAY SEEM UNIMPRESSIVE TODAY, WHAT WITH DOZENS OF COVER ENHANCEMENTS OR PREMIUMS OR TRADING-CARD INSERTS AVAILABLE, AT THE TIME IT TURNED HEADS. AND THAT WAS JUST WHAT DENNY WANTED.

NOT THAT "TEN NIGHTS" WAS THE FIRST "MINISERIES-WITHIN-A-SERIES," OF COURSE. WITH "BATMAN: YEAR ONE," FOR EXAMPLE, A FOUR-PART STORY ARC IN BATMAN A YEAR EARLIER, THE CREATIVE TEAM OF FRANK MILLER AND DAVID MAZZUCCHELLI WORKED ON THE BOOK FOR THOSE FOUR ISSUES ALONE. WHAT MADE BATMAN: TEN NIGHTS OF THE BEAST (ISSUES #417-#420 OF BATMAN) A FIRST, THOUGH, WAS THE FACT THAT THIS SPECIAL SAGA WAS PRODUCED BY THE REGULAR MONTHLY CREATIVE TEAM: JIM STARLIN, JIM APARO AND MIKE DECARLO.

THUS TEN NIGHTS OF THE BEAST PASSED INTO COMIC-BOOK LEGEND.

JIM STARLIN'S STORY, PERHAPS THE STRONGEST OF HIS RUN ON BATMAN, TYPIFIES HIS VISION OF THE DARK KNIGHT AND THE WORLD HE INHABITS. STARLIN'S BATMAN WAS THE GRIMMEST POST-DARK KNIGHT RETURNS PORTRAYAL UP TO THAT TIME IN THE MONTHLY SERIES, AND FANS THRILLED TO HIS LACONIC, ALMOST BITTER DIALOGUE. THE CURRENT INTERNATIONAL POLITICAL SITUATION WAS WELL REFLECTED, TOO, AS THE BEAST'S DARK AGENDA CONCERNS THEN-PRESIDENT REAGAN AND HIS STRATEGIC DEFENSE INITIATIVE. STARLIN'S GREATEST ACHIEVEMENT IN THIS STORYLINE, THOUGH, WAS THE UNSTOPPABLE, UNFATHOMABLE BEAST. THE ROOFTOP SEQUENCE IN PART 3 LEFT FANS CHILLED TO THE BONE, AND THE ENIGMATIC CONCLUSION ALLOWED (AS ENIGMATIC CONCLUSIONS USUALLY DO IN COMICS), FOR A SEQUEL OF SORTS, WHICH TURNED THE BEAST, AND THE STORY YOU'RE HOLDING, INTO SOMETHING OF A FRANCHISE.

AND WHAT CAN BE SAID OF THE JIM APARO VISION OF BATMAN THAT HASN'T BEEN SAID BEFORE? JIM'S STORYTELLING IS FLAWLESS, HIS BATMAN EXUDES ENERGY AND MENACE (AS THE BEST BATMANS DO), AND HIS CHARACTERIZATION (OR ACTING) IS SO GOOD THAT YOU DON'T NOTICE IT. NOT AN EASY TRICK. MY FAVORITE ASPECT OF THE APARO BATMAN, HOWEVER, IS HIS RENDERING OF BATMAN'S HANDS. CHECK 'EM OUT. THEY'RE HUGE. HUGE ENOUGH TO GRAB FLAGPOLES WHEN HE'S FALLING, HUGE ENOUGH TO INTIMIDATE ANYONE. EXCEPT THE BEAST.

SO WHAT YOU'RE HOLDING IS COMIC-BOOK HISTORY. BECAUSE AFTER THE POPULAR SUCCESS OF THIS STORYLINE, "MINISERIES-WITHIN-SERIES" – STORY ARCS – STARTED POPPING UP ON COMIC-BOOK RACKS WITH ASTOUNDING REGULARITY. AND SALES CONTINUED TO CLIMB AS A RESULT. FOR A LONG WHILE, ALL AN EDITOR WOULD HAVE TO DO WAS FOLLOW THE SIMPLE STEPS LISTED ABOVE TO GUARANTEE A SIGNIFICANT BOOST IN HIS TITLE'S POPULARITY.

AND DENNY O'NEIL, OF COURSE, WENT ON TO DREAM OF BIGGER AND BETTER THINGS. CHECK OUT ANY BATMAN COMIC ON THE STANDS TODAY TO SEE WHAT I'M TALKING ABOUT. THAT'S ASSUMING YOU DON'T READ THEM REGULARLY, OF COURSE, WHICH YOU PROBABLY DO.

WHICH MEANS THAT MOST OF ALL THIS IS PROBABLY NOT NEWS TO YOU.

WHICH MEANS THAT YOU PROBABLY SKIPPED OVER THIS WHOLE INTRO TO GET TO THE STORY.

WHICH IS PROBABLY A PRETTY GOOD MOVE, IF YOU ASK ME...

DAN RASPLER

SENIOR EDITOR

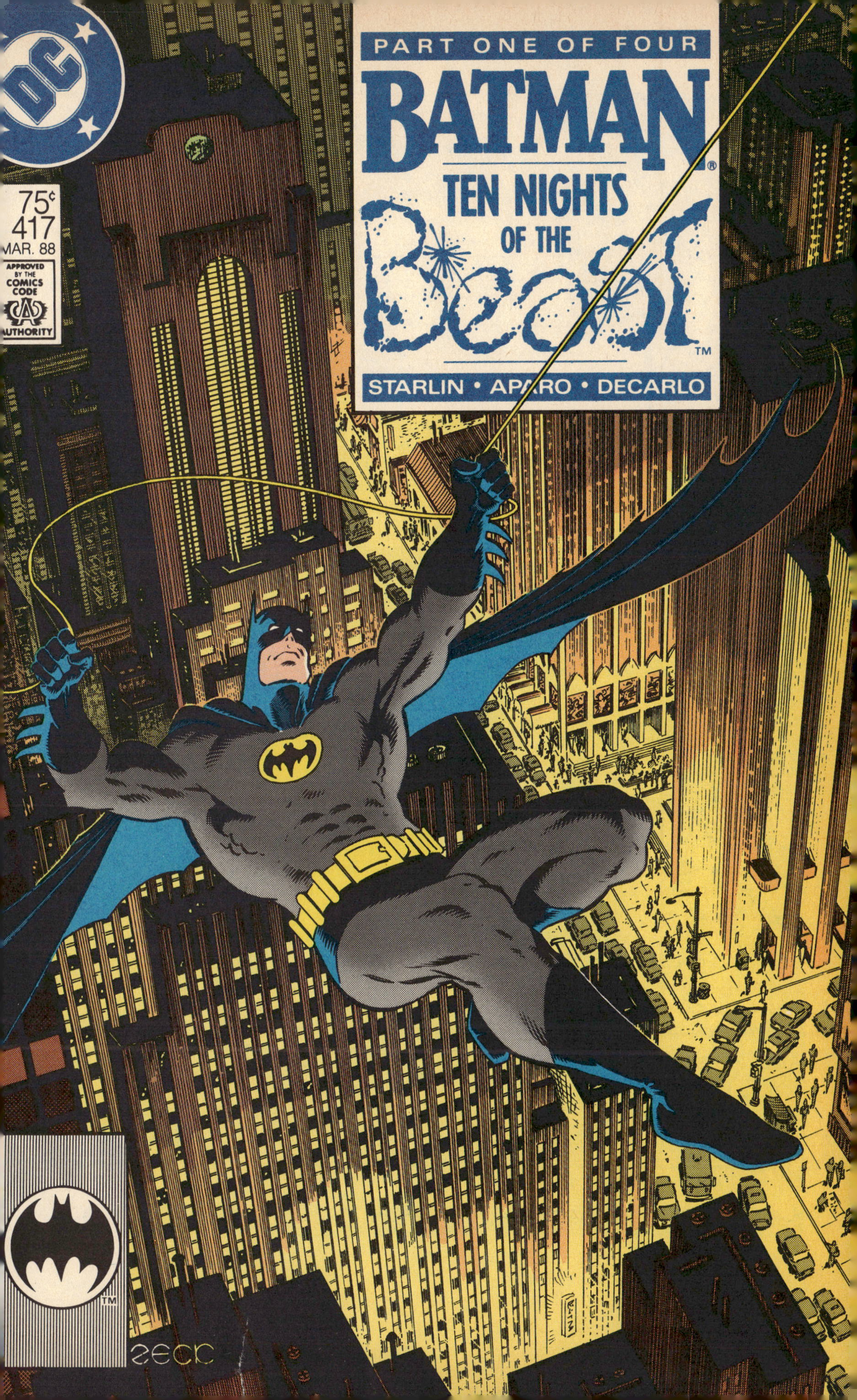
DC
PART ONE OF FOUR
BATMAN
TEN NIGHTS
OF THE
BEAST
STARLIN • APARO • DECARLO
75¢
417
MAR. 88
APPROVED BY THE COMICS CODE AUTHORITY

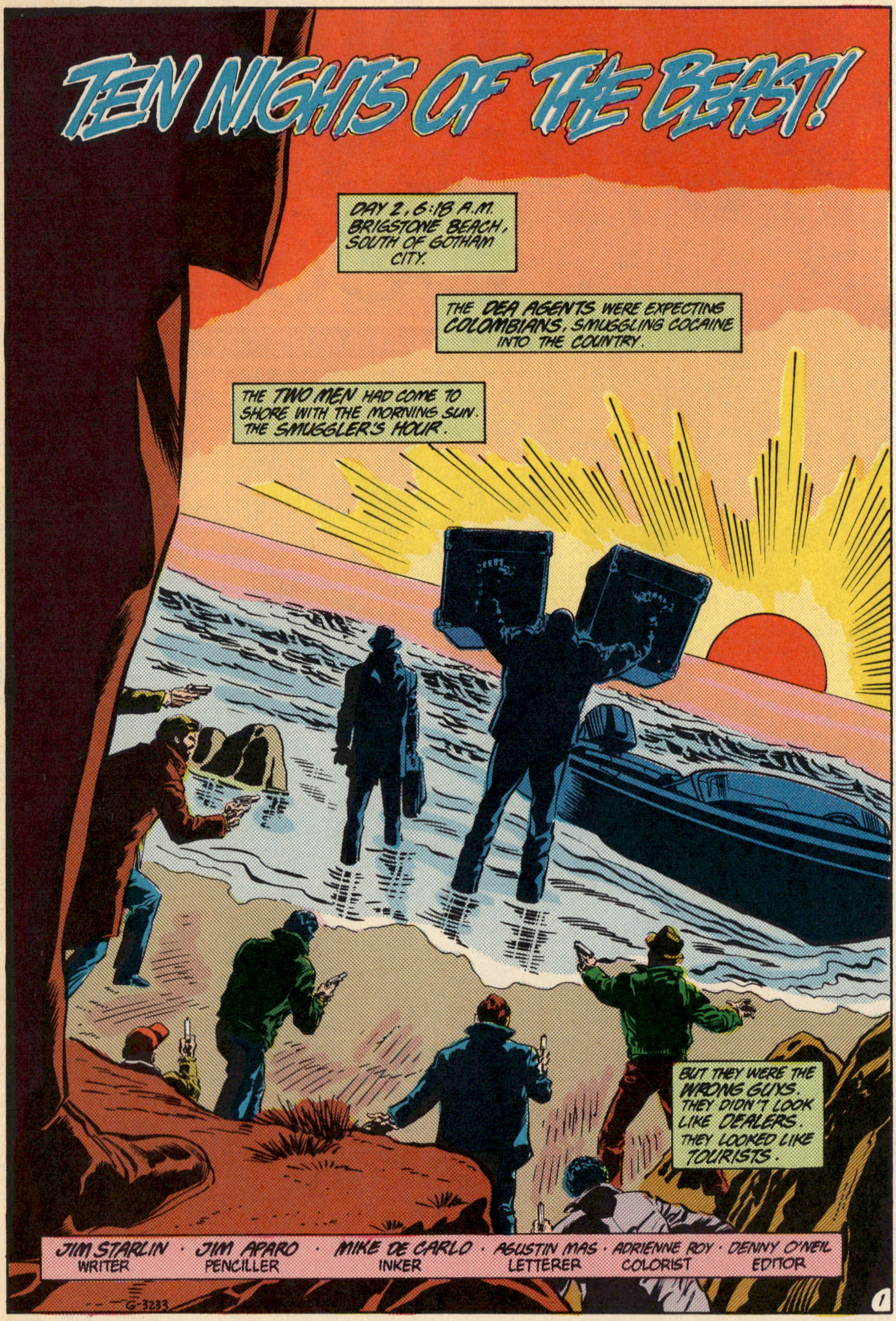
TEN NIGHTS OF THE BEAST!
DAY 2, 6:18 A.M. BRIGSTONE BEACH, SOUTH OF GOTHAM CITY.
THE DEA AGENTS WERE EXPECTING COLOMBIANS, SMUGGLING COCAINE INTO THE COUNTRY.
THE TWO MEN HAD COME TO SHORE WITH THE MORNING SUN. THE SMUGGLER'S HOUR.
BUT THEY WERE THE WRONG GUYS. THEY DIDN'T LOOK LIKE DEALERS. THEY LOOKED LIKE TOURISTS.
JIM STARLIN · WRITER
JIM APARO · PENCILLER
MIKE DE CARLO · INKER
AGUSTIN MAS · LETTERER
ADRIENNE ROY · COLORIST
DENNY O'NEIL · EDITOR
G-3233
1

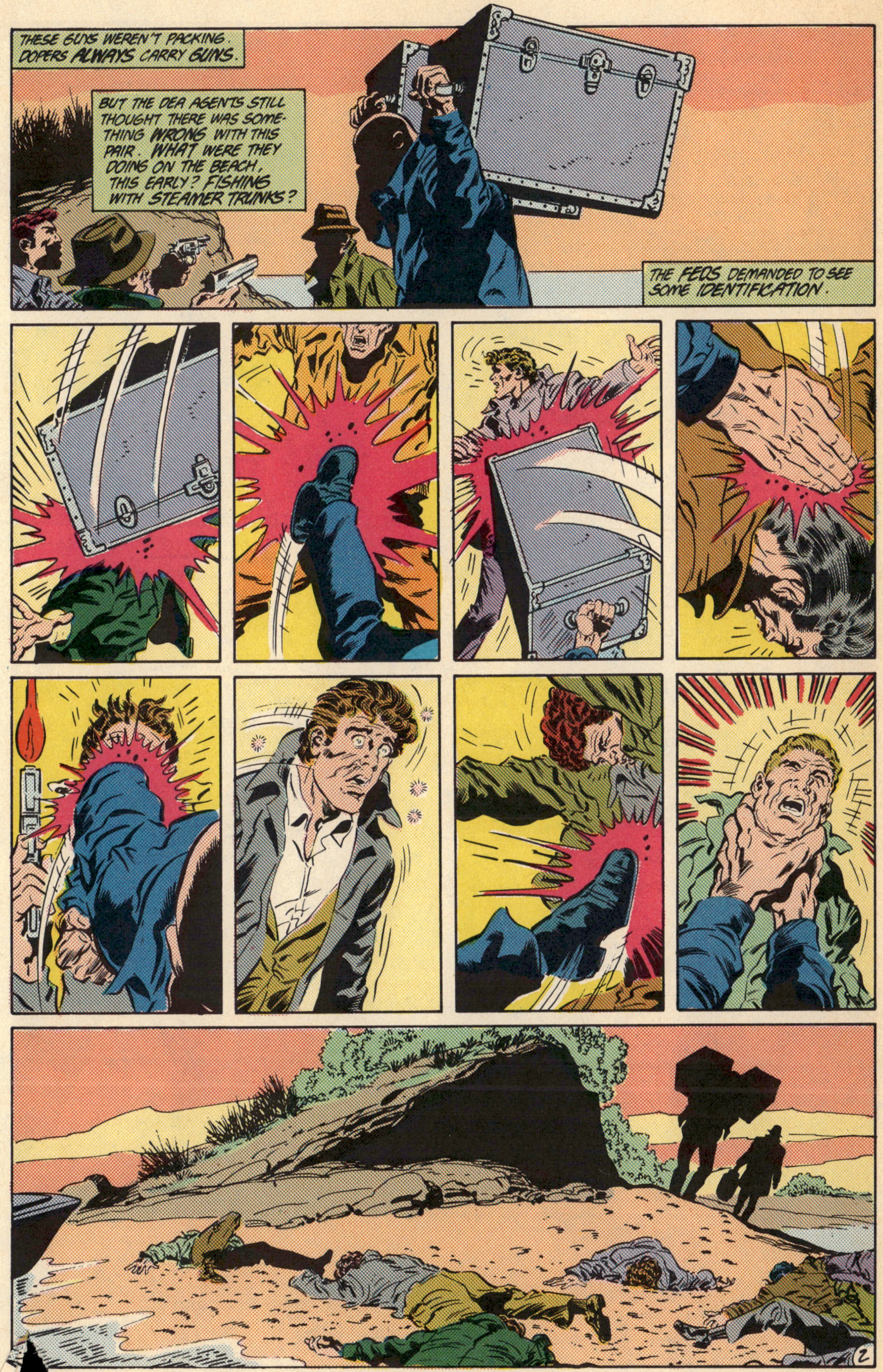
THESE GUYS WEREN'T PACKING. DOPERS ALWAYS CARRY GUNS.
BUT THE DEA AGENTS STILL THOUGHT THERE WAS SOMETHING WRONG WITH THIS PAIR. WHAT WERE THEY DOING ON THE BEACH, THIS EARLY? FISHING WITH STEAMER TRUNKS?
THE FEDS DEMANDED TO SEE SOME IDENTIFICATION.
2

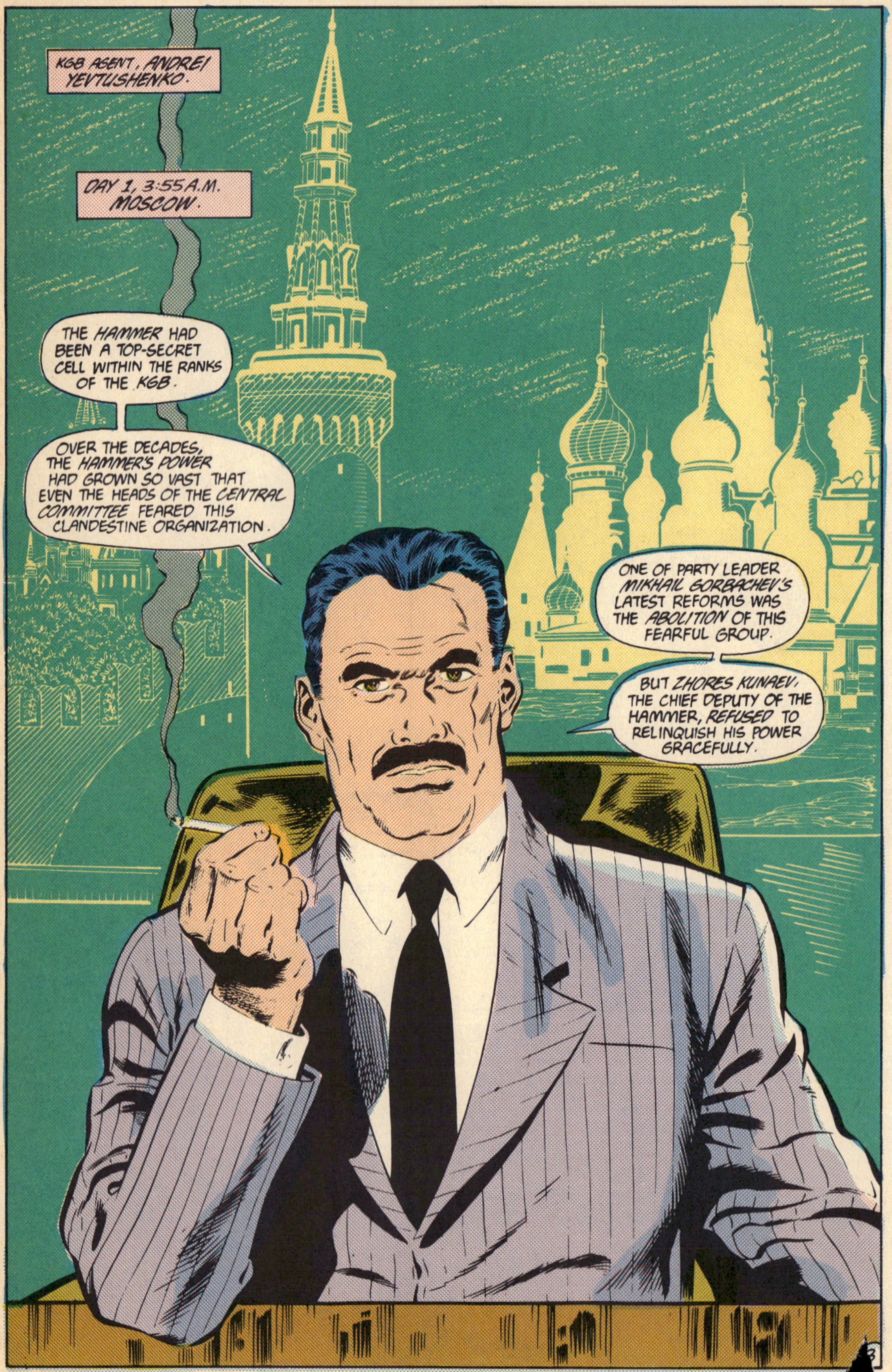
KGB AGENT, ANDREI YEVTUSHENKO.
DAY 1, 3:55 A.M. MOSCOW.
THE HAMMER HAD BEEN A TOP-SECRET CELL WITHIN THE RANKS OF THE KGB.
OVER THE DECADES, THE HAMMER'S POWER HAD GROWN SO VAST THAT EVEN THE HEADS OF THE CENTRAL COMMITTEE FEARED THIS CLANDESTINE ORGANIZATION.
ONE OF PARTY LEADER MIKHAIL GORBACHEV'S LATEST REFORMS WAS THE ABOLITION OF THIS FEARFUL GROUP.
BUT ZHORES KUNAEV, THE CHIEF DEPUTY OF THE HAMMER, REFUSED TO RELINQUISH HIS POWER GRACEFULLY.

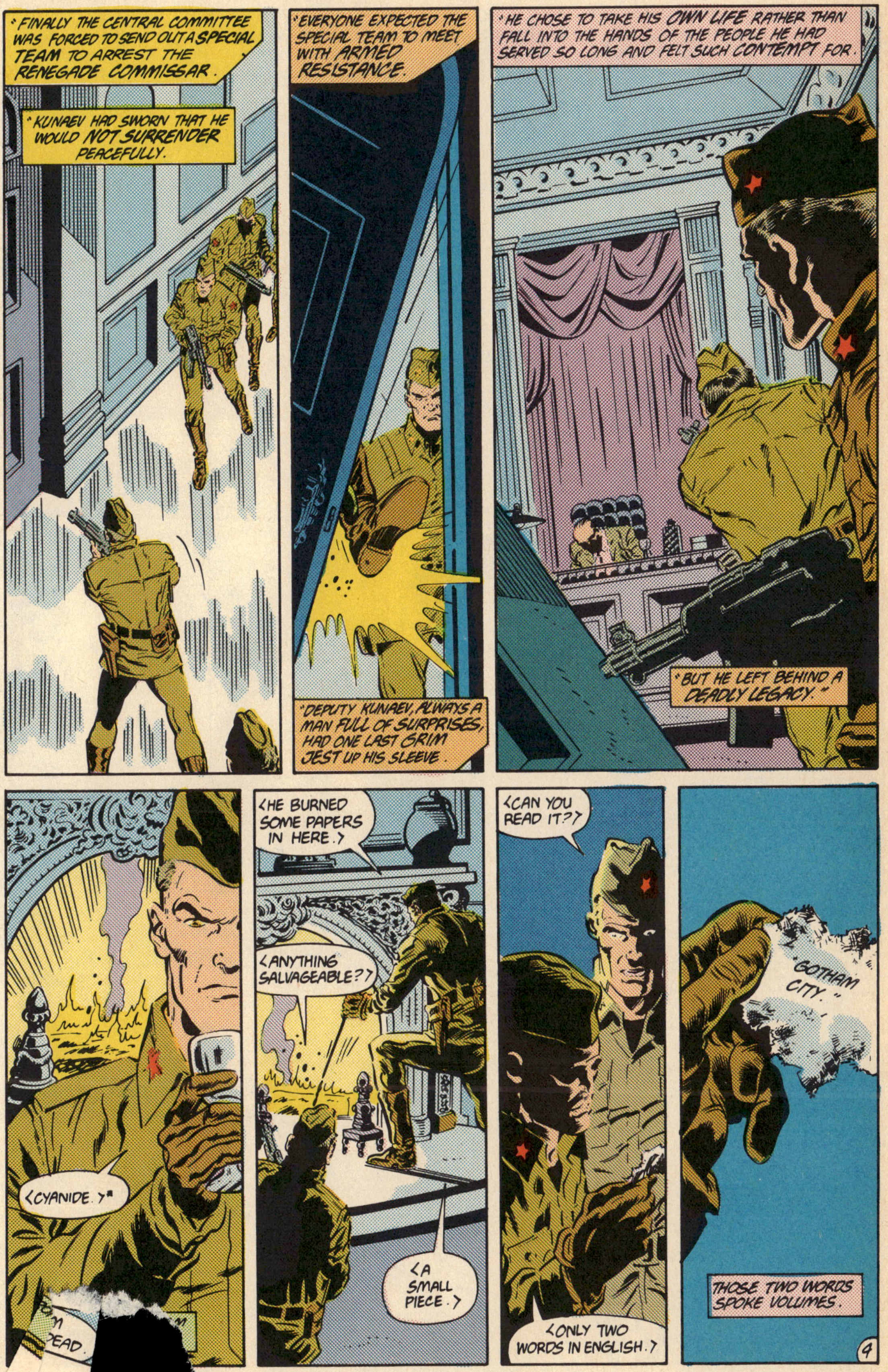
"FINALLY THE CENTRAL COMMITTEE WAS FORCED TO SEND OUT A SPECIAL TEAM TO ARREST THE RENEGADE COMMISSAR.
"KUNAEV HAD SWORN THAT HE WOULD NOT SURRENDER PEACEFULLY.
"EVERYONE EXPECTED THE SPECIAL TEAM TO MEET WITH ARMED RESISTANCE.
"DEPUTY KUNAEV, ALWAYS A MAN FULL OF SURPRISES, HAD ONE LAST GRIM JEST UP HIS SLEEVE.
"HE CHOSE TO TAKE HIS OWN LIFE RATHER THAN FALL INTO THE HANDS OF THE PEOPLE HE HAD SERVED SO LONG AND FELT SUCH CONTEMPT FOR.
"BUT HE LEFT BEHIND A DEADLY LEGACY."
<CYANIDE.>*
<HE BURNED SOME PAPERS IN HERE.>
<ANYTHING SALVAGEABLE?>
<A SMALL PIECE.>
<CAN YOU READ IT?>
<ONLY TWO WORDS IN ENGLISH.>
"GOTHAM CITY."
THOSE TWO WORDS SPOKE VOLUMES.
4

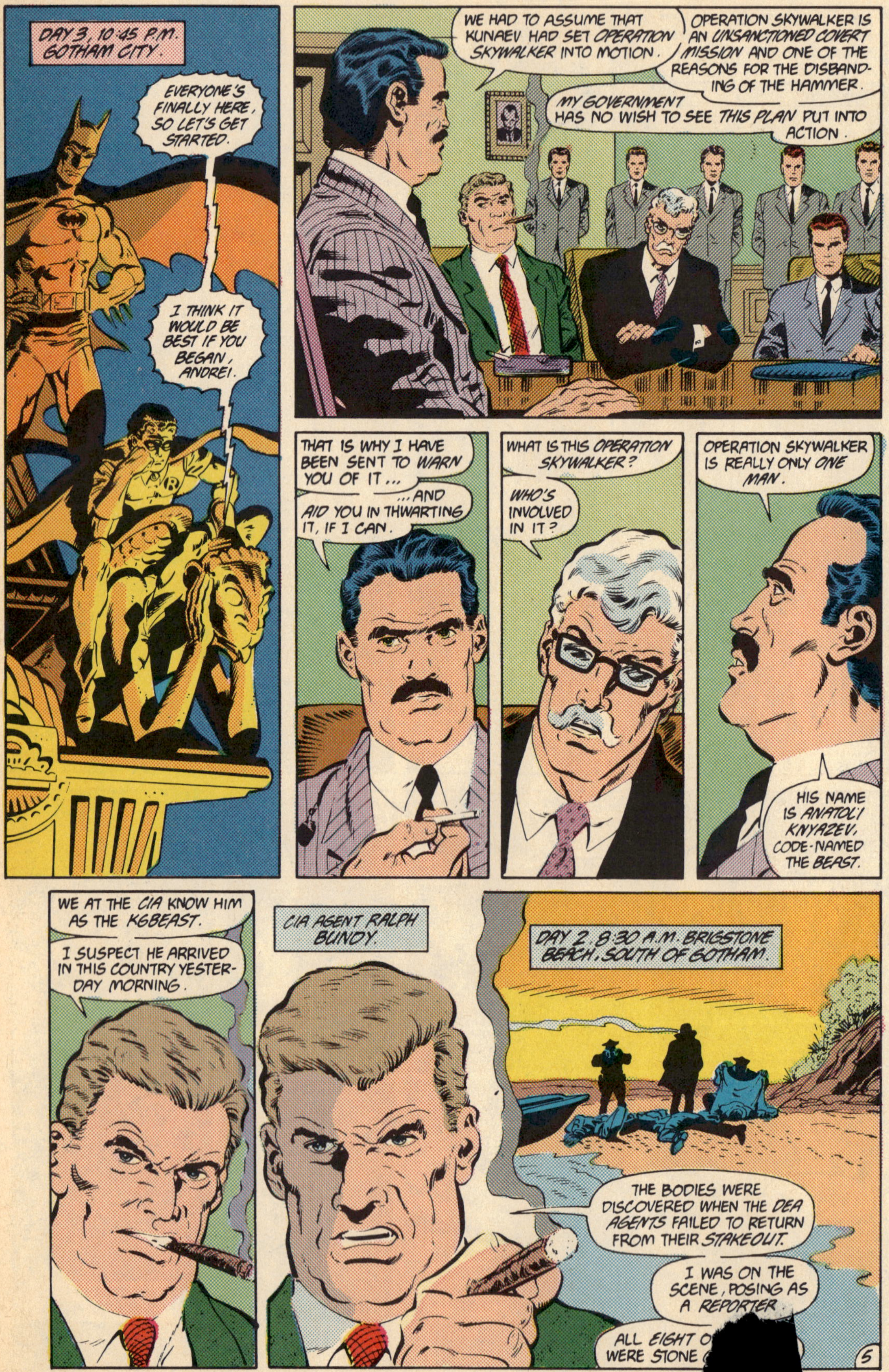
DAY 3, 10:45 P.M. GOTHAM CITY.
EVERYONE'S FINALLY HERE, SO LET'S GET STARTED.
I THINK IT WOULD BE BEST IF YOU BEGAN, ANDREI.
WE HAD TO ASSUME THAT KUNAEV HAD SET OPERATION SKYWALKER INTO MOTION.
OPERATION SKYWALKER IS AN UNSANCTIONED COVERT MISSION AND ONE OF THE REASONS FOR THE DISBANDING OF THE HAMMER.
MY GOVERNMENT HAS NO WISH TO SEE THIS PLAN PUT INTO ACTION.
THAT IS WHY I HAVE BEEN SENT TO WARN YOU OF IT...
...AND AID YOU IN THWARTING IT, IF I CAN.
WHAT IS THIS OPERATION SKYWALKER?
WHO'S INVOLVED IN IT?
OPERATION SKYWALKER IS REALLY ONLY ONE MAN.
HIS NAME IS ANATOLI KNYAZEV, CODE-NAMED THE BEAST.
WE AT THE CIA KNOW HIM AS THE KGBEAST.
I SUSPECT HE ARRIVED IN THIS COUNTRY YESTERDAY MORNING.
CIA AGENT RALPH BUNDY.
DAY 2, 8:30 A.M. BRIGSTONE BEACH, SOUTH OF GOTHAM.
THE BODIES WERE DISCOVERED WHEN THE DEA AGENTS FAILED TO RETURN FROM THEIR STAKEOUT.
I WAS ON THE SCENE, POSING AS A REPORTER.
ALL EIGHT O
WERE STONE
5

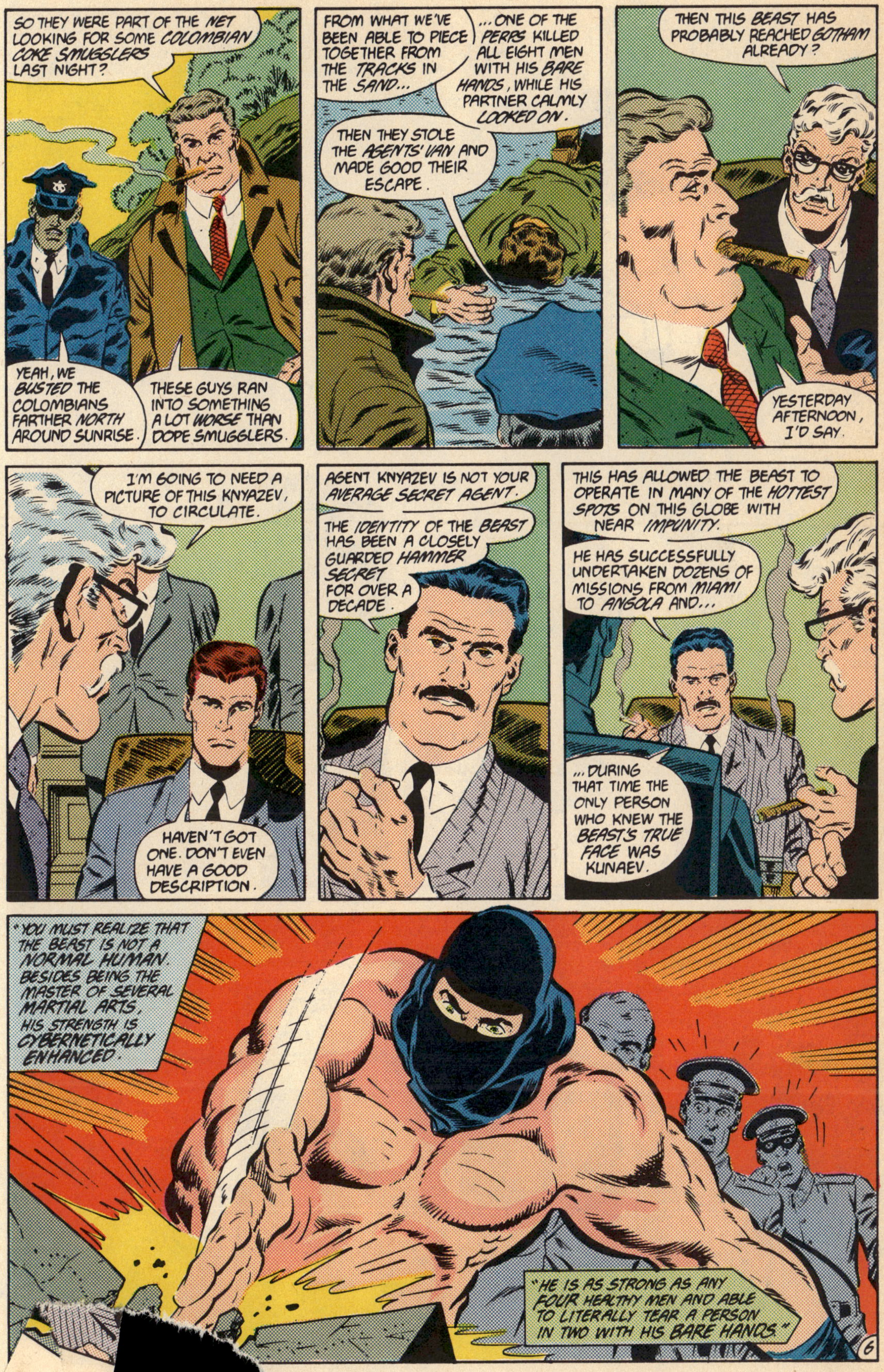
SO THEY WERE PART OF THE NET LOOKING FOR SOME COLOMBIAN COKE SMUGGLERS LAST NIGHT?
YEAH, WE BUSTED THE COLOMBIANS FARTHER NORTH AROUND SUNRISE.
THESE GUYS RAN INTO SOMETHING A LOT WORSE THAN DOPE SMUGGLERS.
FROM WHAT WE'VE BEEN ABLE TO PIECE TOGETHER FROM THE TRACKS IN THE SAND...
...ONE OF THE PERPS KILLED ALL EIGHT MEN WITH HIS BARE HANDS, WHILE HIS PARTNER CALMLY LOOKED ON.
THEN THEY STOLE THE AGENTS' VAN AND MADE GOOD THEIR ESCAPE.
THEN THIS BEAST HAS PROBABLY REACHED GOTHAM ALREADY?
YESTERDAY AFTERNOON, I'D SAY.
I'M GOING TO NEED A PICTURE OF THIS KNYAZEV, TO CIRCULATE.
HAVEN'T GOT ONE. DON'T EVEN HAVE A GOOD DESCRIPTION.
AGENT KNYAZEV IS NOT YOUR AVERAGE SECRET AGENT.
THE IDENTITY OF THE BEAST HAS BEEN A CLOSELY GUARDED HAMMER SECRET FOR OVER A DECADE.
THIS HAS ALLOWED THE BEAST TO OPERATE IN MANY OF THE HOTTEST SPOTS ON THIS GLOBE WITH NEAR IMPUNITY.
HE HAS SUCCESSFULLY UNDERTAKEN DOZENS OF MISSIONS FROM MIAMI TO ANGOLA AND...
...DURING THAT TIME THE ONLY PERSON WHO KNEW THE BEAST'S TRUE FACE WAS KUNAEV.
"YOU MUST REALIZE THAT THE BEAST IS NOT A NORMAL HUMAN. BESIDES BEING THE MASTER OF SEVERAL MARTIAL ARTS, HIS STRENGTH IS CYBERNETICALLY ENHANCED.
"HE IS AS STRONG AS ANY FOUR HEALTHY MEN AND ABLE TO LITERALLY TEAR A PERSON IN TWO WITH HIS BARE HANDS."
6

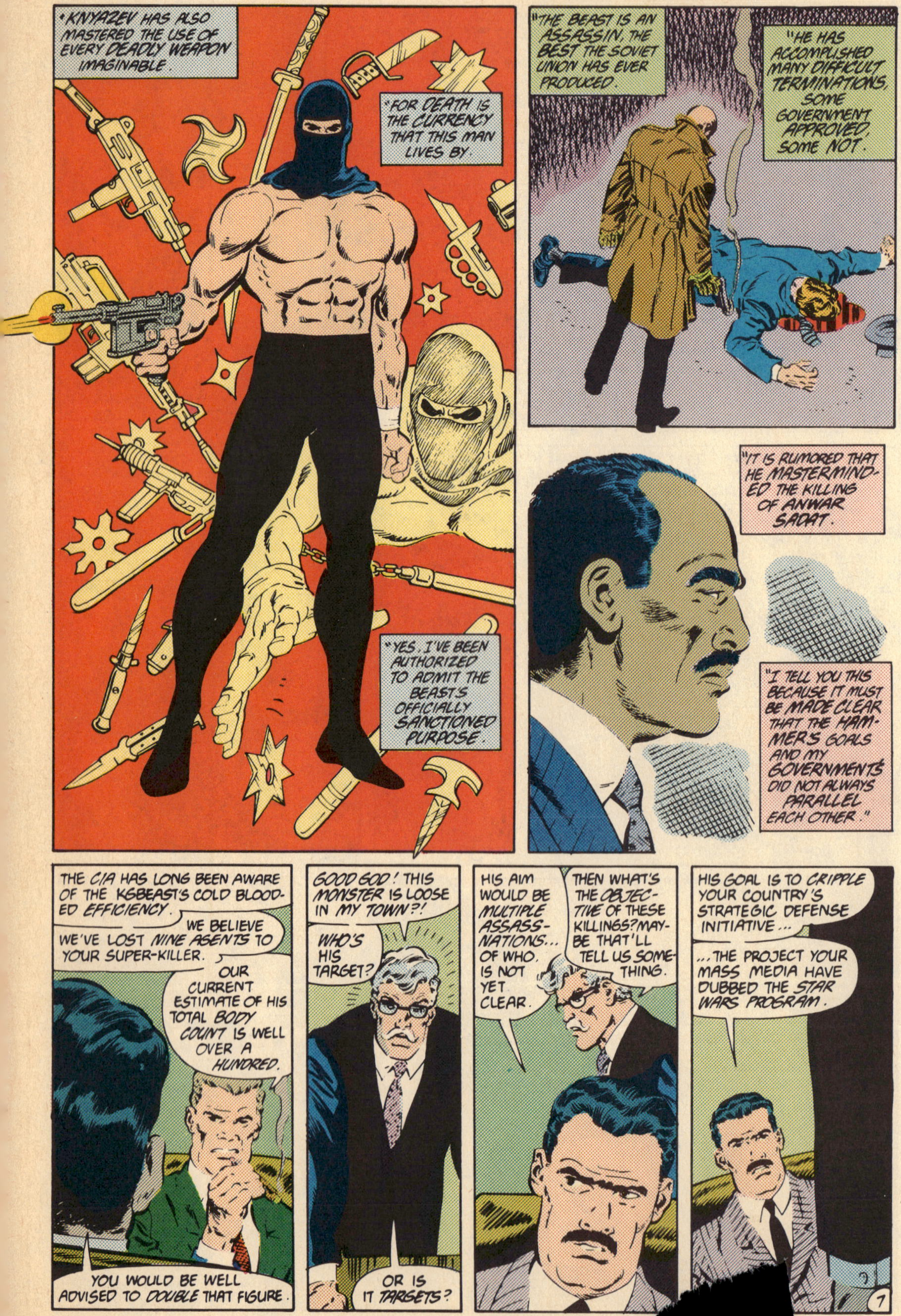

"KNYAZEV HAS ALSO MASTERED THE USE OF EVERY DEADLY WEAPON IMAGINABLE.
"FOR DEATH IS THE CURRENCY THAT THIS MAN LIVES BY.
"YES, I'VE BEEN AUTHORIZED TO ADMIT THE BEAST'S OFFICIALLY SANCTIONED PURPOSE.
"THE BEAST IS AN ASSASSIN, THE BEST THE SOVIET UNION HAS EVER PRODUCED.
"HE HAS ACCOMPLISHED MANY DIFFICULT TERMINATIONS, SOME GOVERNMENT APPROVED, SOME NOT.
"IT IS RUMORED THAT HE MASTERMINDED THE KILLING OF ANWAR SADAT.
"I TELL YOU THIS BECAUSE IT MUST BE MADE CLEAR THAT THE HAMMER'S GOALS AND MY GOVERNMENT'S DID NOT ALWAYS PARALLEL EACH OTHER."
THE CIA HAS LONG BEEN AWARE OF THE KGBEAST'S COLD BLOODED EFFICIENCY.
WE BELIEVE WE'VE LOST NINE AGENTS TO YOUR SUPER-KILLER.
OUR CURRENT ESTIMATE OF HIS TOTAL BODY COUNT IS WELL OVER A HUNDRED.
YOU WOULD BE WELL ADVISED TO DOUBLE THAT FIGURE.
GOOD GOD! THIS MONSTER IS LOOSE IN MY TOWN?!
WHO'S HIS TARGET?
OR IS IT TARGETS?
HIS AIM WOULD BE MULTIPLE ASSASSINATIONS... OF WHO, IS NOT YET CLEAR.
THEN WHAT'S THE OBJECTIVE OF THESE KILLINGS? MAYBE THAT'LL TELL US SOMETHING.
HIS GOAL IS TO CRIPPLE YOUR COUNTRY'S STRATEGIC DEFENSE INITIATIVE...
...THE PROJECT YOUR MASS MEDIA HAVE DUBBED THE STAR WARS PROGRAM.
7

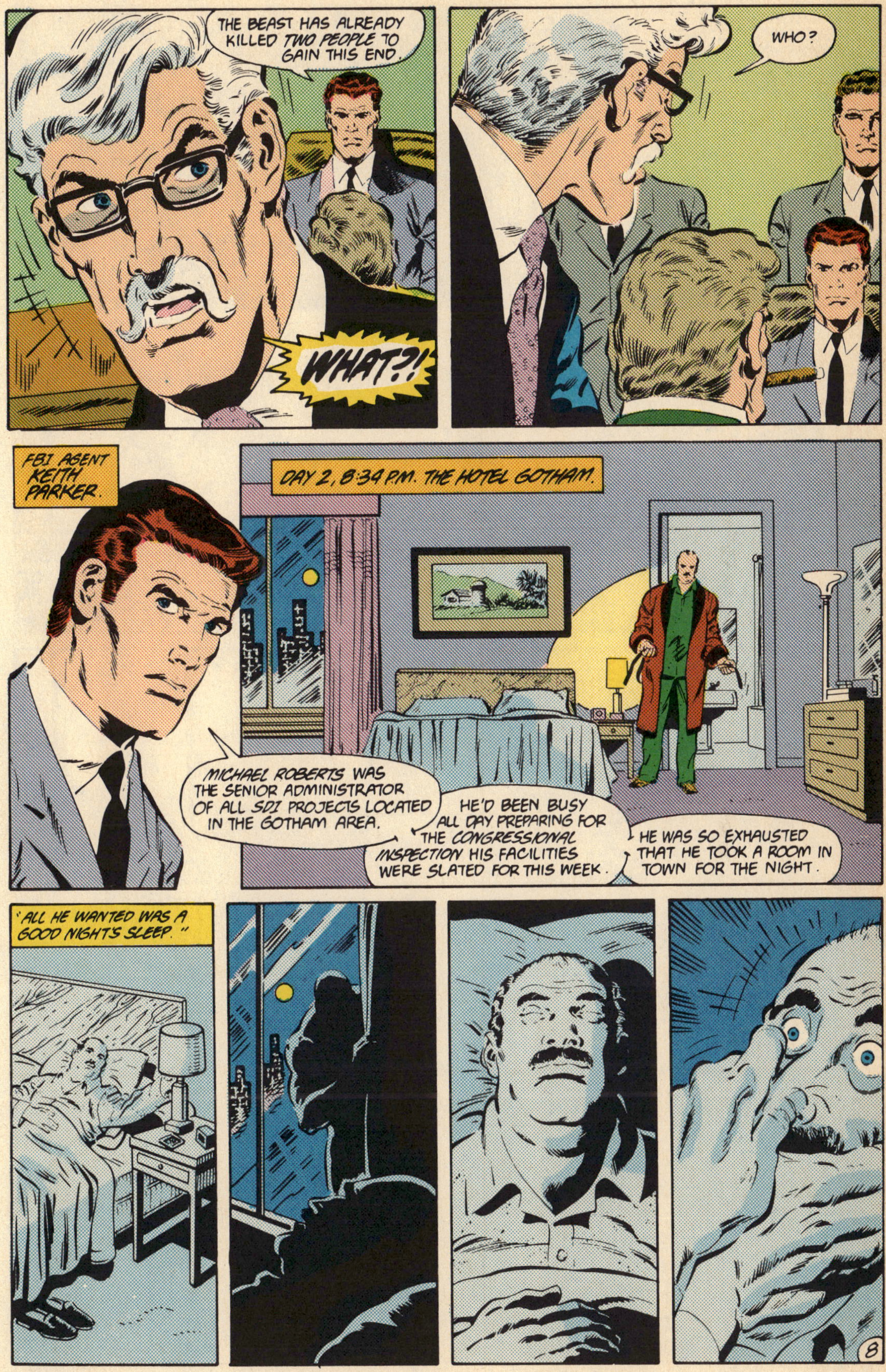
THE BEAST HAS ALREADY KILLED TWO PEOPLE TO GAIN THIS END.
WHAT?!
WHO?
FBI AGENT KEITH PARKER.
DAY 2, 8:34 P.M. THE HOTEL GOTHAM.
MICHAEL ROBERTS WAS THE SENIOR ADMINISTRATOR OF ALL SDI PROJECTS LOCATED IN THE GOTHAM AREA.
HE'D BEEN BUSY ALL DAY PREPARING FOR THE CONGRESSIONAL INSPECTION HIS FACILITIES WERE SLATED FOR THIS WEEK.
HE WAS SO EXHAUSTED THAT HE TOOK A ROOM IN TOWN FOR THE NIGHT.
"ALL HE WANTED WAS A GOOD NIGHT'S SLEEP."
8

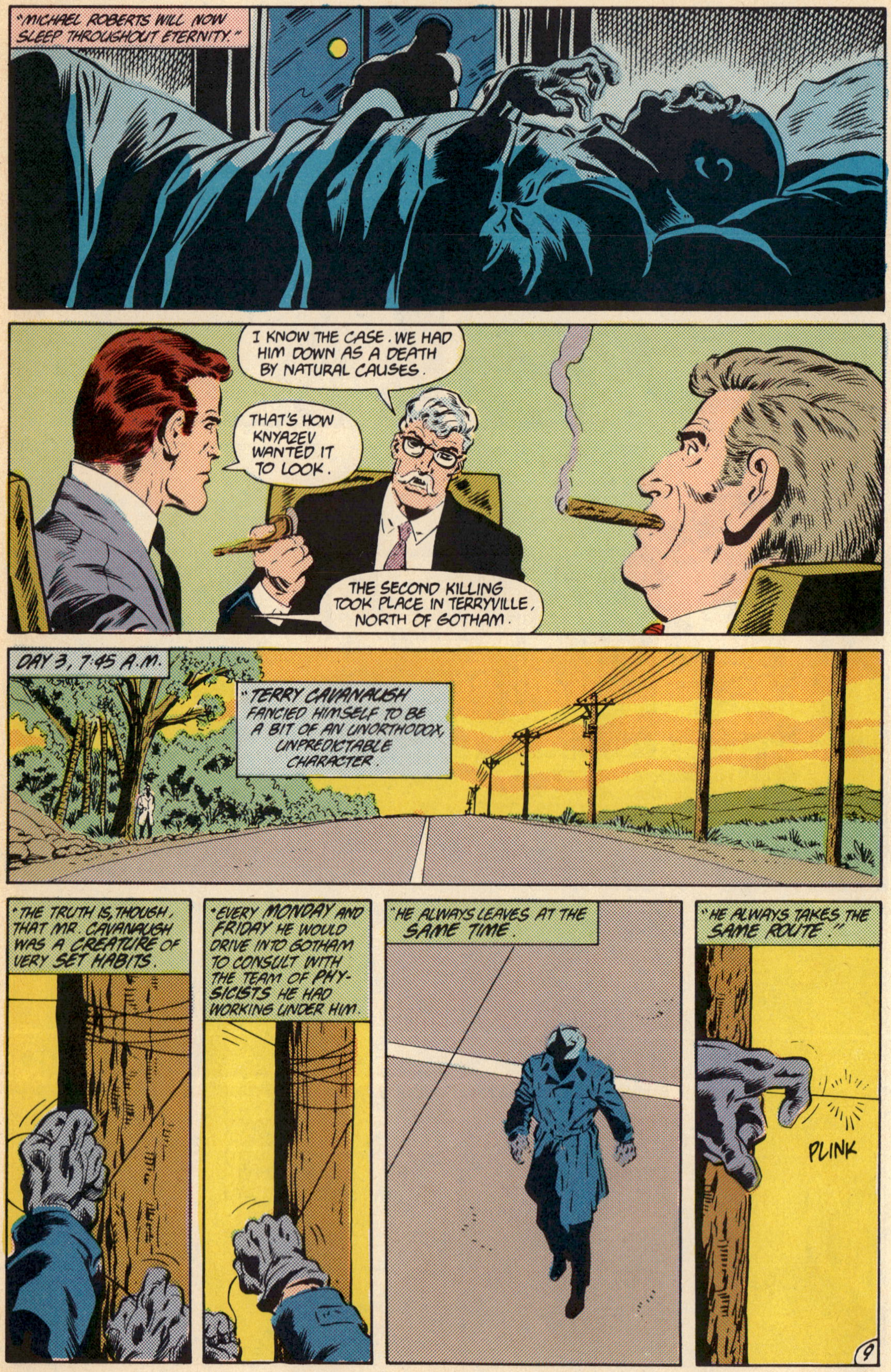
"MICHAEL ROBERTS WILL NOW SLEEP THROUGHOUT ETERNITY."
I KNOW THE CASE. WE HAD HIM DOWN AS A DEATH BY NATURAL CAUSES.
THAT'S HOW KNYAZEV WANTED IT TO LOOK.
THE SECOND KILLING TOOK PLACE IN TERRYVILLE, NORTH OF GOTHAM.
DAY 3, 7:45 A.M.
"TERRY CAVANAUGH FANCIED HIMSELF TO BE A BIT OF AN UNORTHODOX, UNPREDICTABLE CHARACTER.
"THE TRUTH IS, THOUGH, THAT MR. CAVANAUGH WAS A CREATURE OF VERY SET HABITS.
"EVERY MONDAY AND FRIDAY HE WOULD DRIVE INTO GOTHAM TO CONSULT WITH THE TEAM OF PHYSICISTS HE HAD WORKING UNDER HIM.
"HE ALWAYS LEAVES AT THE SAME TIME.
"HE ALWAYS TAKES THE SAME ROUTE."
PLINK
9

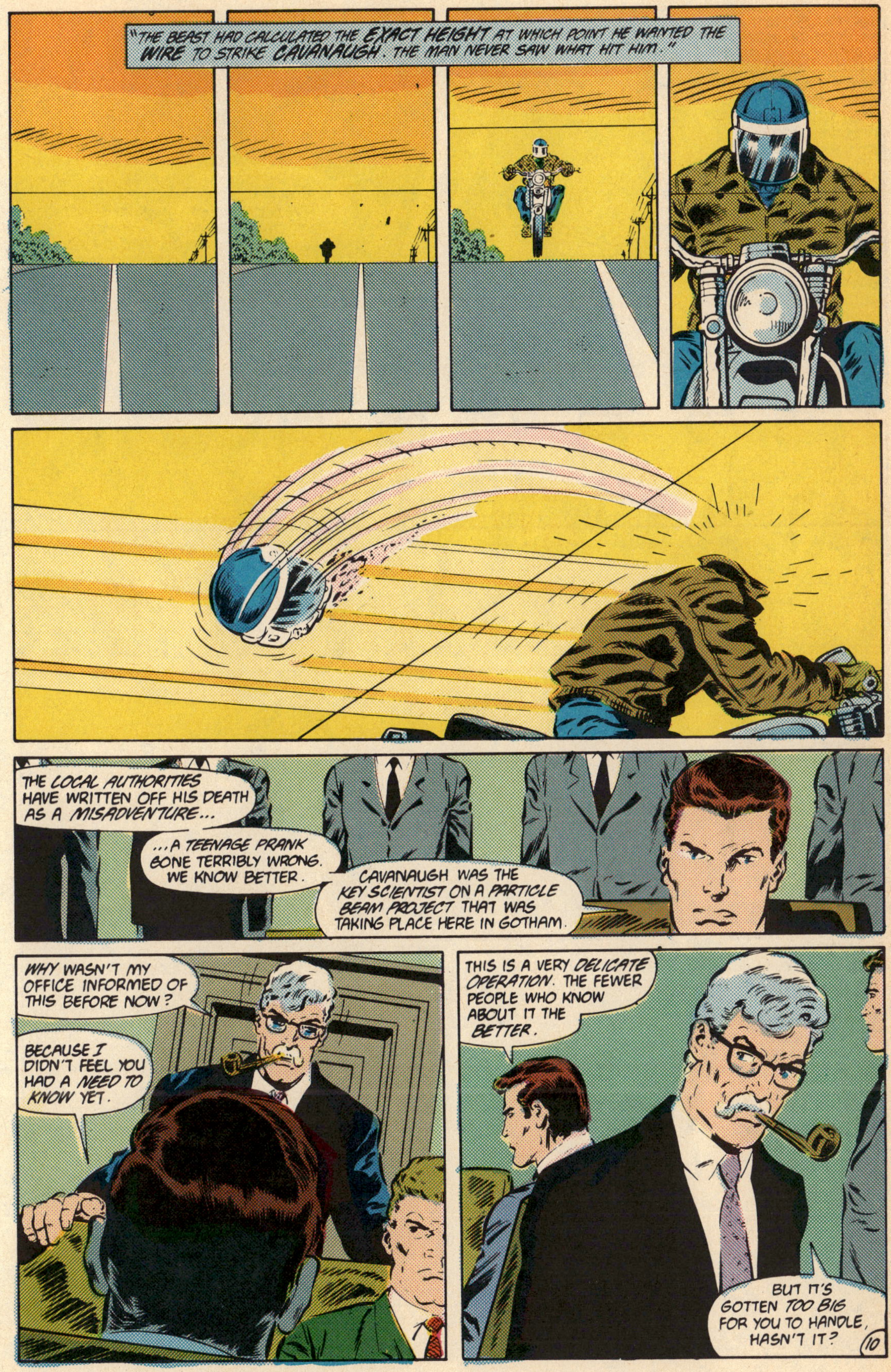
"THE BEAST HAD CALCULATED THE EXACT HEIGHT AT WHICH POINT HE WANTED THE WIRE TO STRIKE CAVANAUGH. THE MAN NEVER SAW WHAT HIT HIM."
THE LOCAL AUTHORITIES HAVE WRITTEN OFF HIS DEATH AS A MISADVENTURE...
...A TEENAGE PRANK GONE TERRIBLY WRONG. WE KNOW BETTER.
CAVANAUGH WAS THE KEY SCIENTIST ON A PARTICLE BEAM PROJECT THAT WAS TAKING PLACE HERE IN GOTHAM.
WHY WASN'T MY OFFICE INFORMED OF THIS BEFORE NOW?
BECAUSE I DIDN'T FEEL YOU HAD A NEED TO KNOW YET.
THIS IS A VERY DELICATE OPERATION. THE FEWER PEOPLE WHO KNOW ABOUT IT THE BETTER.
BUT IT'S GOTTEN TOO BIG FOR YOU TO HANDLE, HASN'T IT?
10

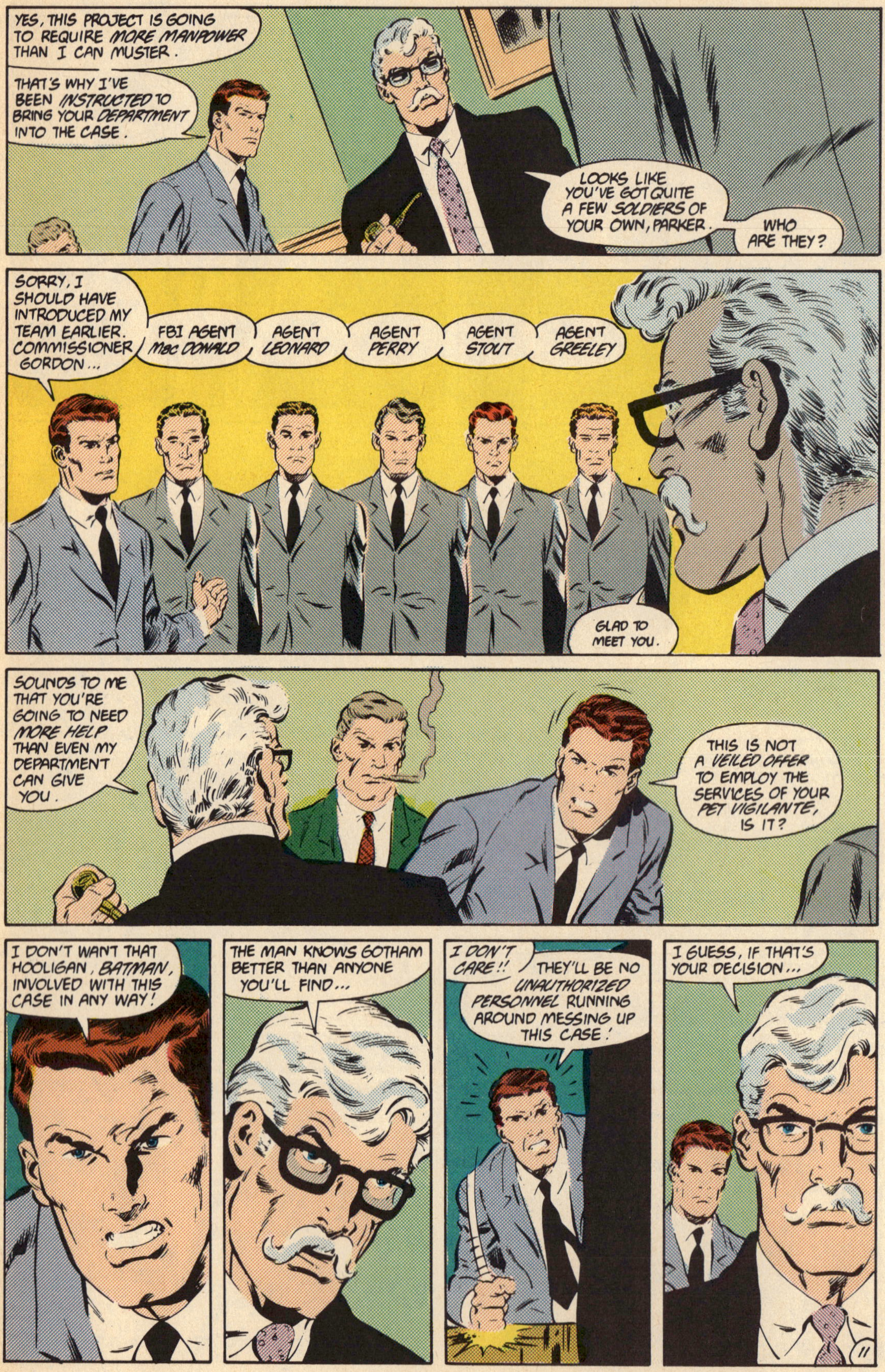
YES, THIS PROJECT IS GOING TO REQUIRE MORE MANPOWER THAN I CAN MUSTER.
THAT'S WHY I'VE BEEN INSTRUCTED TO BRING YOUR DEPARTMENT INTO THE CASE.
LOOKS LIKE YOU'VE GOT QUITE A FEW SOLDIERS OF YOUR OWN, PARKER.
WHO ARE THEY?
SORRY, I SHOULD HAVE INTRODUCED MY TEAM EARLIER. COMMISSIONER GORDON...
FBI AGENT MacDONALD
AGENT LEONARD
AGENT PERRY
AGENT STOUT
AGENT GREELEY
GLAD TO MEET YOU.
SOUNDS TO ME THAT YOU'RE GOING TO NEED MORE HELP THAN EVEN MY DEPARTMENT CAN GIVE YOU.
THIS IS NOT A VEILED OFFER TO EMPLOY THE SERVICES OF YOUR PET VIGILANTE, IS IT?
I DON'T WANT THAT HOOLIGAN, BATMAN, INVOLVED WITH THIS CASE IN ANY WAY!
THE MAN KNOWS GOTHAM BETTER THAN ANYONE YOU'LL FIND...
I DON'T CARE!!
THEY'LL BE NO UNAUTHORIZED PERSONNEL RUNNING AROUND MESSING UP THIS CASE!
I GUESS, IF THAT'S YOUR DECISION...
11

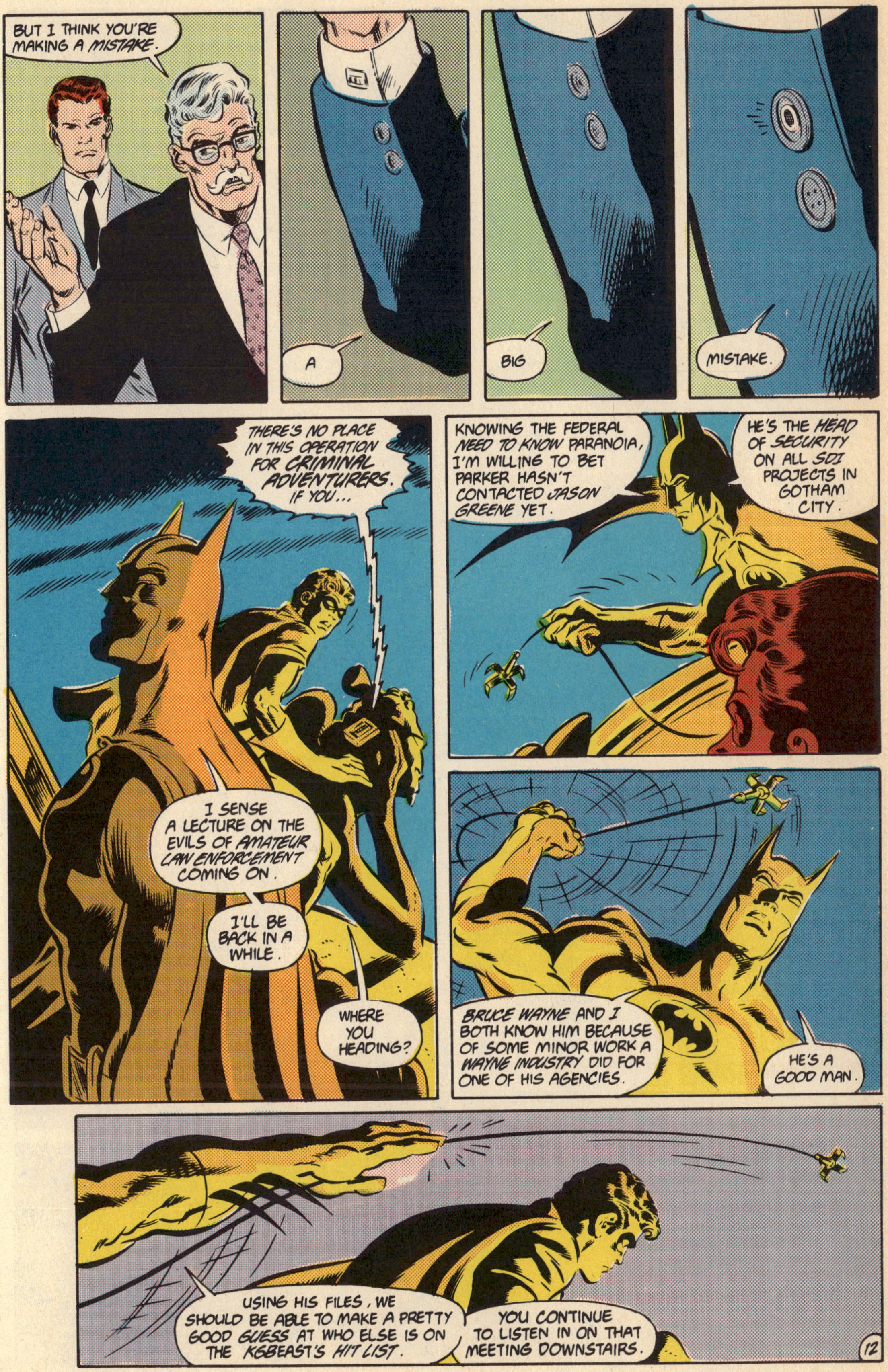
BUT I THINK YOU'RE MAKING A MISTAKE.
A
BIG
MISTAKE.
THERE'S NO PLACE IN THIS OPERATION FOR CRIMINAL ADVENTURERS. IF YOU...
I SENSE A LECTURE ON THE EVILS OF AMATEUR LAW ENFORCEMENT COMING ON.
I'LL BE BACK IN A WHILE.
WHERE YOU HEADING?
KNOWING THE FEDERAL NEED TO KNOW PARANOIA, I'M WILLING TO BET PARKER HASN'T CONTACTED JASON GREENE YET.
HE'S THE HEAD OF SECURITY ON ALL SDI PROJECTS IN GOTHAM CITY.
BRUCE WAYNE AND I BOTH KNOW HIM BECAUSE OF SOME MINOR WORK A WAYNE INDUSTRY DID FOR ONE OF HIS AGENCIES.
HE'S A GOOD MAN.
USING HIS FILES, WE SHOULD BE ABLE TO MAKE A PRETTY GOOD GUESS AT WHO ELSE IS ON THE KGBEAST'S HIT LIST.
YOU CONTINUE TO LISTEN IN ON THAT MEETING DOWNSTAIRS.
12

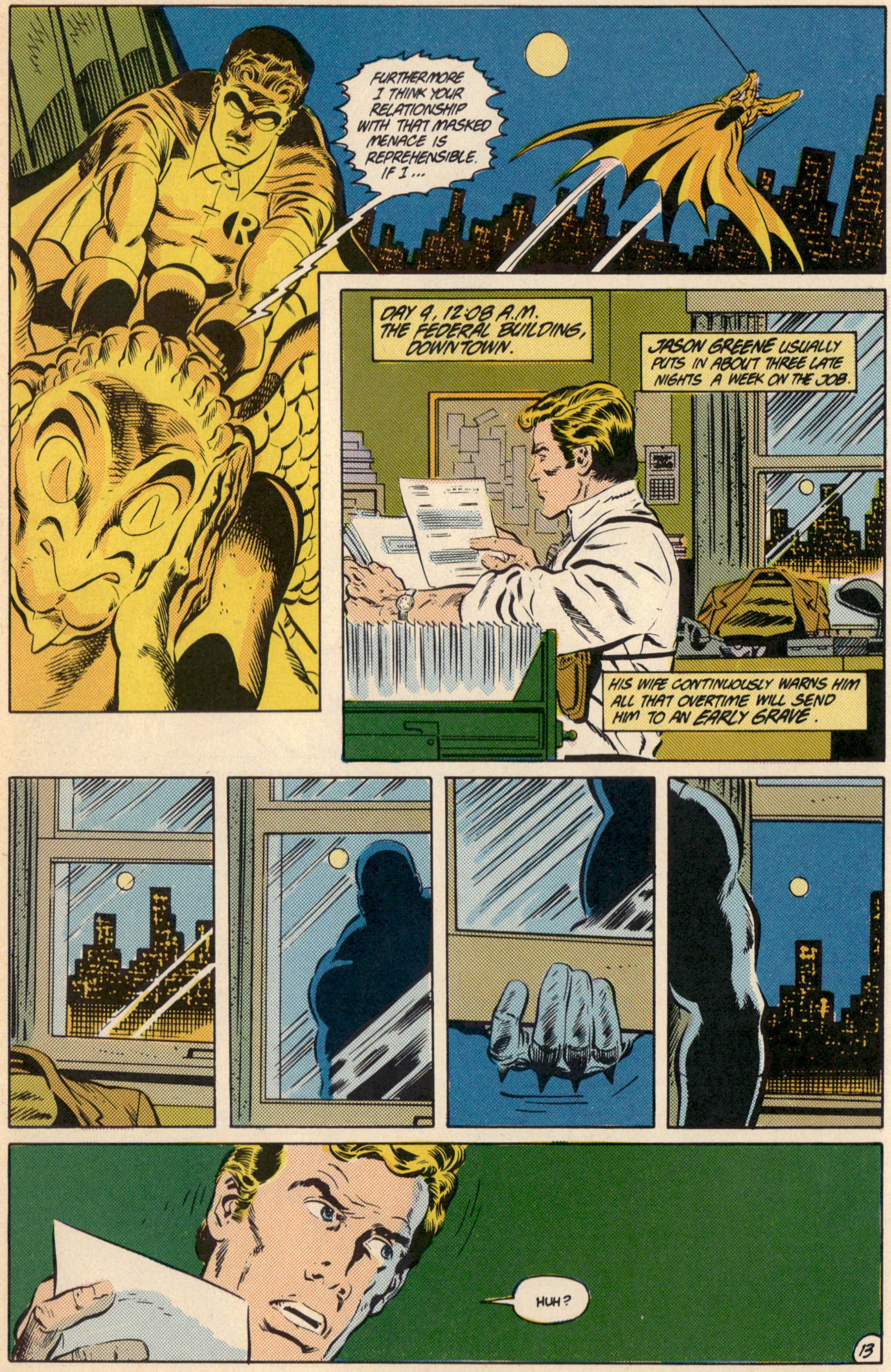
FURTHERMORE I THINK YOUR RELATIONSHIP WITH THAT MASKED MENACE IS REPREHENSIBLE. IF I...
DAY 4, 12:08 A.M. THE FEDERAL BUILDINGS, DOWNTOWN.
JASON GREENE USUALLY PUTS IN ABOUT THREE LATE NIGHTS A WEEK ON THE JOB.
HIS WIFE CONTINUOUSLY WARNS HIM ALL THAT OVERTIME WILL SEND HIM TO AN EARLY GRAVE.
HUH?
13

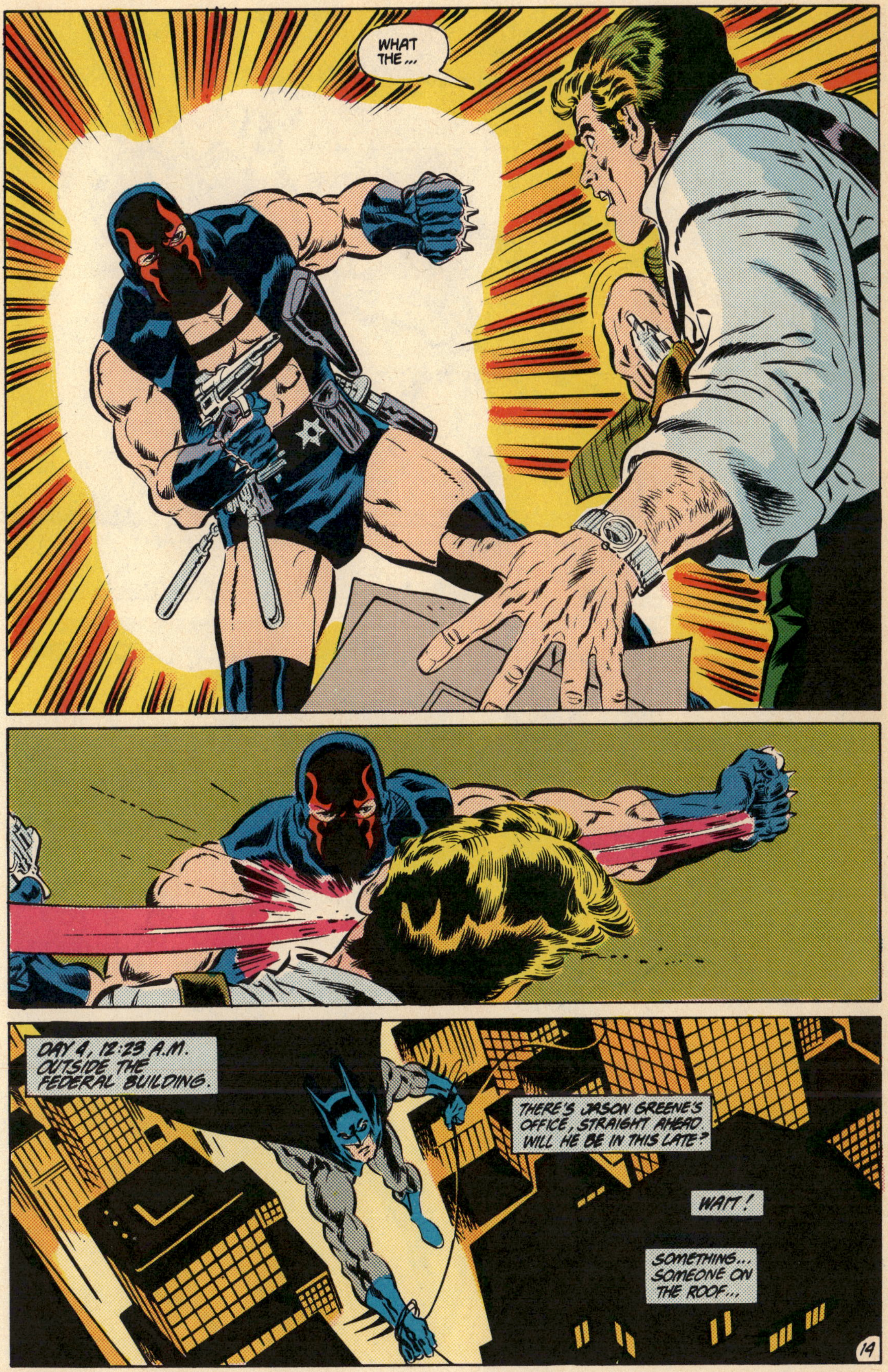
WHAT THE...
DAY 4, 12:23 A.M. OUTSIDE THE FEDERAL BUILDING.
THERE'S JASON GREENE'S OFFICE, STRAIGHT AHEAD. WILL HE BE IN THIS LATE?
WAIT!
SOMETHING... SOMEONE ON THE ROOF...
14

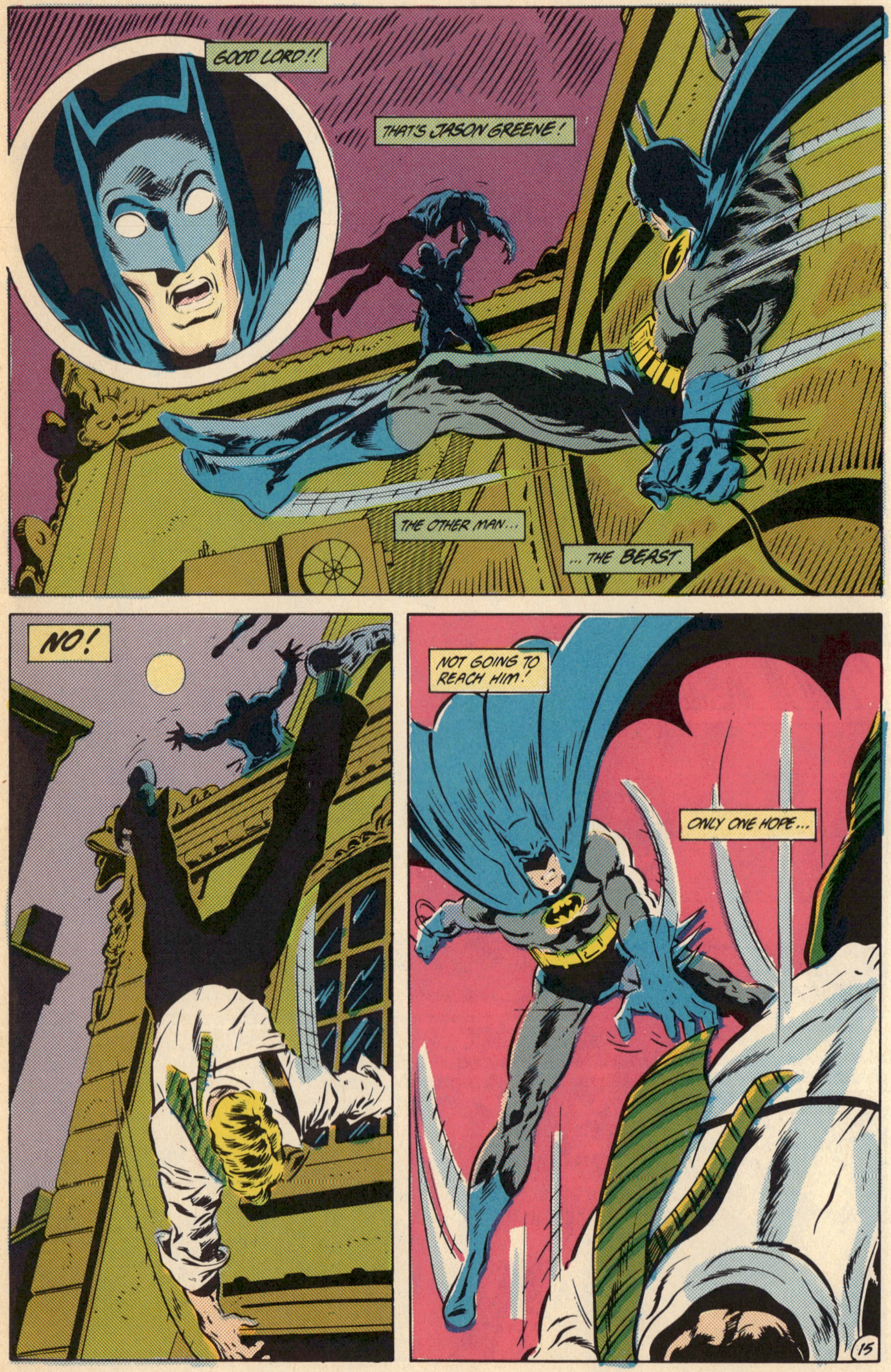
GOOD LORD!!
THAT'S JASON GREENE!
THE OTHER MAN...
...THE BEAST.
NO!
NOT GOING TO REACH HIM!
ONLY ONE HOPE...
15

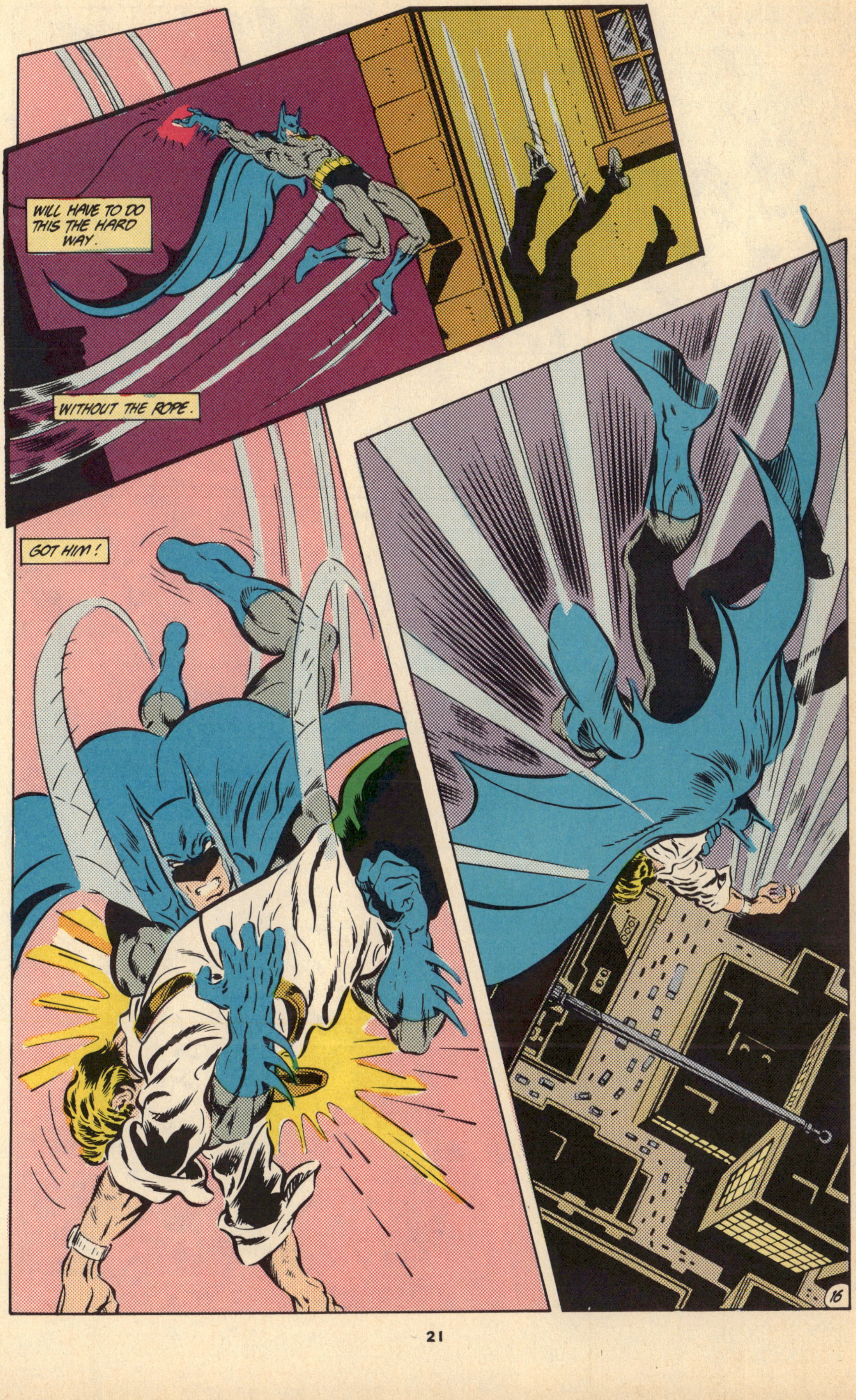
WILL HAVE TO DO THIS THE HARD WAY.
WITHOUT THE ROPE.
GOT HIM!
16

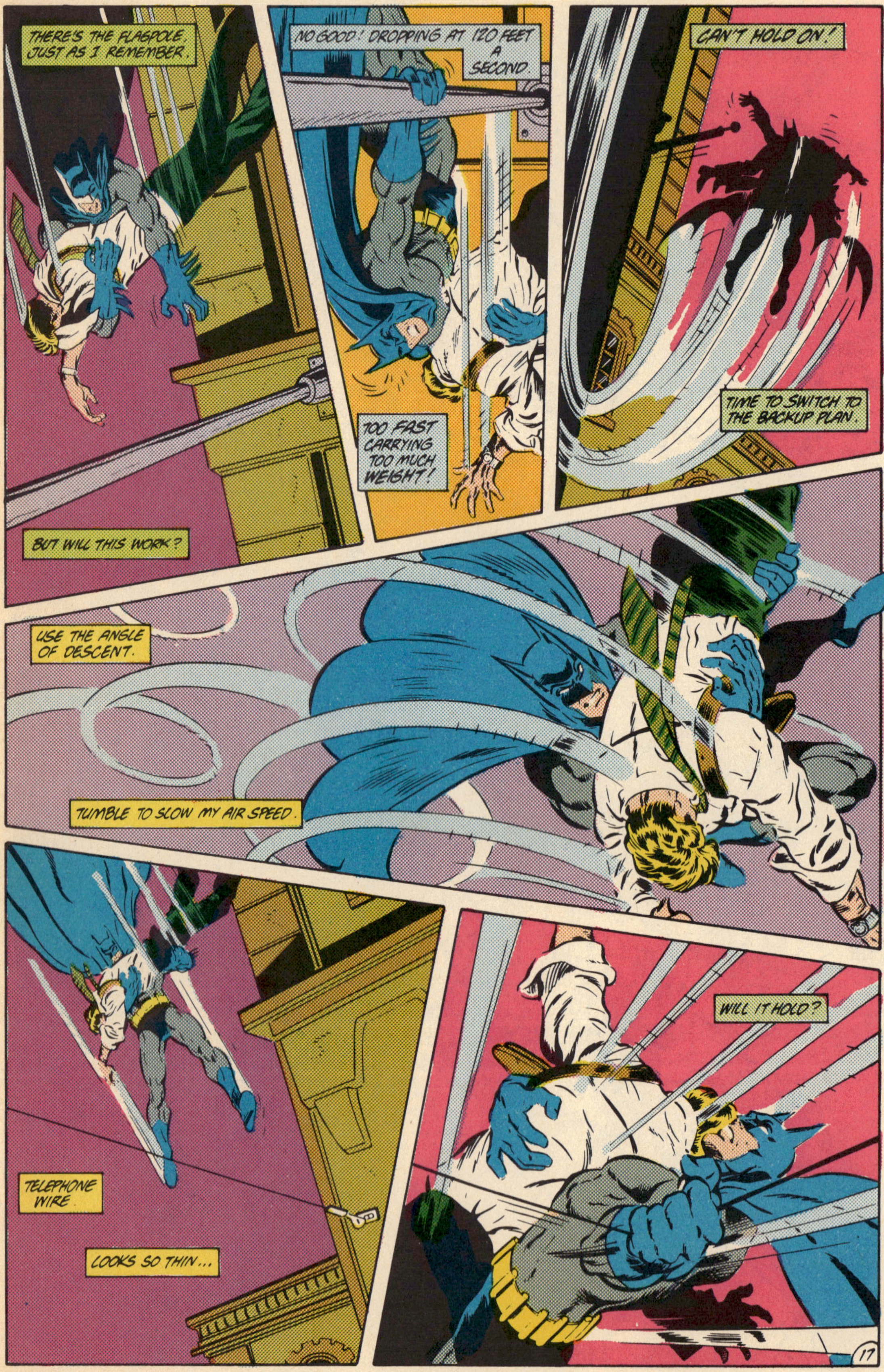
THERE'S THE FLAGPOLE JUST AS I REMEMBER.
NO GOOD! DROPPING AT 120 FEET A SECOND.
TOO FAST CARRYING TOO MUCH WEIGHT!
CAN'T HOLD ON!
TIME TO SWITCH TO THE BACKUP PLAN.
BUT WILL THIS WORK?
USE THE ANGLE OF DESCENT.
TUMBLE TO SLOW MY AIR SPEED.
TELEPHONE WIRE.
LOOKS SO THIN...
WILL IT HOLD?
17

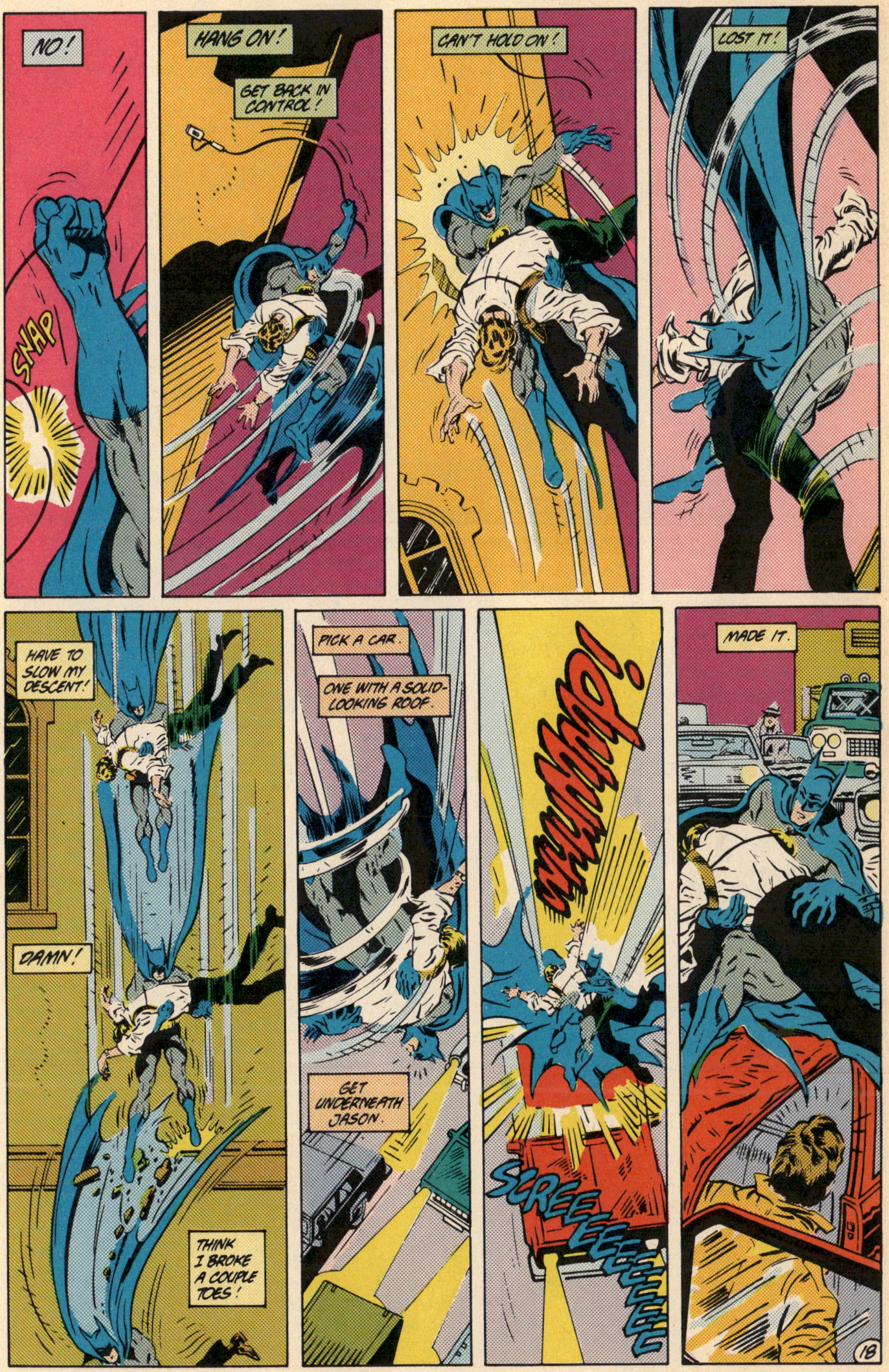
NO!
SNAP
HANG ON!
GET BACK IN CONTROL!
CAN'T HOLD ON!
LOST IT!
HAVE TO SLOW MY DESCENT!
DAMN!
THINK I BROKE A COUPLE TOES!
PICK A CAR.
ONE WITH A SOLID-LOOKING ROOF
GET UNDERNEATH JASON.
WHAMMP!
SCREEEEEEEEEE
MADE IT.
18

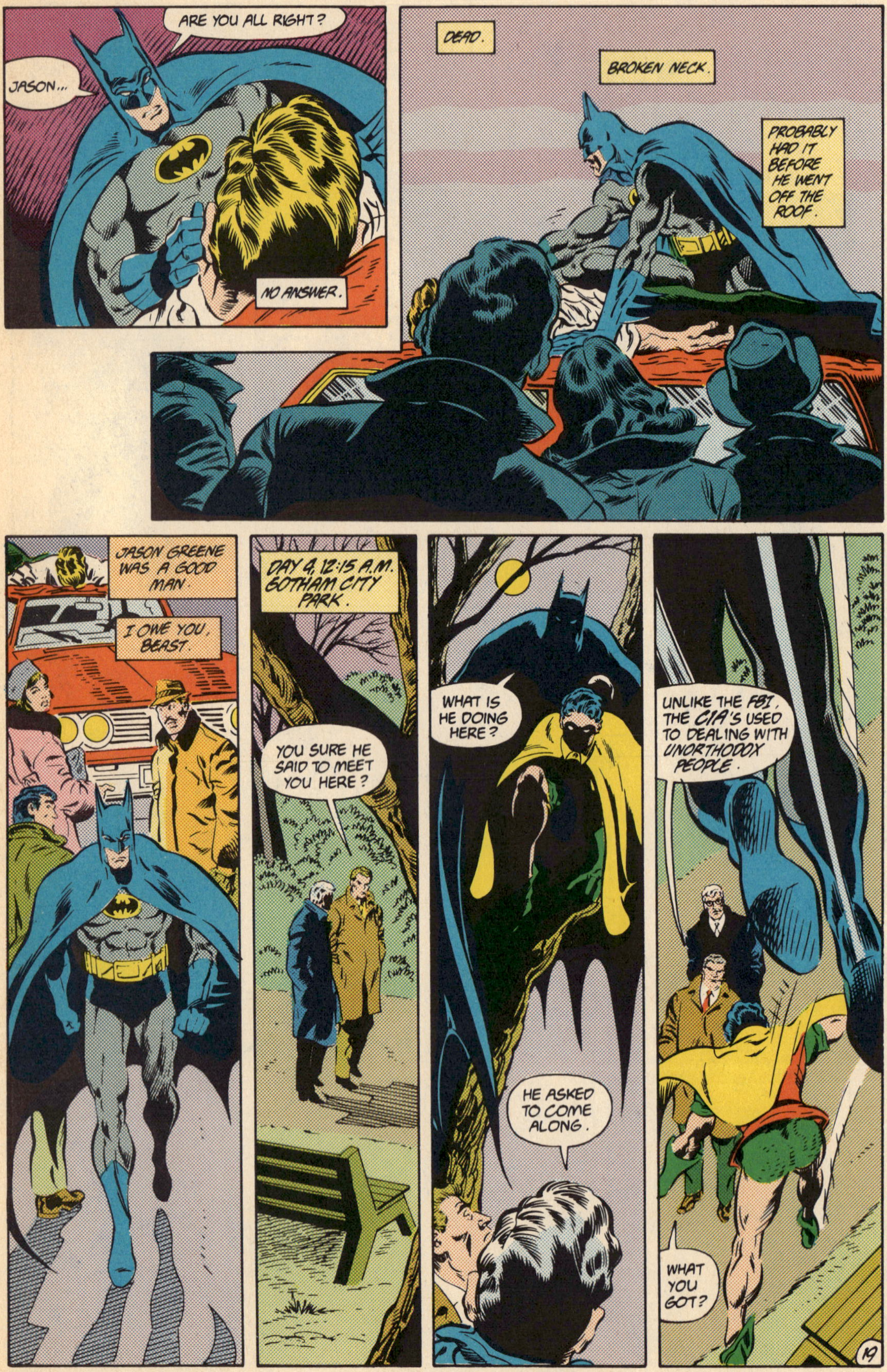
JASON...
ARE YOU ALL RIGHT?
NO ANSWER.
DEAD.
BROKEN NECK.
PROBABLY HAD IT BEFORE HE WENT OFF THE ROOF.
JASON GREENE WAS A GOOD MAN.
I OWE YOU, BEAST.
DAY 4, 12:15 A.M. GOTHAM CITY PARK.
YOU SURE HE SAID TO MEET YOU HERE?
WHAT IS HE DOING HERE?
HE ASKED TO COME ALONG.
UNLIKE THE FBI, THE CIA'S USED TO DEALING WITH UNORTHODOX PEOPLE.
WHAT YOU GOT?
19

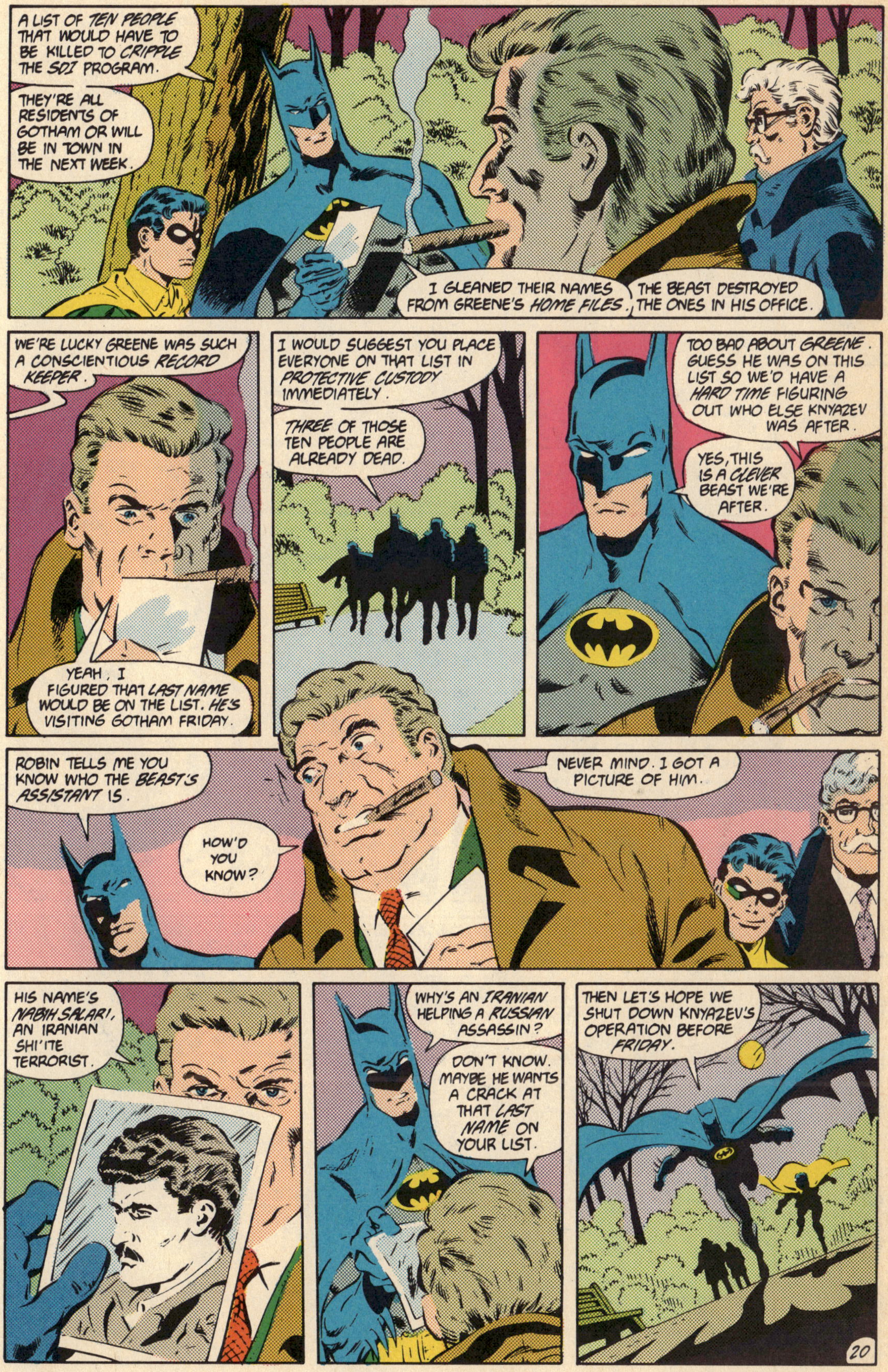
A LIST OF TEN PEOPLE THAT WOULD HAVE TO BE KILLED TO CRIPPLE THE SDI PROGRAM.
THEY'RE ALL RESIDENTS OF GOTHAM OR WILL BE IN TOWN IN THE NEXT WEEK.
I GLEANED THEIR NAMES FROM GREENE'S HOME FILES.
THE BEAST DESTROYED THE ONES IN HIS OFFICE.
WE'RE LUCKY GREENE WAS SUCH A CONSCIENTIOUS RECORD KEEPER.
YEAH. I FIGURED THAT LAST NAME WOULD BE ON THE LIST. HE'S VISITING GOTHAM FRIDAY.
I WOULD SUGGEST YOU PLACE EVERYONE ON THAT LIST IN PROTECTIVE CUSTODY IMMEDIATELY.
THREE OF THOSE TEN PEOPLE ARE ALREADY DEAD.
TOO BAD ABOUT GREENE. GUESS HE WAS ON THIS LIST SO WE'D HAVE A HARD TIME FIGURING OUT WHO ELSE KNYAZEV WAS AFTER.
YES, THIS IS A CLEVER BEAST WE'RE AFTER.
ROBIN TELLS ME YOU KNOW WHO THE BEAST'S ASSISTANT IS.
HOW'D YOU KNOW?
NEVER MIND. I GOT A PICTURE OF HIM.
HIS NAME'S NABIH SALARI, AN IRANIAN SHI'ITE TERRORIST.
WHY'S AN IRANIAN HELPING A RUSSIAN ASSASSIN?
DON'T KNOW. MAYBE HE WANTS A CRACK AT THAT LAST NAME ON YOUR LIST.
THEN LET'S HOPE WE SHUT DOWN KNYAZEV'S OPERATION BEFORE FRIDAY.
20

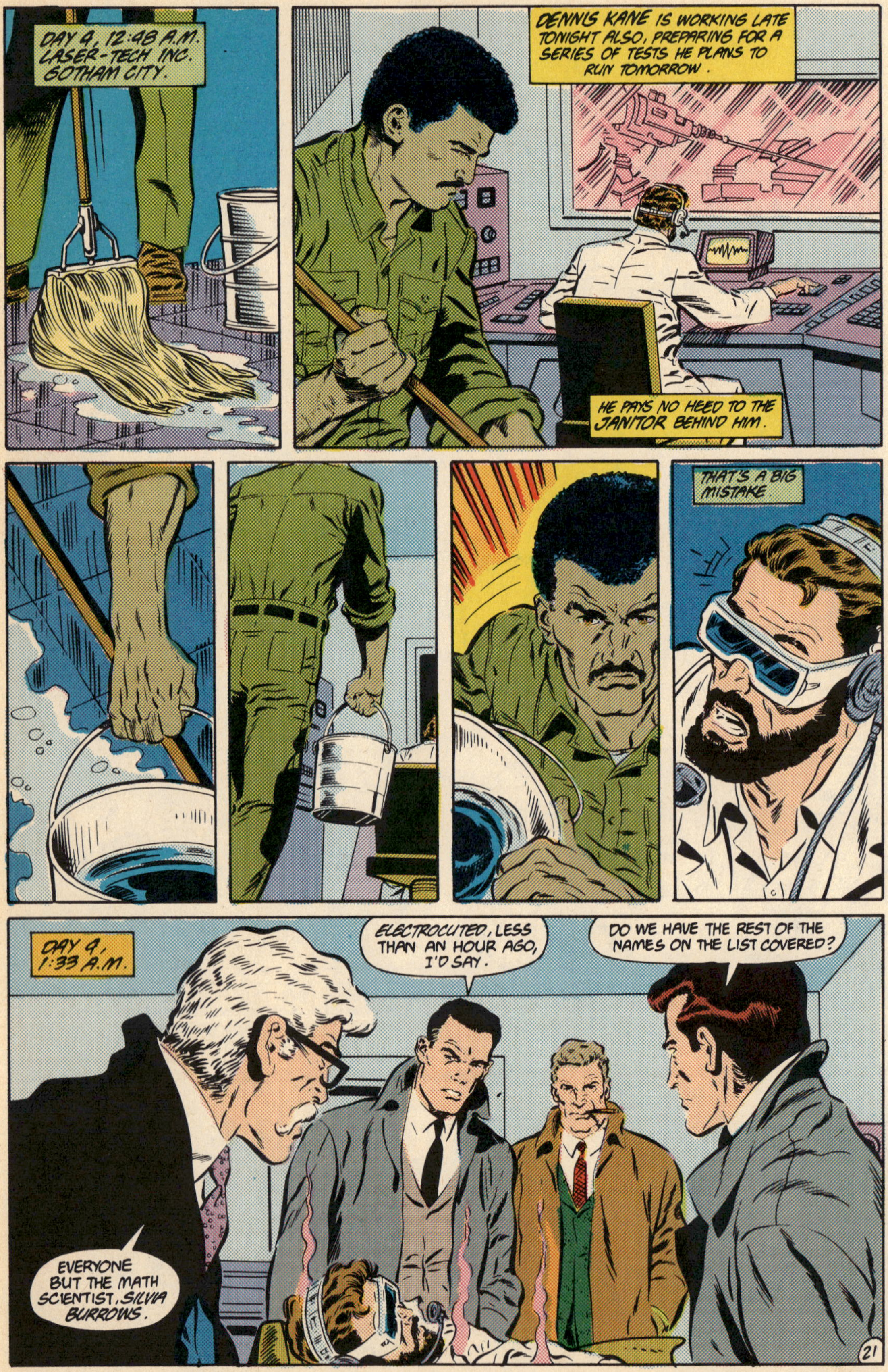
DAY 4, 12:48 A.M. LASER-TECH INC. GOTHAM CITY.
DENNIS KANE IS WORKING LATE TONIGHT ALSO, PREPARING FOR A SERIES OF TESTS HE PLANS TO RUN TOMORROW.
HE PAYS NO HEED TO THE JANITOR BEHIND HIM.
THAT'S A BIG MISTAKE.
DAY 4, 1:33 A.M.
ELECTROCUTED, LESS THAN AN HOUR AGO, I'D SAY.
DO WE HAVE THE REST OF THE NAMES ON THE LIST COVERED?
EVERYONE BUT THE MATH SCIENTIST, SILVIA BURROWS.
21

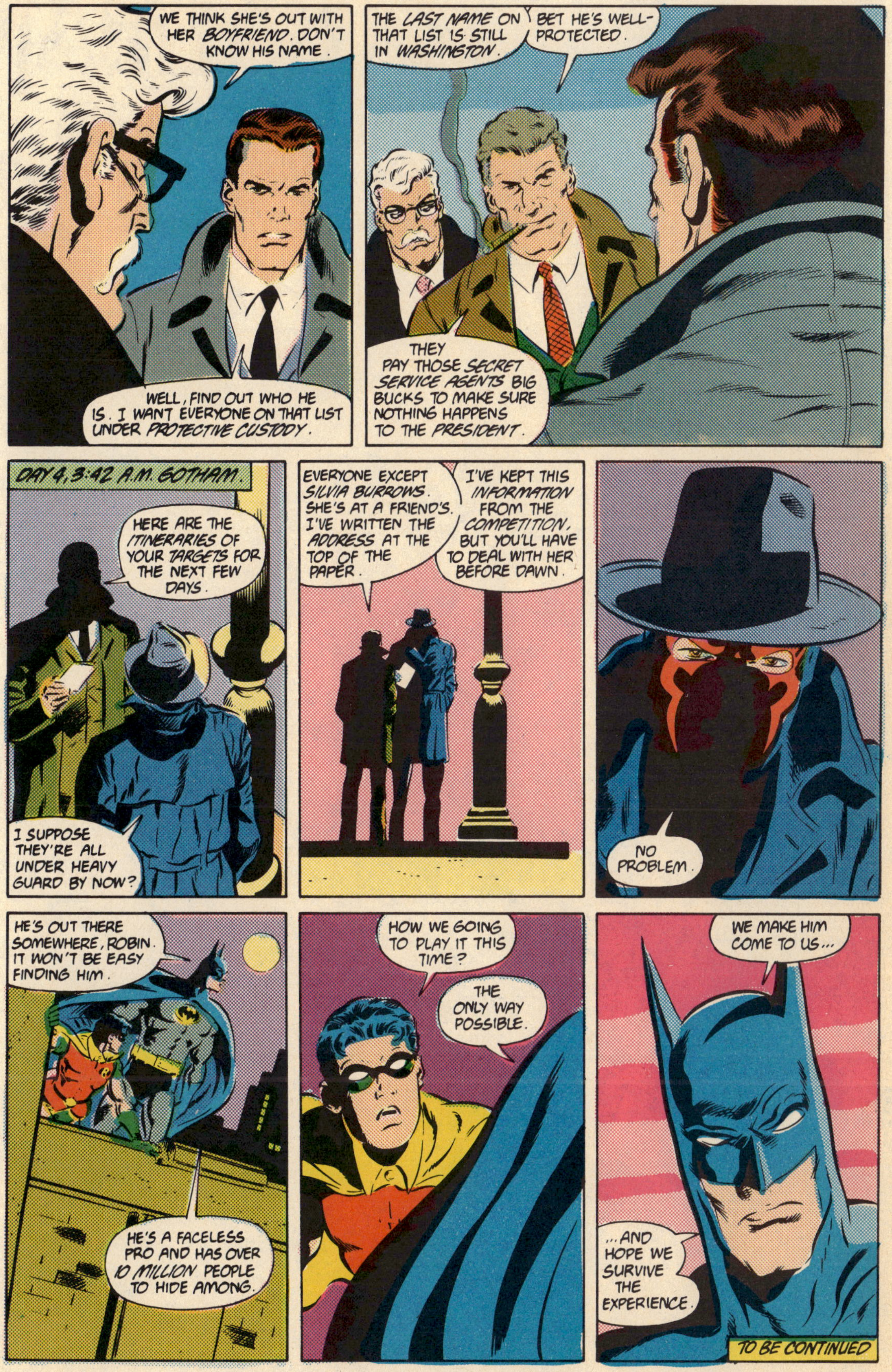
WE THINK SHE'S OUT WITH HER BOYFRIEND. DON'T KNOW HIS NAME.
WELL, FIND OUT WHO HE IS. I WANT EVERYONE ON THAT LIST UNDER PROTECTIVE CUSTODY.
THE LAST NAME ON THAT LIST IS STILL IN WASHINGTON.
BET HE'S WELL-PROTECTED.
THEY PAY THOSE SECRET SERVICE AGENTS BIG BUCKS TO MAKE SURE NOTHING HAPPENS TO THE PRESIDENT.
DAY 4, 3:42 A.M. GOTHAM.
HERE ARE THE ITINERARIES OF YOUR TARGETS FOR THE NEXT FEW DAYS.
I SUPPOSE THEY'RE ALL UNDER HEAVY GUARD BY NOW?
EVERYONE EXCEPT SILVIA BURROWS. SHE'S AT A FRIEND'S. I'VE WRITTEN THE ADDRESS AT THE TOP OF THE PAPER.
I'VE KEPT THIS INFORMATION FROM THE COMPETITION, BUT YOU'LL HAVE TO DEAL WITH HER BEFORE DAWN.
NO PROBLEM.
HE'S OUT THERE SOMEWHERE, ROBIN. IT WON'T BE EASY FINDING HIM.
HE'S A FACELESS PRO AND HAS OVER 10 MILLION PEOPLE TO HIDE AMONG.
HOW WE GOING TO PLAY IT THIS TIME?
THE ONLY WAY POSSIBLE.
WE MAKE HIM COME TO US...
...AND HOPE WE SURVIVE THE EXPERIENCE.
TO BE CONTINUED

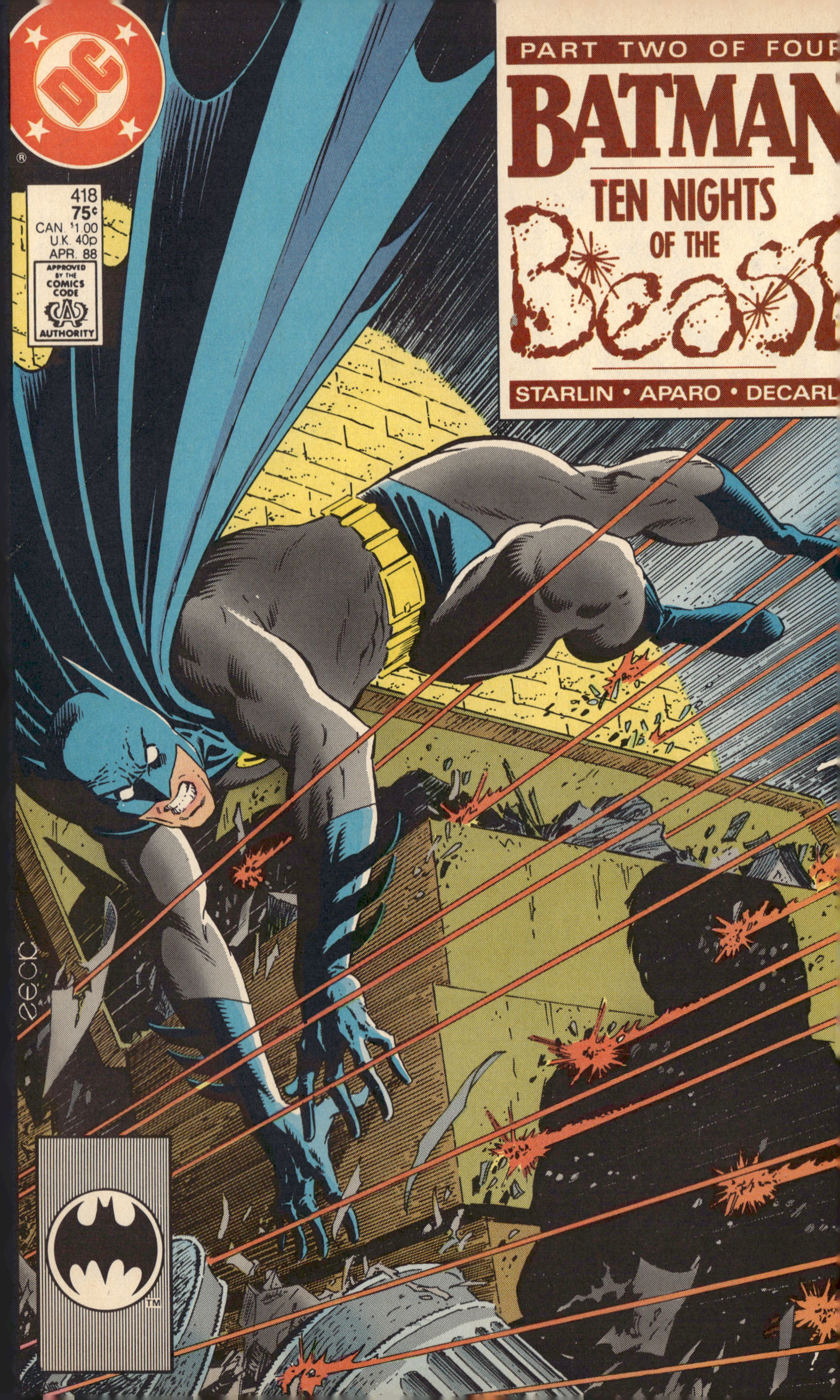
DC
418
75¢
CAN. $1.00
U.K. 40p
APR. 88
APPROVED BY THE COMICS CODE AUTHORITY
PART TWO OF FOUR
BATMAN
TEN NIGHTS OF THE BEAST
STARLIN • APARO • DECARLO
ZECK

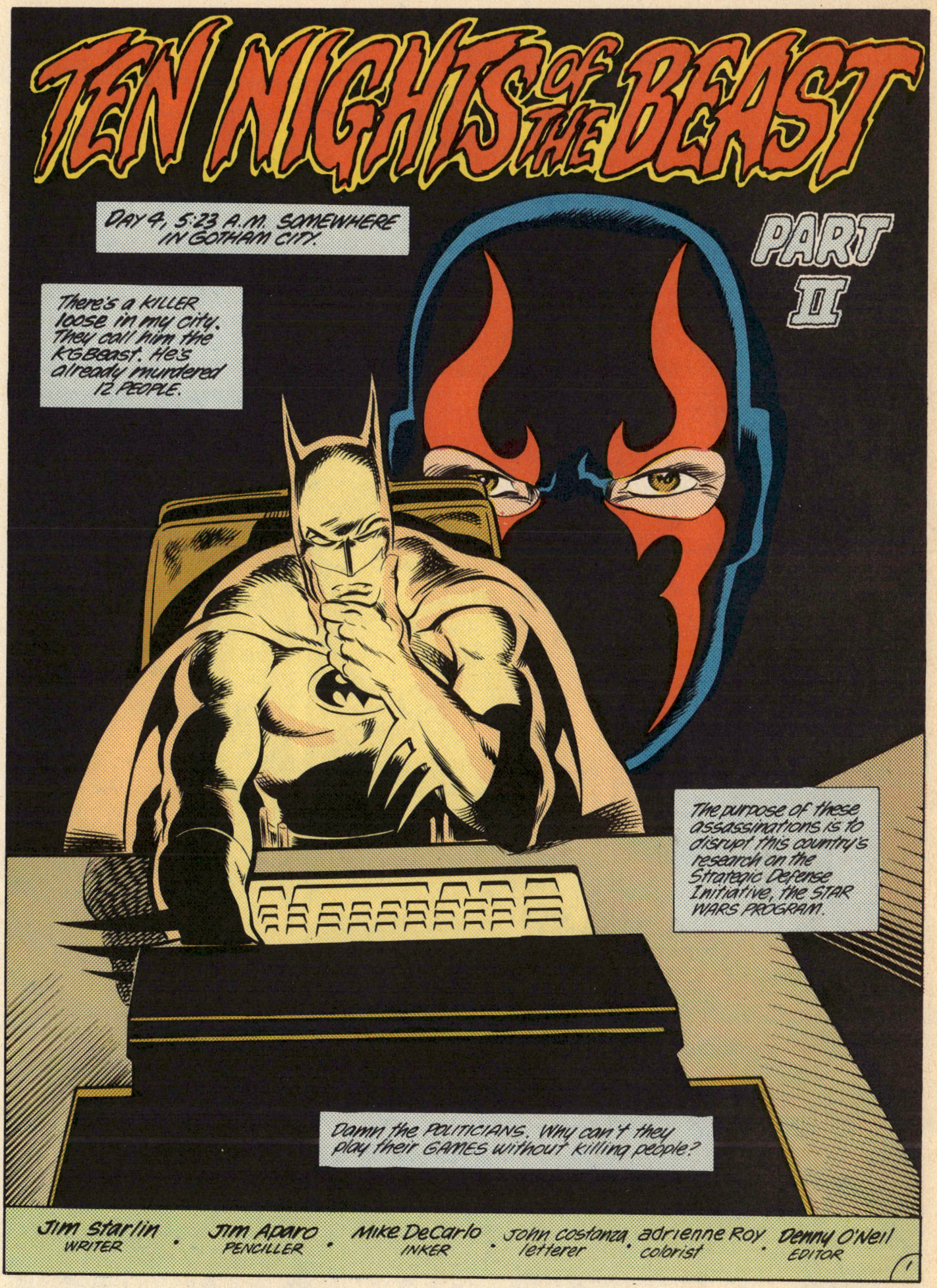

TEN NIGHTS OF THE BEAST
DAY 4, 5:23 A.M. SOMEWHERE IN GOTHAM CITY.
PART II
There's a KILLER loose in my city. They call him the KGBeast. He's already murdered 12 PEOPLE.
The purpose of these assassinations is to disrupt this country's research on the Strategic Defense Initiative, the STAR WARS PROGRAM.
Damn the POLITICIANS. Why can't they play their GAMES without killing people?
Jim Starlin WRITER • Jim Aparo PENCILLER • Mike DeCarlo INKER • John Costanza letterer • adrienne Roy colorist • Denny O'Neil EDITOR
1

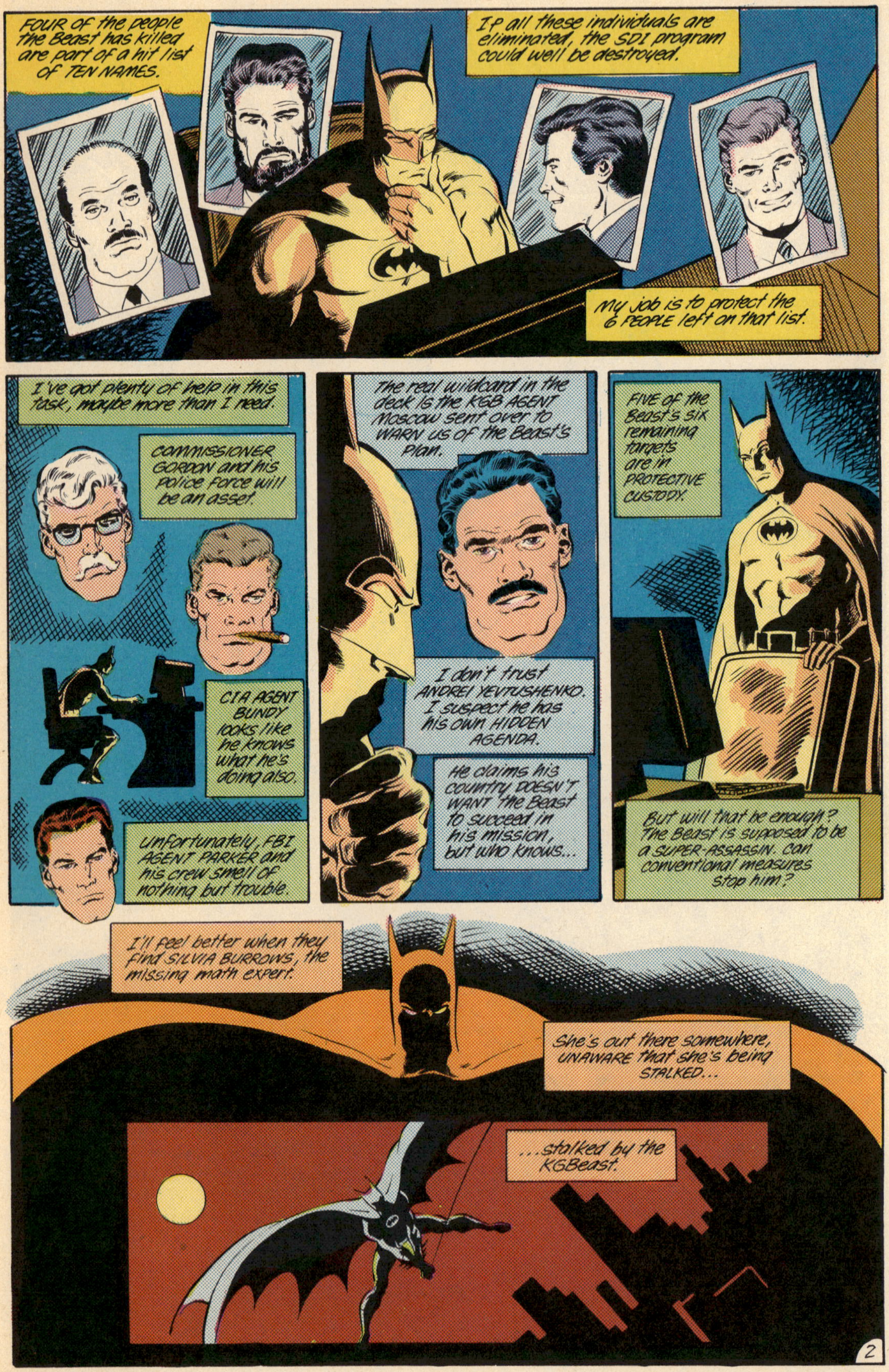
FOUR OF the people the Beast has killed are part of a hit list of TEN NAMES.
IF all these individuals are eliminated, the SDI program could well be destroyed.
My job is to protect the 6 PEOPLE left on that list.
I've got plenty of help in this task, maybe more than I need.
COMMISSIONER GORDON and his police force will be an asset.
C.I.A. AGENT BUNDY looks like he knows what he's doing also.
Unfortunately, FBI AGENT PARKER and his crew smell of nothing but trouble.
The real wildcard in the deck is the KGB AGENT Moscow sent over to WARN us of the Beast's plan.
I don't trust ANDREI YEVTUSHENKO. I suspect he has his own HIDDEN AGENDA.
He claims his country DOESN'T WANT the Beast to succeed in his mission, but who knows...
FIVE of the Beast's six remaining targets are in PROTECTIVE CUSTODY.
But will that be enough? The Beast is supposed to be a SUPER-ASSASSIN. Can conventional measures stop him?
I'll feel better when they find SILVIA BURROWS, the missing math expert.
She's out there somewhere, UNAWARE that she's being STALKED...
...stalked by the KGBeast.
2

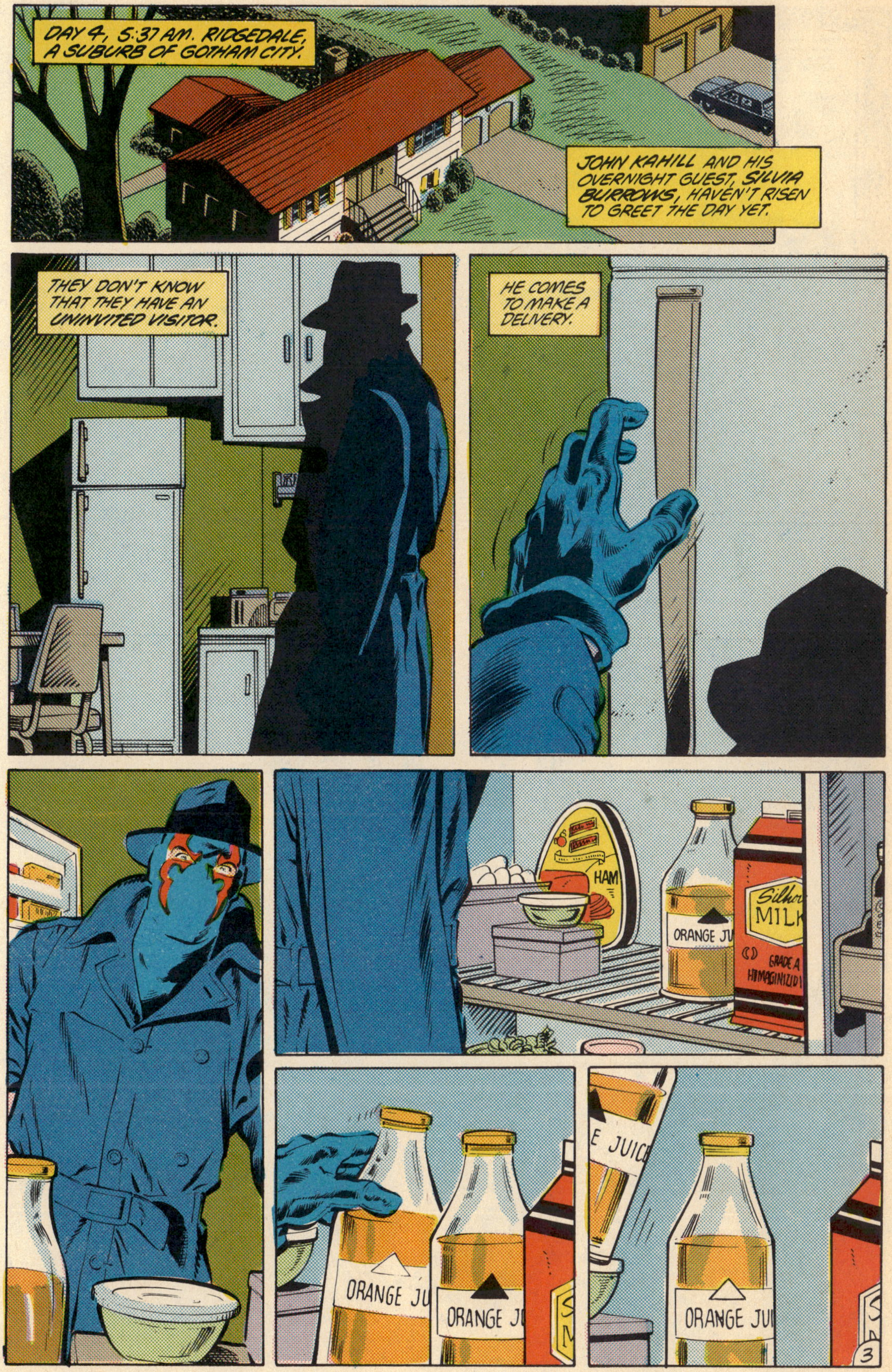

DAY 4, 5:37 AM. RIDGEDALE, A SUBURB OF GOTHAM CITY.
JOHN KAHILL AND HIS OVERNIGHT GUEST, SILVIA BURROWS, HAVEN'T RISEN TO GREET THE DAY YET.
THEY DON'T KNOW THAT THEY HAVE AN UNINVITED VISITOR.
HE COMES TO MAKE A DELIVERY.
HAM
ORANGE JU
MILK
GRADE A
ORANGE JU
ORANGE JU
E JUIC
ORANGE JU

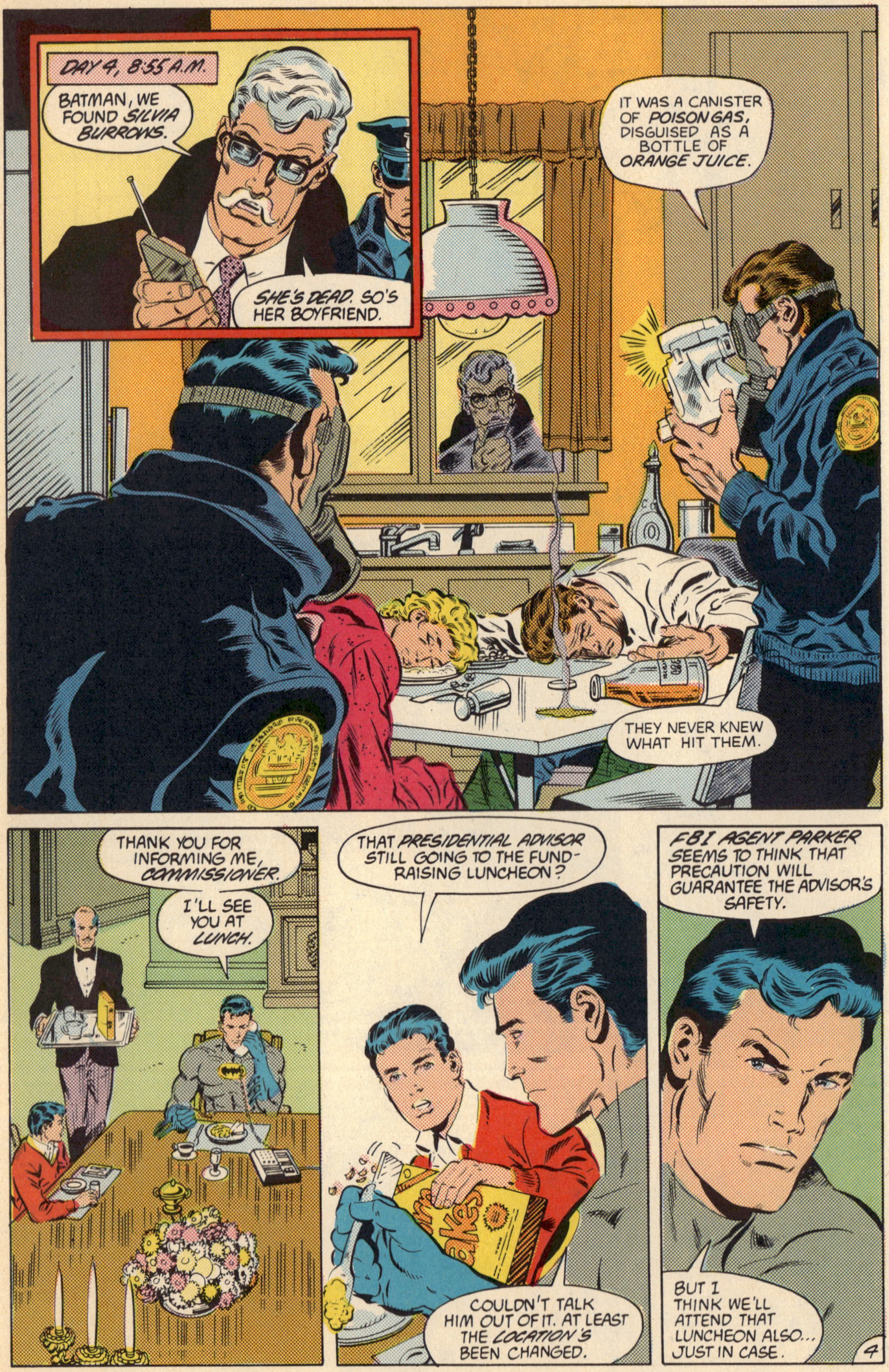

DAY 4, 8:55 A.M.
BATMAN, WE FOUND SILVIA BURROWS.
SHE'S DEAD. SO'S HER BOYFRIEND.
IT WAS A CANISTER OF POISON GAS, DISGUISED AS A BOTTLE OF ORANGE JUICE.
THEY NEVER KNEW WHAT HIT THEM.
THANK YOU FOR INFORMING ME, COMMISSIONER.
I'LL SEE YOU AT LUNCH.
THAT PRESIDENTIAL ADVISOR STILL GOING TO THE FUND-RAISING LUNCHEON?
COULDN'T TALK HIM OUT OF IT. AT LEAST THE LOCATION'S BEEN CHANGED.
FBI AGENT PARKER SEEMS TO THINK THAT PRECAUTION WILL GUARANTEE THE ADVISOR'S SAFETY.
BUT I THINK WE'LL ATTEND THAT LUNCHEON ALSO... JUST IN CASE.
4

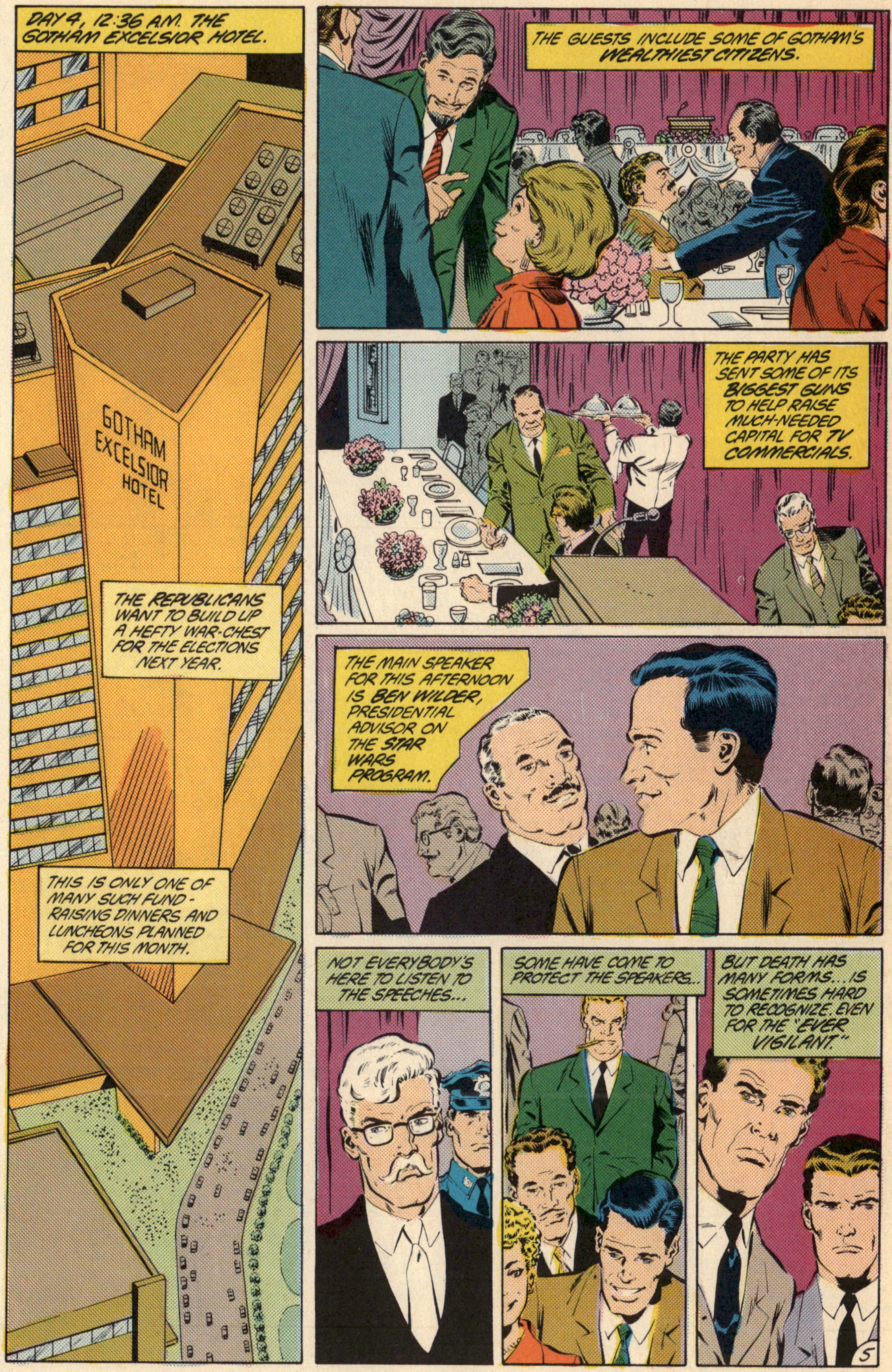

DAY 4, 12:36 A.M. THE GOTHAM EXCELSIOR HOTEL.
GOTHAM EXCELSIOR HOTEL
THE REPUBLICANS WANT TO BUILD UP A HEFTY WAR-CHEST FOR THE ELECTIONS NEXT YEAR.
THIS IS ONLY ONE OF MANY SUCH FUND-RAISING DINNERS AND LUNCHEONS PLANNED FOR THIS MONTH.
THE GUESTS INCLUDE SOME OF GOTHAM'S WEALTHIEST CITIZENS.
THE PARTY HAS SENT SOME OF ITS BIGGEST GUNS TO HELP RAISE MUCH-NEEDED CAPITAL FOR TV COMMERCIALS.
THE MAIN SPEAKER FOR THIS AFTERNOON IS BEN WILDER, PRESIDENTIAL ADVISOR ON THE STAR WARS PROGRAM.
NOT EVERYBODY'S HERE TO LISTEN TO THE SPEECHES...
SOME HAVE COME TO PROTECT THE SPEAKERS...
BUT DEATH HAS MANY FORMS... IS SOMETIMES HARD TO RECOGNIZE. EVEN FOR THE "EVER VIGILANT."
5

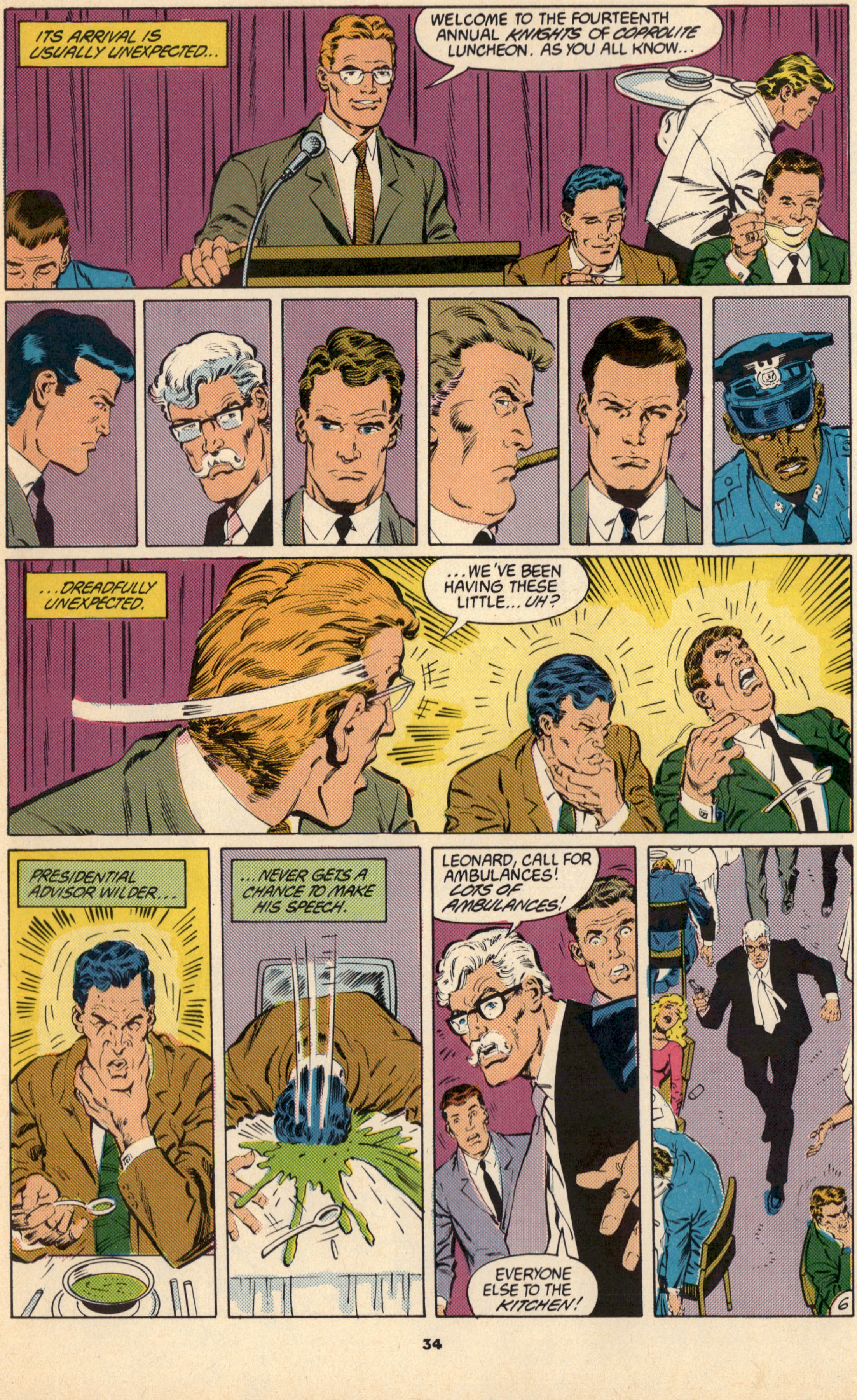
ITS ARRIVAL IS USUALLY UNEXPECTED...
WELCOME TO THE FOURTEENTH ANNUAL KNIGHTS OF COPROLITE LUNCHEON. AS YOU ALL KNOW...
...DREADFULLY UNEXPECTED.
...WE'VE BEEN HAVING THESE LITTLE... UH?
PRESIDENTIAL ADVISOR WILDER...
...NEVER GETS A CHANCE TO MAKE HIS SPEECH.
LEONARD, CALL FOR AMBULANCES! LOTS OF AMBULANCES!
EVERYONE ELSE TO THE KITCHEN!
6

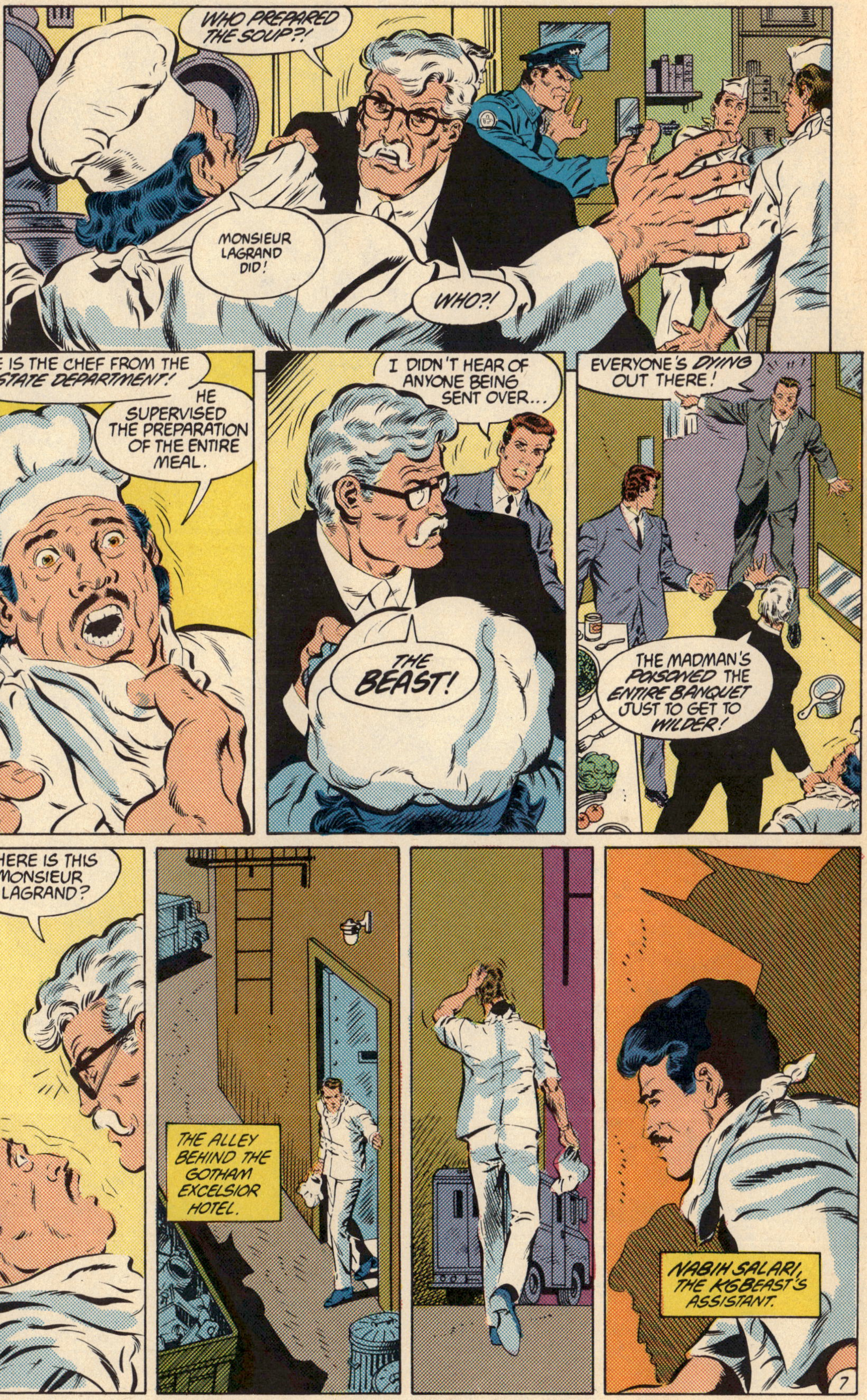

WHO PREPARED THE SOUP?!
MONSIEUR LAGRAND DID!
WHO?!
HE IS THE CHEF FROM THE STATE DEPARTMENT!
HE SUPERVISED THE PREPARATION OF THE ENTIRE MEAL.
I DIDN'T HEAR OF ANYONE BEING SENT OVER...
THE BEAST!
EVERYONE'S DYING OUT THERE!
THE MADMAN'S POISONED THE ENTIRE BANQUET JUST TO GET TO WILDER!
WHERE IS THIS MONSIEUR LAGRAND?
THE ALLEY BEHIND THE GOTHAM EXCELSIOR HOTEL.
NABIH SALARI, THE KGBEAST'S ASSISTANT.
7

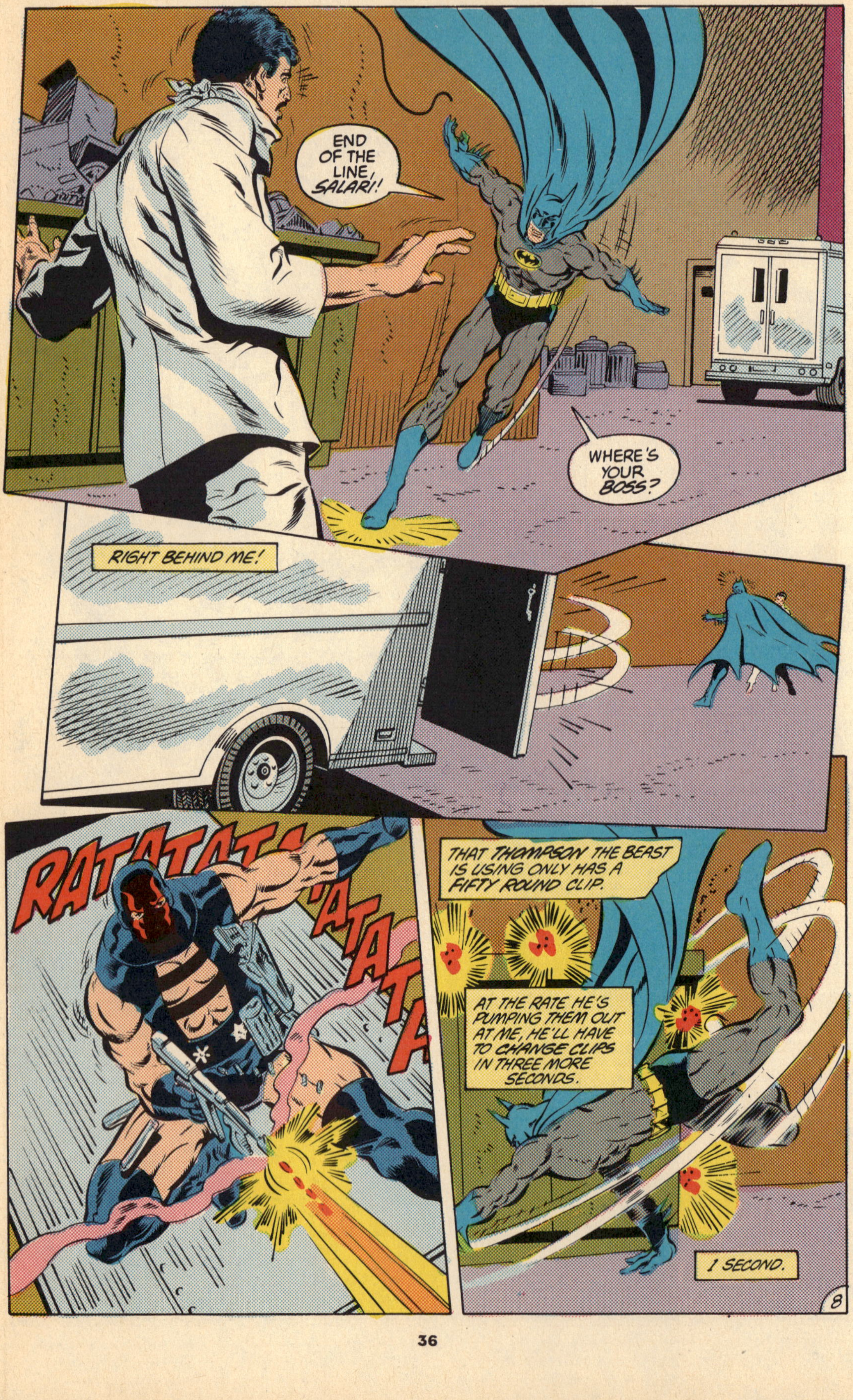

END OF THE LINE, SALARI!
WHERE'S YOUR BOSS?
RIGHT BEHIND ME!
RATATATATATATATA
THAT THOMPSON THE BEAST IS USING ONLY HAS A FIFTY ROUND CLIP.
AT THE RATE HE'S PUMPING THEM OUT AT ME, HE'LL HAVE TO CHANGE CLIPS IN THREE MORE SECONDS.
1 SECOND.
8

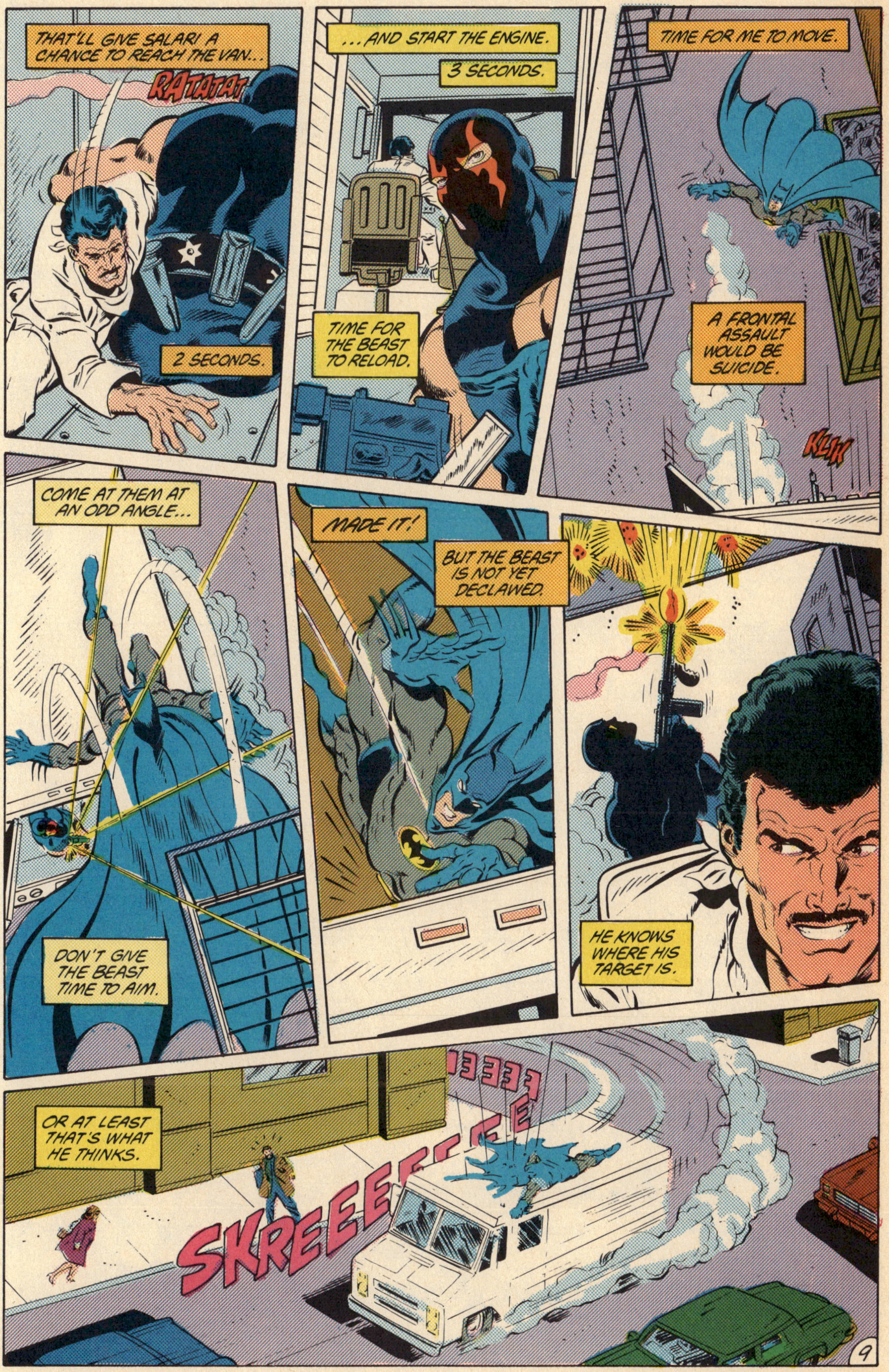
THAT'LL GIVE SALARI A CHANCE TO REACH THE VAN...
RATATAT
2 SECONDS.
...AND START THE ENGINE.
3 SECONDS.
TIME FOR THE BEAST TO RELOAD.
TIME FOR ME TO MOVE.
A FRONTAL ASSAULT WOULD BE SUICIDE.
KLIK
COME AT THEM AT AN ODD ANGLE...
DON'T GIVE THE BEAST TIME TO AIM.
MADE IT!
BUT THE BEAST IS NOT YET DECLAWED.
HE KNOWS WHERE HIS TARGET IS.
OR AT LEAST THAT'S WHAT HE THINKS.
SKREEEEEEEE
9

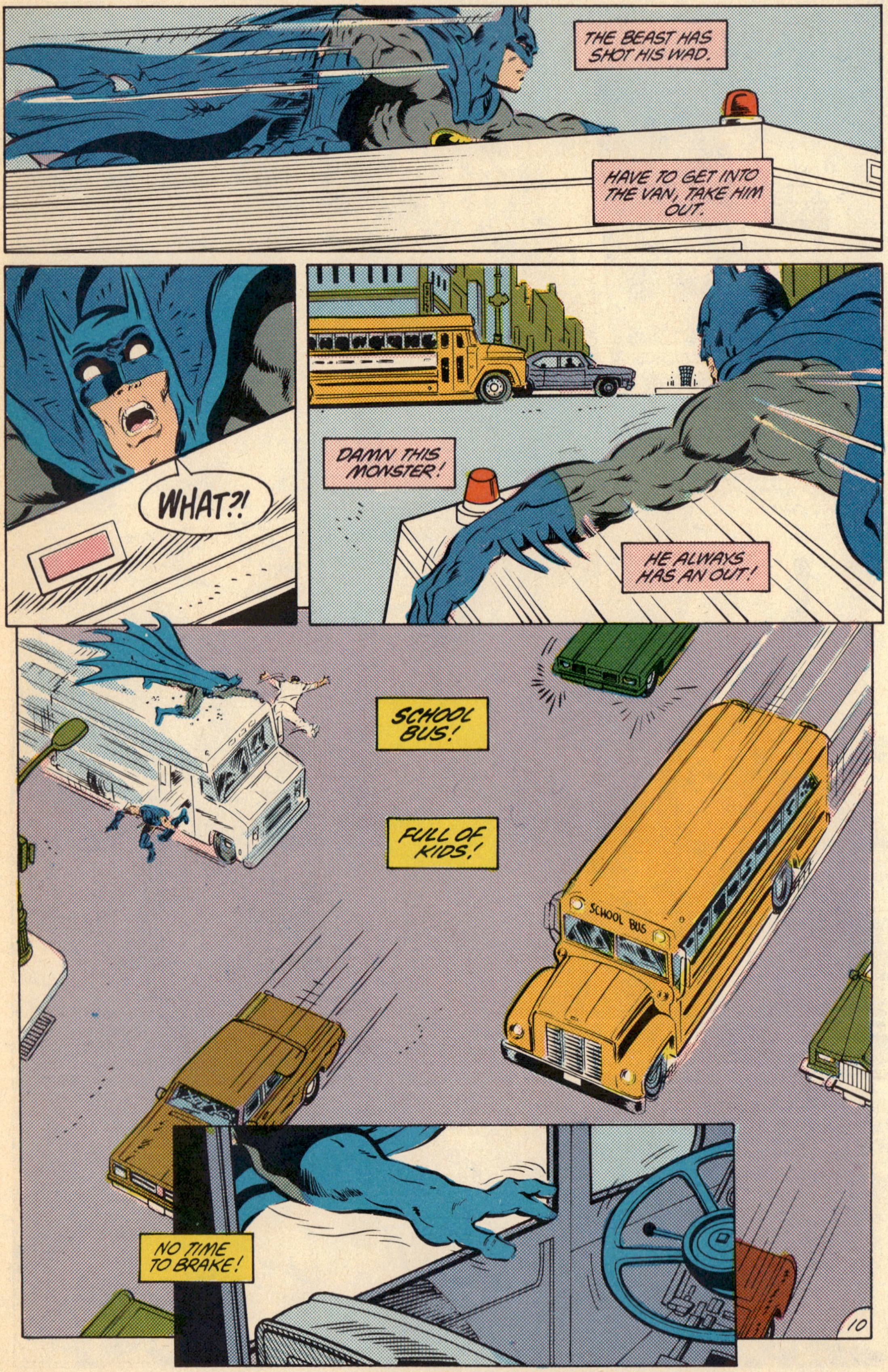
THE BEAST HAS SHOT HIS WAD.
HAVE TO GET INTO THE VAN, TAKE HIM OUT.
WHAT?!
DAMN THIS MONSTER!
HE ALWAYS HAS AN OUT!
SCHOOL BUS!
FULL OF KIDS!
SCHOOL BUS
NO TIME TO BRAKE!
10

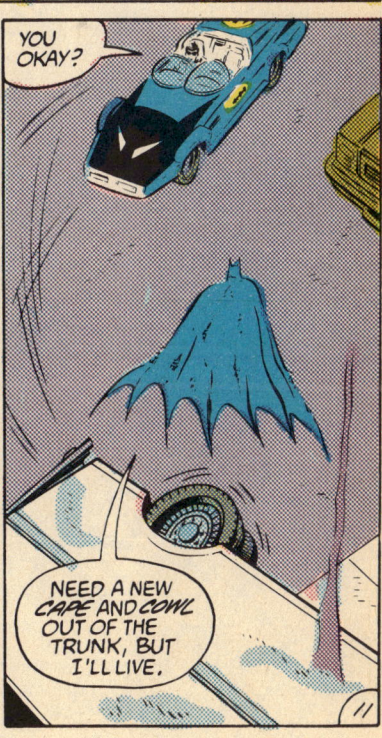

| GOT TO YANK THE WHEEL TO THE LEFT.

HARD! |

CLOSE.

SKREEEE

TOO CLOSE.

IT ONLY TOOK *SECONDS* TO SAVE THOSE CHILDREN.

MORE THAN *ENOUGH* TIME FOR THE BEAST AND HIS PAL TO *DISAPPEAR*.

YOU OKAY?

NEED A NEW *CAPE* AND *COWL* OUT OF THE TRUNK, BUT I'LL LIVE.

"THAT'S MORE THAN ANY OF THOSE PEOPLE AT THE LUNCHEON CAN SAY."

"I HEARD OVER THE POLICE BAND THEY ALL DIED."

"HOW MANY WERE THERE?"

"40 COUPLES... 80 PEOPLE."

"HE DIDN'T HAVE TO MURDER ALL THOSE PEOPLE TO GET TO WILDER."

"THAT SLAUGHTER WAS THE BEAST'S WAY OF MAKING A STATEMENT."

"HE'S TELLING US THAT NOTHING WILL STAND IN THE WAY OF HIM ACCOMPLISHING HIS MISSION."

"HE'S DECLARED WAR ON GOTHAM."

"HE MUST HAVE A GREAT INTELLIGENCE-GATHERING SETUP."

"HOW'D HE FIND OUT ABOUT THE CHANGE IN THE LUNCHEON'S LOCATION, IN TIME TO GET HIS MAN SET UP IN THE KITCHEN?"

"ALL THE GUESTS WERE LIMOED FROM THE LUNCH'S ORIGINAL LOCATION."

"ONLY THE SECURITY FORCE KNEW WHERE THE NEW SITE WOULD BE BEFOREHAND."

"THEN THAT MEANS..."

"...THE BEAST HAS A SECRET AGENT WITHIN OUR CAMP."

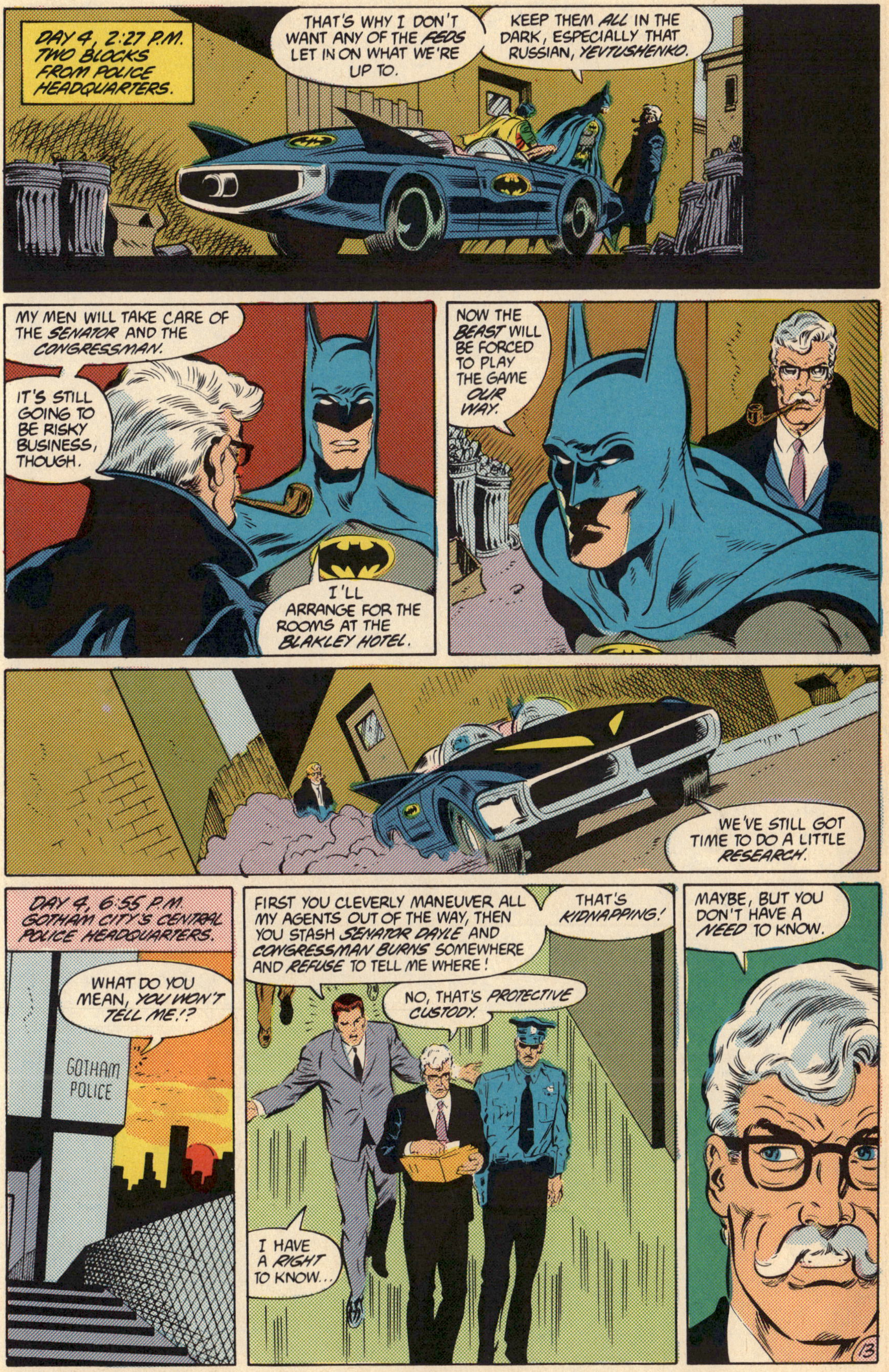
DAY 4, 2:27 P.M. TWO BLOCKS FROM POLICE HEADQUARTERS.
THAT'S WHY I DON'T WANT ANY OF THE FEDS LET IN ON WHAT WE'RE UP TO.
KEEP THEM ALL IN THE DARK, ESPECIALLY THAT RUSSIAN, YEVTUSHENKO.
MY MEN WILL TAKE CARE OF THE SENATOR AND THE CONGRESSMAN.
IT'S STILL GOING TO BE RISKY BUSINESS, THOUGH.
I'LL ARRANGE FOR THE ROOMS AT THE BLAKLEY HOTEL.
NOW THE BEAST WILL BE FORCED TO PLAY THE GAME OUR WAY.
WE'VE STILL GOT TIME TO DO A LITTLE RESEARCH.
DAY 4, 6:55 P.M. GOTHAM CITY'S CENTRAL POLICE HEADQUARTERS.
WHAT DO YOU MEAN, YOU WON'T TELL ME!?
GOTHAM POLICE
FIRST YOU CLEVERLY MANEUVER ALL MY AGENTS OUT OF THE WAY, THEN YOU STASH SENATOR DAYLE AND CONGRESSMAN BURNS SOMEWHERE AND REFUSE TO TELL ME WHERE!
THAT'S KIDNAPPING!
NO, THAT'S PROTECTIVE CUSTODY.
I HAVE A RIGHT TO KNOW...
MAYBE, BUT YOU DON'T HAVE A NEED TO KNOW.
13

— THINK YOU'RE PRETTY FUNNY, DON'T YOU?

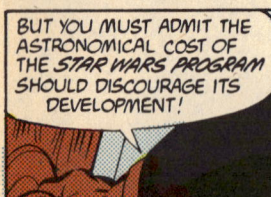

— YOU'RE GOING TO END UP WITH YOUR *TAIL* IN A *GRINDER* ON THIS ONE, GORDON!

— WHERE'S *BUNDY*?
— IN YOUR OFFICE WITH THE RUSSIAN. I THINK THEY'RE HAVING A *DEBATE*.

— BUT YOU MUST ADMIT THE ASTRONOMICAL COST OF THE *STAR WARS* PROGRAM SHOULD DISCOURAGE ITS DEVELOPMENT!
— SUCH A NEW *ARMS RACE* WILL *BANKRUPT* BOTH OUR COUNTRIES!
— THERE ARE BETTER USES FOR THIS MONEY!

— BUT IT MIGHT BE THE ONLY WAY TO STOP THE *NUCLEAR BUILD-UP*! THERE ARE POWERFUL *VESTED INTERESTS*, IN BOTH OUR SOCIETIES, THAT WANT THE PROLIFERATION OF *ATOMIC WARHEADS* TO CONTINUE!
— MAKING NUCLEAR WEAPONS *OBSOLETE* MAY BE OUR ONLY OUT!

— *NONE* OF THE *EXPERTS* WILL GUARANTEE THAT *SDI* WILL ACCOMPLISH THAT! STAR WARS MAY BE A *FALSE HOPE*, THAT COULD ACTUALLY TRIGGER *ATOMIC ANNIHILATION*! DISARMAMENT IS THE ONLY ANSWER!

— IF YOU WANT DISARMAMENT, YOU HAVE TO ALLOW *ON SITE VERIFICATION*!
— AND ALLOW YOUR *CIA AGENTS* FREE REIGN ALL OVER OUR COUNTRY? *NEVER*!

— YEAH, YEAH, IT'S THE SAME OLD STORY...
— YES...THE SAME OLD STORY...

DAY 4, 7:15 P.M.
— THEY'VE GOT THE SENATOR STASHED AT THE *REGENCY HOTEL*, ROOM 714.

14

42

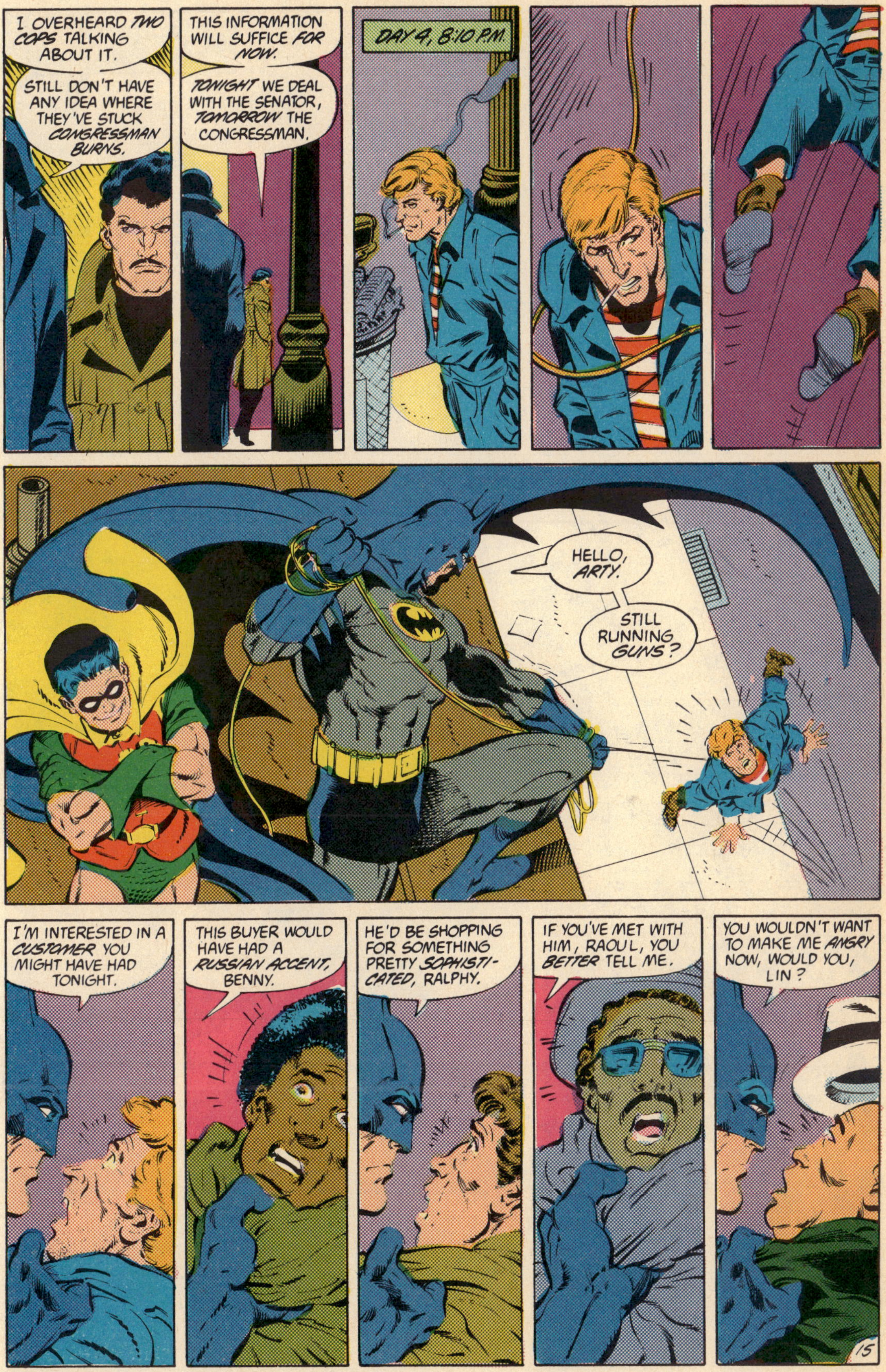
I OVERHEARD TWO COPS TALKING ABOUT IT.
STILL DON'T HAVE ANY IDEA WHERE THEY'VE STUCK CONGRESSMAN BURNS.
THIS INFORMATION WILL SUFFICE FOR NOW.
TONIGHT WE DEAL WITH THE SENATOR, TOMORROW THE CONGRESSMAN.
DAY 4, 8:10 P.M.
HELLO, ARTY.
STILL RUNNING GUNS?
I'M INTERESTED IN A CUSTOMER YOU MIGHT HAVE HAD TONIGHT.
THIS BUYER WOULD HAVE HAD A RUSSIAN ACCENT, BENNY.
HE'D BE SHOPPING FOR SOMETHING PRETTY SOPHISTI-CATED, RALPHY.
IF YOU'VE MET WITH HIM, RAOUL, YOU BETTER TELL ME.
YOU WOULDN'T WANT TO MAKE ME ANGRY NOW, WOULD YOU, LIN?
15

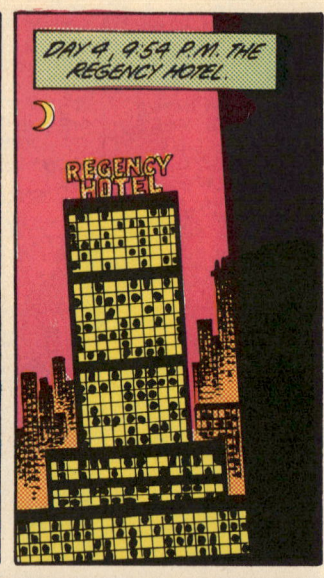

44

Panel 1: "I...I sold him a bazooka...one rocket... Please...don't drop me..."

Panel 2: "Now we know what the BEAST will be coming at us with. A LITTLE RESEARCH does make the job a lot easier, doesn't it?"

Panel 3: DAY 4, 9:54 P.M. THE REGENCY HOTEL

Panel 4: ROOM 714

SENATOR DAYLE'S DISTINCTIVE SILVER MANE MAKES HIM EASY TO SPOT.

ONLY ONE PROBLEM: IT'S ALL TOO EASY.

Panel 5: THE WHOLE SETUP IS WRONG. ONLY ONE MAN IN THE ROOM WITH THE TARGET, THE CURTAINS LEFT OPEN.

IT'S AS IF THEY'RE INVITING HIM TO KILL SENATOR DAYLE. THE BEAST SUSPECTS A TRAP.

Panel 6: BUT HE'S COME TOO FAR TO BACK OFF NOW.

IF HE PASSES UP THIS OPPORTUNITY, HE MAY NOT GET ANOTHER CRACK AT THE MAN.

BESIDES, EVEN IF IT IS A TRAP, HE HAS SEVERAL ESCAPE ROUTES MAPPED OUT FOR JUST SUCH AN EVENTUALITY.

16

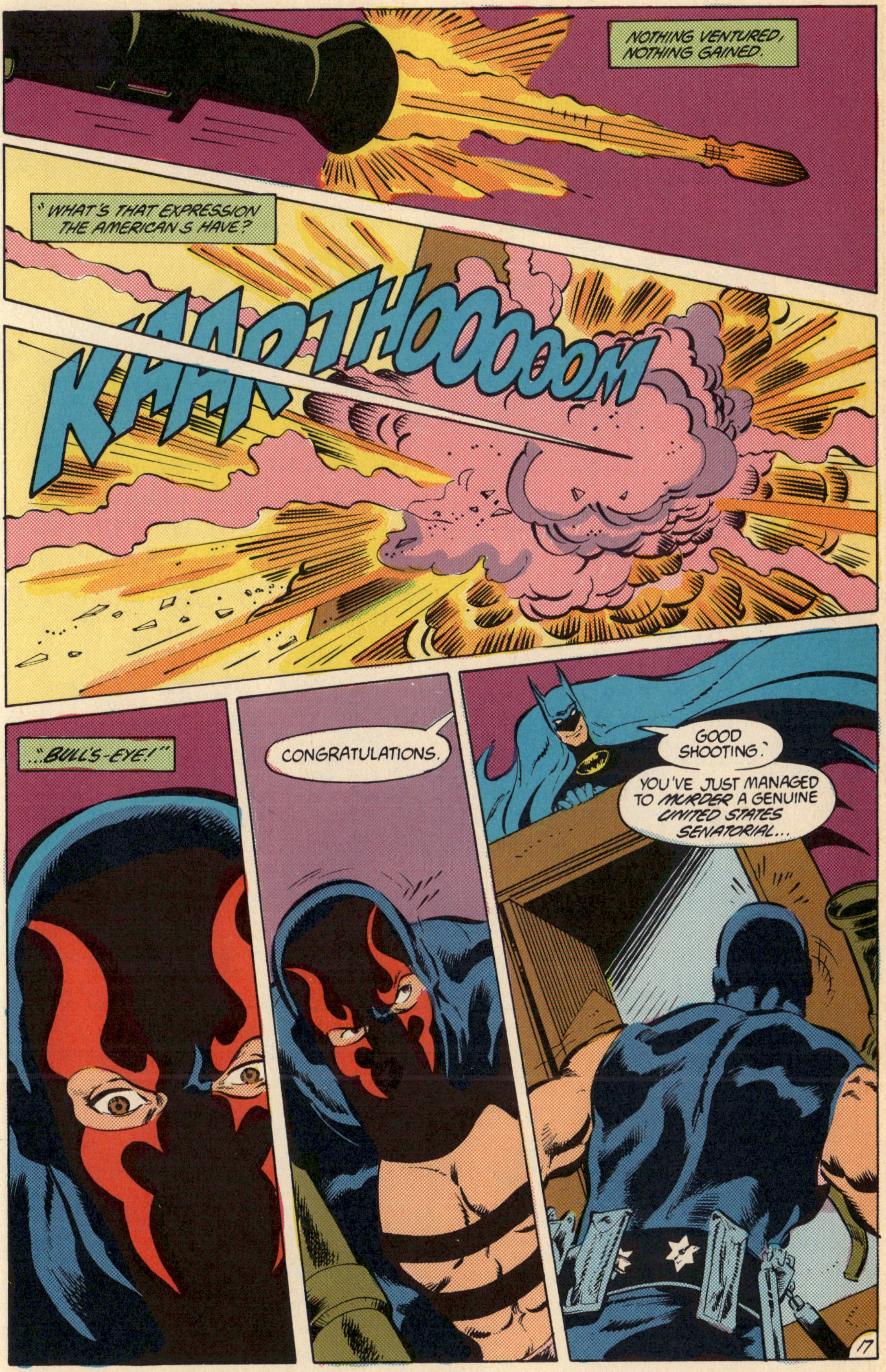
NOTHING VENTURED, NOTHING GAINED.
"WHAT'S THAT EXPRESSION THE AMERICAN'S HAVE?
KAAR THOOOOOOM
..."BULL'S-EYE!"
CONGRATULATIONS.
GOOD SHOOTING.
YOU'VE JUST MANAGED TO MURDER A GENUINE UNITED STATES SENATORIAL...
17

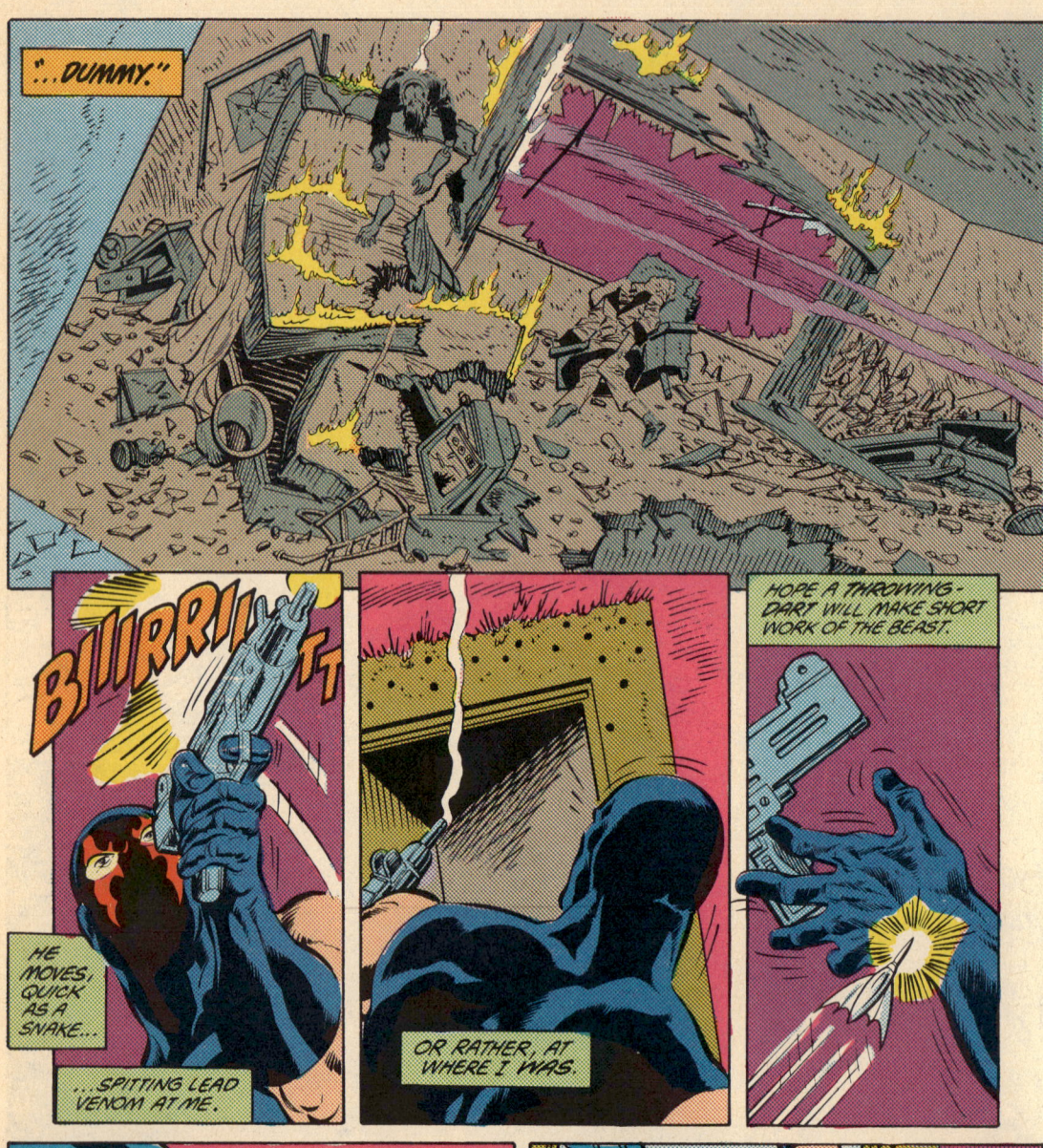

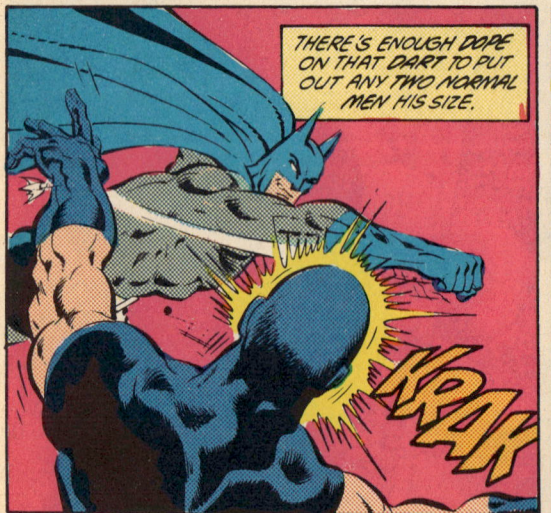

"...DUMMY."

He moves, quick as a snake...

...spitting lead venom at me.

Or rather, at where I was.

Hope a throwing-dart will make short work of the beast.

There's enough dope on that dart to put out any two normal men his size.

KRAK

Unfortunately, the KGBeast is no ordinary man.

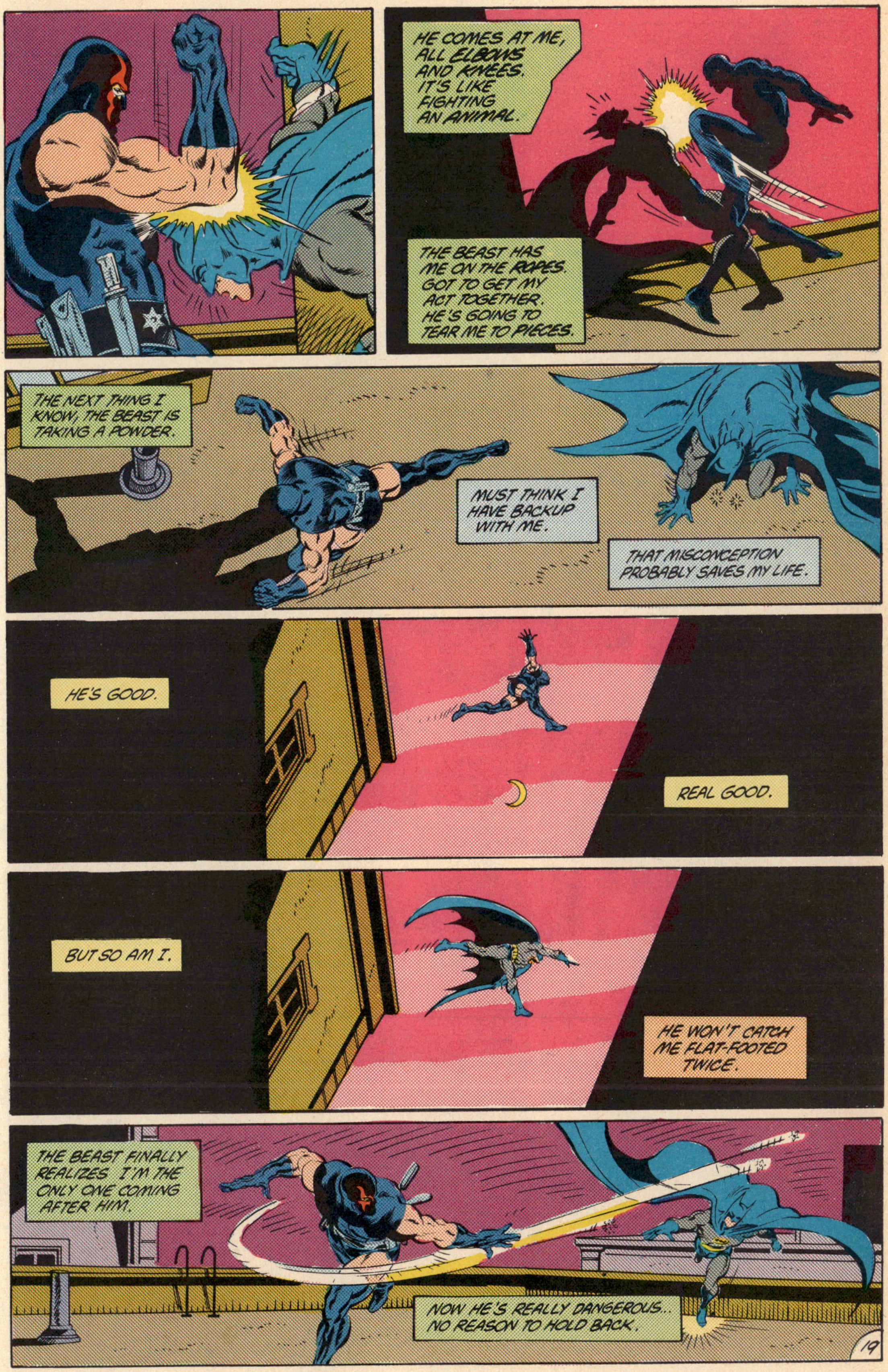
HE COMES AT ME, ALL ELBOWS AND KNEES. IT'S LIKE FIGHTING AN ANIMAL.
THE BEAST HAS ME ON THE ROPES. GOT TO GET MY ACT TOGETHER. HE'S GOING TO TEAR ME TO PIECES.
THE NEXT THING I KNOW, THE BEAST IS TAKING A POWDER.
MUST THINK I HAVE BACKUP WITH ME.
THAT MISCONCEPTION PROBABLY SAVES MY LIFE.
HE'S GOOD.
REAL GOOD.
BUT SO AM I.
HE WON'T CATCH ME FLAT-FOOTED TWICE.
THE BEAST FINALLY REALIZES I'M THE ONLY ONE COMING AFTER HIM.
NOW HE'S REALLY DANGEROUS... NO REASON TO HOLD BACK.
19

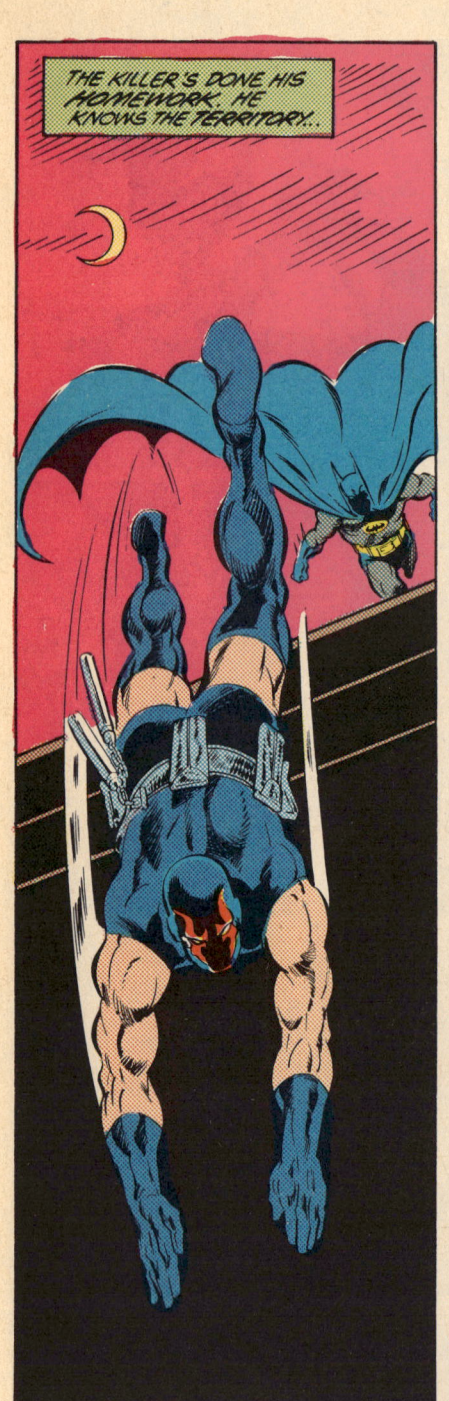

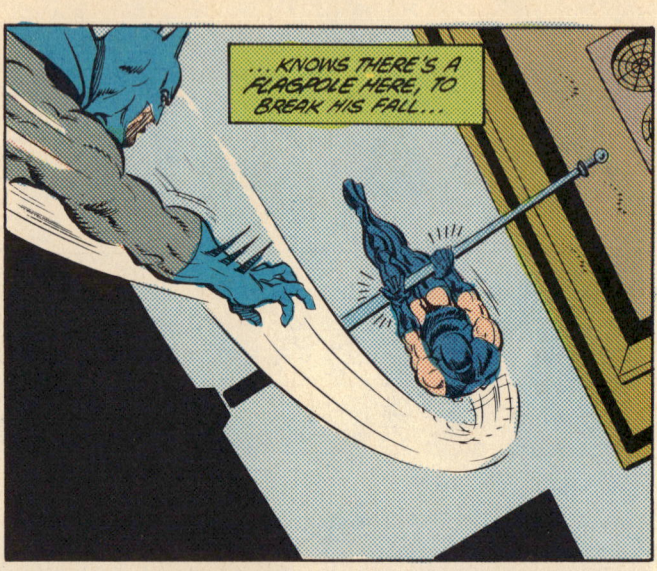

THE KILLER'S DONE HIS HOMEWORK. HE KNOWS THE TERRITORY...

...KNOWS THERE'S A FLAGPOLE HERE, TO BREAK HIS FALL...

...AND A NEARBY ROOF TO LAND ON.

AS SOON AS WE TOUCH DOWN, HE'LL STRIKE.

HE NEVER MISSES A CHANCE.

BUT THEN NEITHER DO I.

20

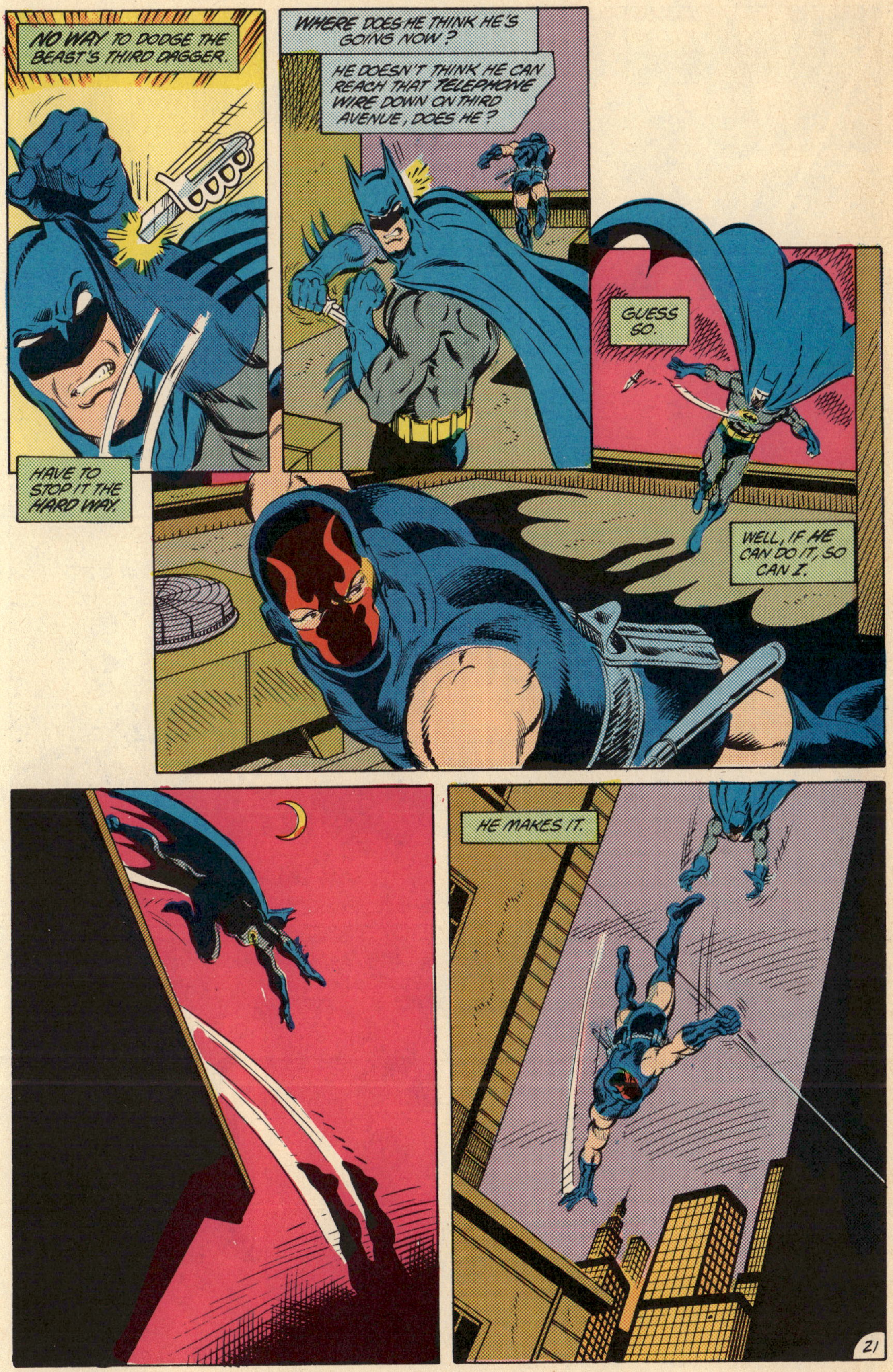
NO WAY TO DODGE THE BEAST'S THIRD DAGGER.
HAVE TO STOP IT THE HARD WAY.
WHERE DOES HE THINK HE'S GOING NOW?
HE DOESN'T THINK HE CAN REACH THAT TELEPHONE WIRE DOWN ON THIRD AVENUE, DOES HE?
GUESS SO.
WELL, IF HE CAN DO IT, SO CAN I.
HE MAKES IT.
21

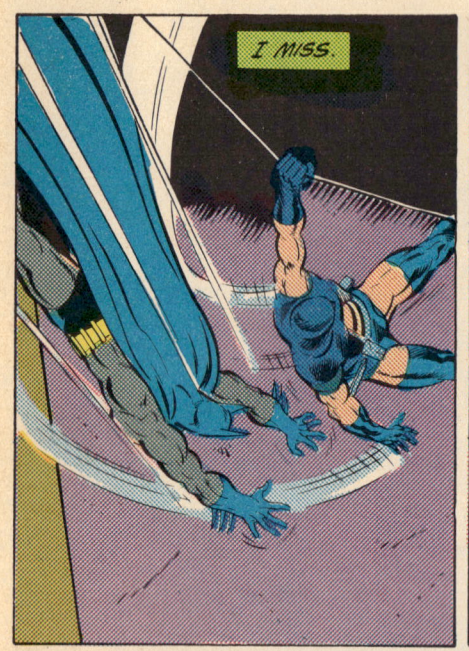

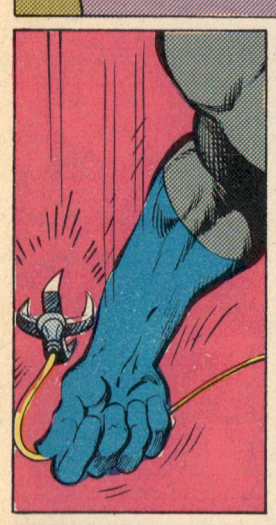

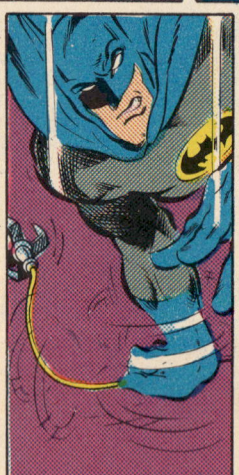

I MISS.

NO NEED TO PANIC.

I'VE BEEN HERE BEFORE.

I SURVIVE, BUT THE BEAST ESCAPES...

...LEAVING A STARTLING REALIZATION IN THE WAKE OF HIS DEPARTURE.

I'VE FINALLY RUN INTO SOMEONE WHO'S BETTER AT THIS GAME THAN I AM.

CONTINUED...

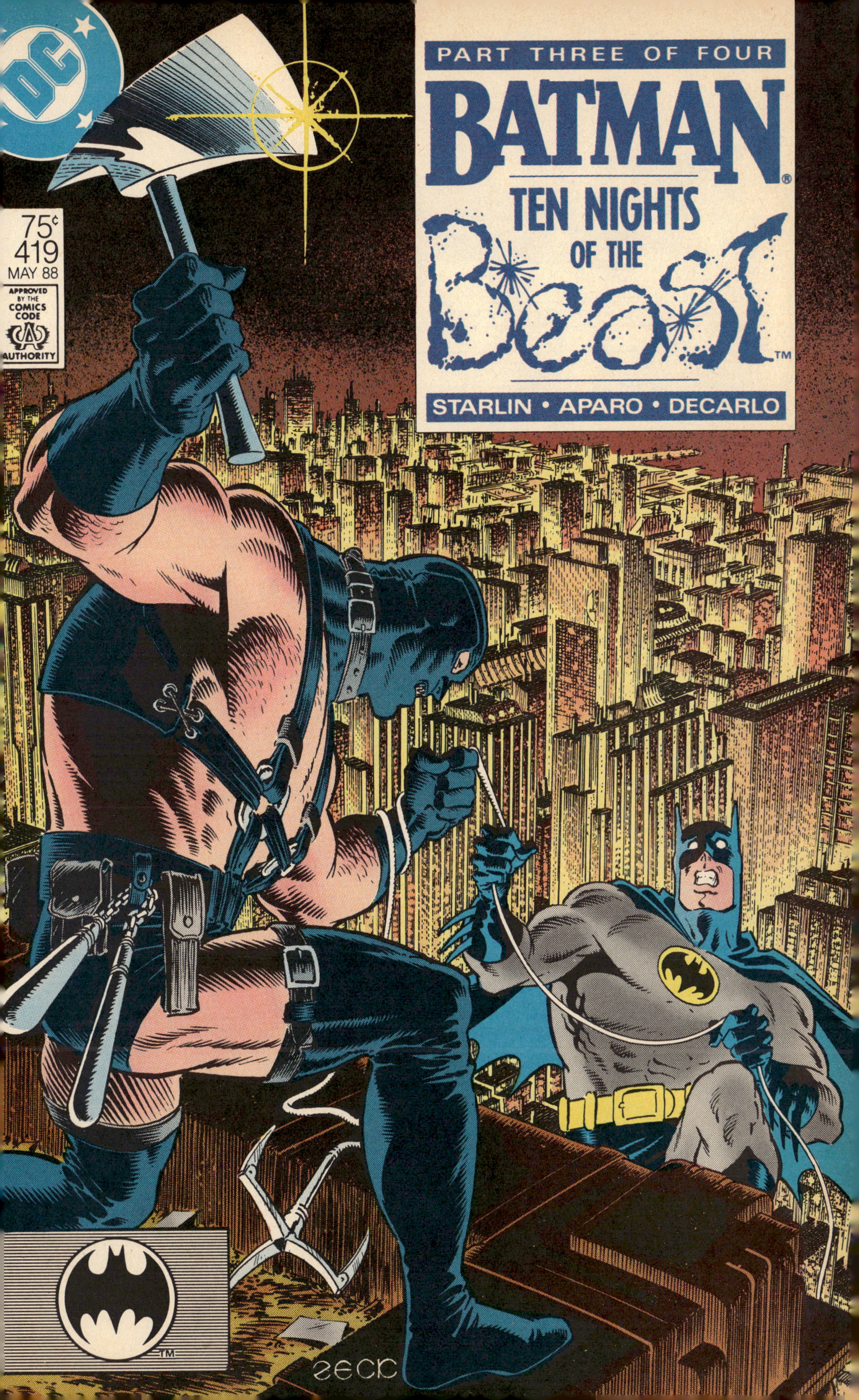
DC
PART THREE OF FOUR
BATMAN
TEN NIGHTS OF THE BEAST
STARLIN • APARO • DECARLO
75¢
419
MAY 88
APPROVED BY THE COMICS CODE AUTHORITY

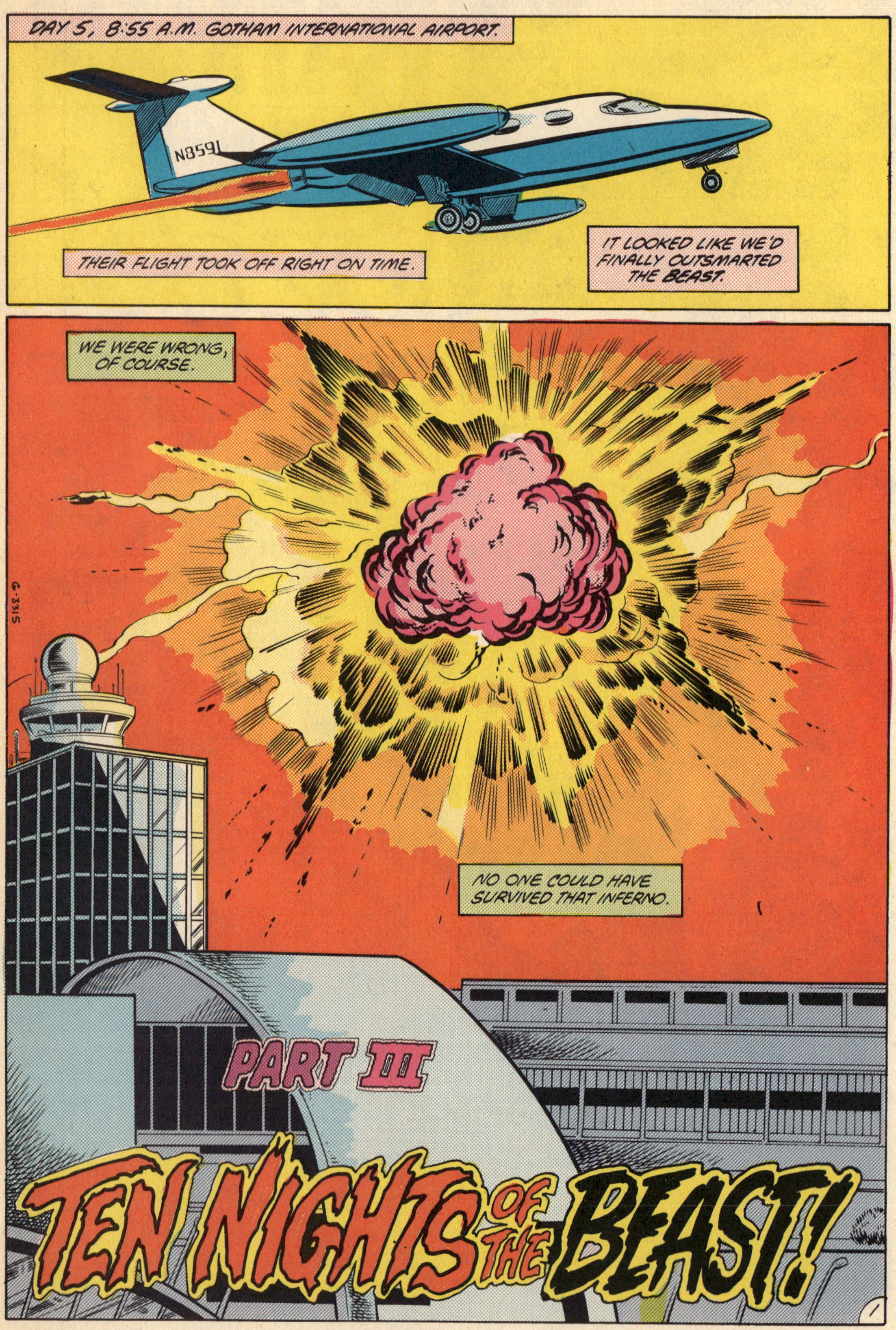
DAY 5, 8:55 A.M. GOTHAM INTERNATIONAL AIRPORT.
N8591
THEIR FLIGHT TOOK OFF RIGHT ON TIME.
IT LOOKED LIKE WE'D FINALLY OUTSMARTED THE BEAST.
WE WERE WRONG, OF COURSE.
NO ONE COULD HAVE SURVIVED THAT INFERNO.
PART III
TEN NIGHTS OF THE BEAST!

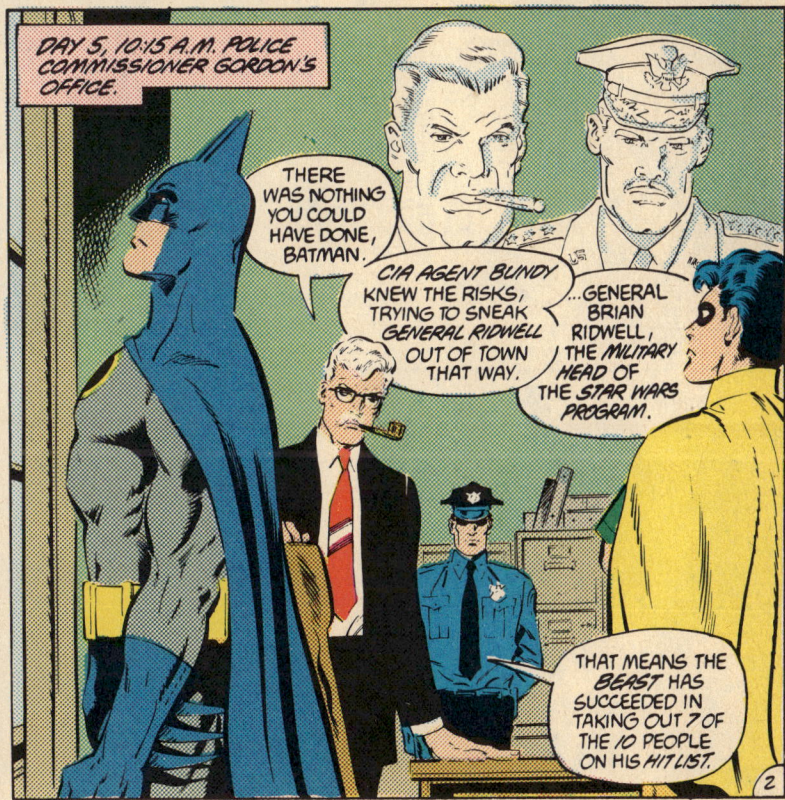

A PASSING MOTORIST SPOTTED TWO STRANGE-LOOKING MEN PARKED ALONGSIDE AIRPORT ROAD.

THE DESCRIPTION HE GAVE US TO THEM LEAVES NO DOUBT IN MY MIND...

...ANATOLI KNYAZEV, THE KGBEAST HAS STRUCK AGAIN.

HIS SHI'ITE TERRORIST ASSISTANT, NABIH SALARI, WAS WITH HIM.

HE USED A PORTABLE STINGER ROCKET LAUNCHER TO KNOCK DOWN THE PLANE.

AN AMERICAN MADE WEAPON... PROBABLY PICKED IT UP ON GOTHAM CITY'S BLACK MARKET.

I SHOULD HAVE BEEN THERE.

DAY 5, 10:15 A.M. POLICE COMMISSIONER GORDON'S OFFICE.

THERE WAS NOTHING YOU COULD HAVE DONE, BATMAN.

CIA AGENT BUNDY KNEW THE RISKS, TRYING TO SNEAK GENERAL RIDWELL OUT OF TOWN THAT WAY.

...GENERAL BRIAN RIDWELL, THE MILITARY HEAD OF THE STAR WARS PROGRAM.

THAT MEANS THE BEAST HAS SUCCEEDED IN TAKING OUT 7 OF THE 10 PEOPLE ON HIS HIT LIST.

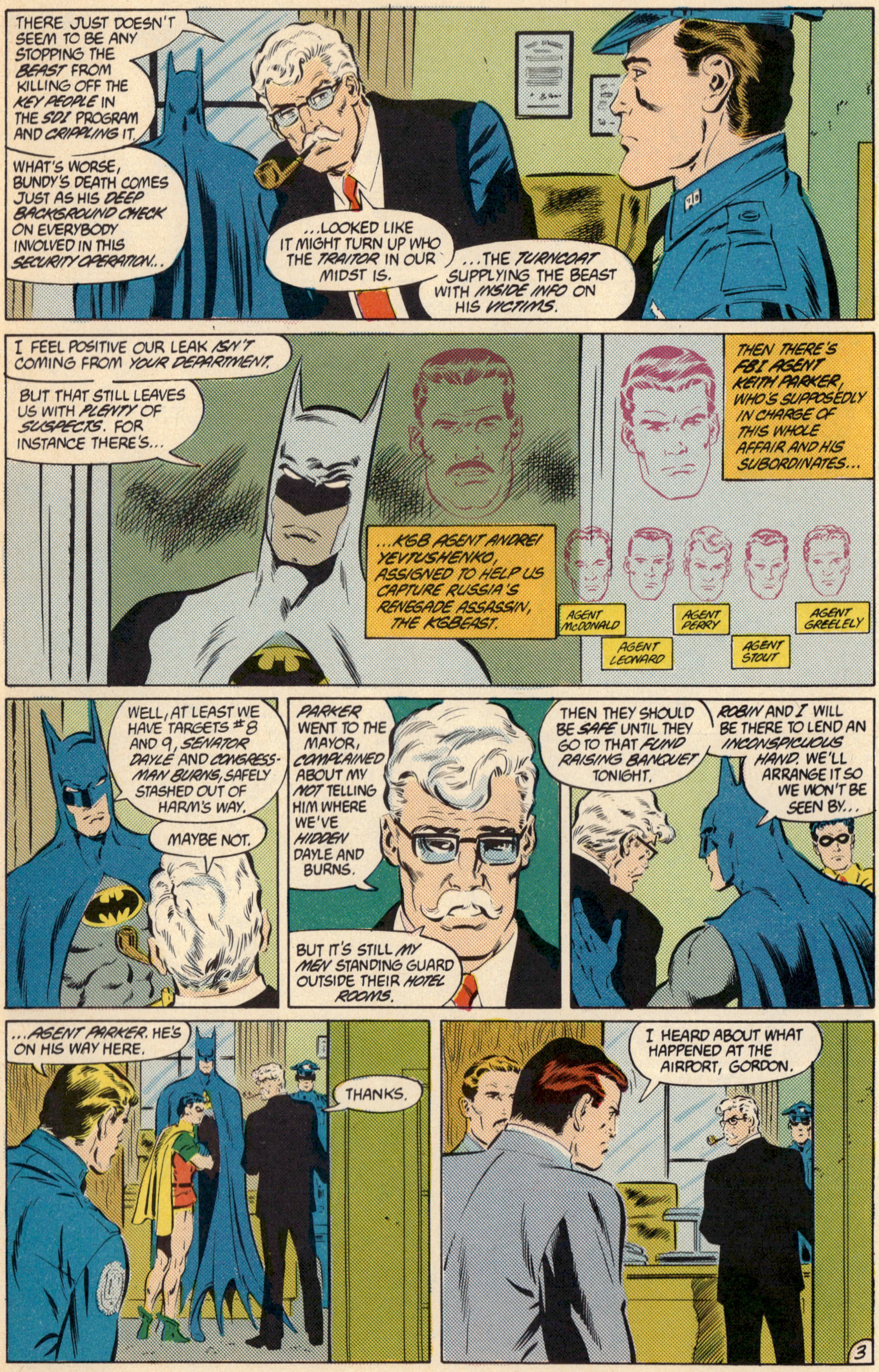
THERE JUST DOESN'T SEEM TO BE ANY STOPPING THE BEAST FROM KILLING OFF THE KEY PEOPLE IN THE SDI PROGRAM AND CRIPPLING IT.
WHAT'S WORSE, BUNDY'S DEATH COMES JUST AS HIS DEEP BACKGROUND CHECK ON EVERYBODY INVOLVED IN THIS SECURITY OPERATION...
...LOOKED LIKE IT MIGHT TURN UP WHO THE TRAITOR IN OUR MIDST IS.
...THE TURNCOAT SUPPLYING THE BEAST WITH INSIDE INFO ON HIS VICTIMS.
I FEEL POSITIVE OUR LEAK ISN'T COMING FROM YOUR DEPARTMENT.
BUT THAT STILL LEAVES US WITH PLENTY OF SUSPECTS. FOR INSTANCE THERE'S...
...KGB AGENT ANDREI YEVTUSHENKO, ASSIGNED TO HELP US CAPTURE RUSSIA'S RENEGADE ASSASSIN, THE KGBEAST.
THEN THERE'S FBI AGENT KEITH PARKER, WHO'S SUPPOSEDLY IN CHARGE OF THIS WHOLE AFFAIR AND HIS SUBORDINATES...
AGENT McDONALD
AGENT LEONARD
AGENT PERRY
AGENT STOUT
AGENT GREELEY
WELL, AT LEAST WE HAVE TARGETS #8 AND 9, SENATOR DAYLE AND CONGRESS-MAN BURNS, SAFELY STASHED OUT OF HARM'S WAY.
MAYBE NOT.
PARKER WENT TO THE MAYOR, COMPLAINED ABOUT MY NOT TELLING HIM WHERE WE'VE HIDDEN DAYLE AND BURNS.
BUT IT'S STILL MY MEN STANDING GUARD OUTSIDE THEIR HOTEL ROOMS.
THEN THEY SHOULD BE SAFE UNTIL THEY GO TO THAT FUND RAISING BANQUET TONIGHT.
ROBIN AND I WILL BE THERE TO LEND AN INCONSPICUOUS HAND. WE'LL ARRANGE IT SO WE WON'T BE SEEN BY...
...AGENT PARKER. HE'S ON HIS WAY HERE.
THANKS.
I HEARD ABOUT WHAT HAPPENED AT THE AIRPORT, GORDON.
3

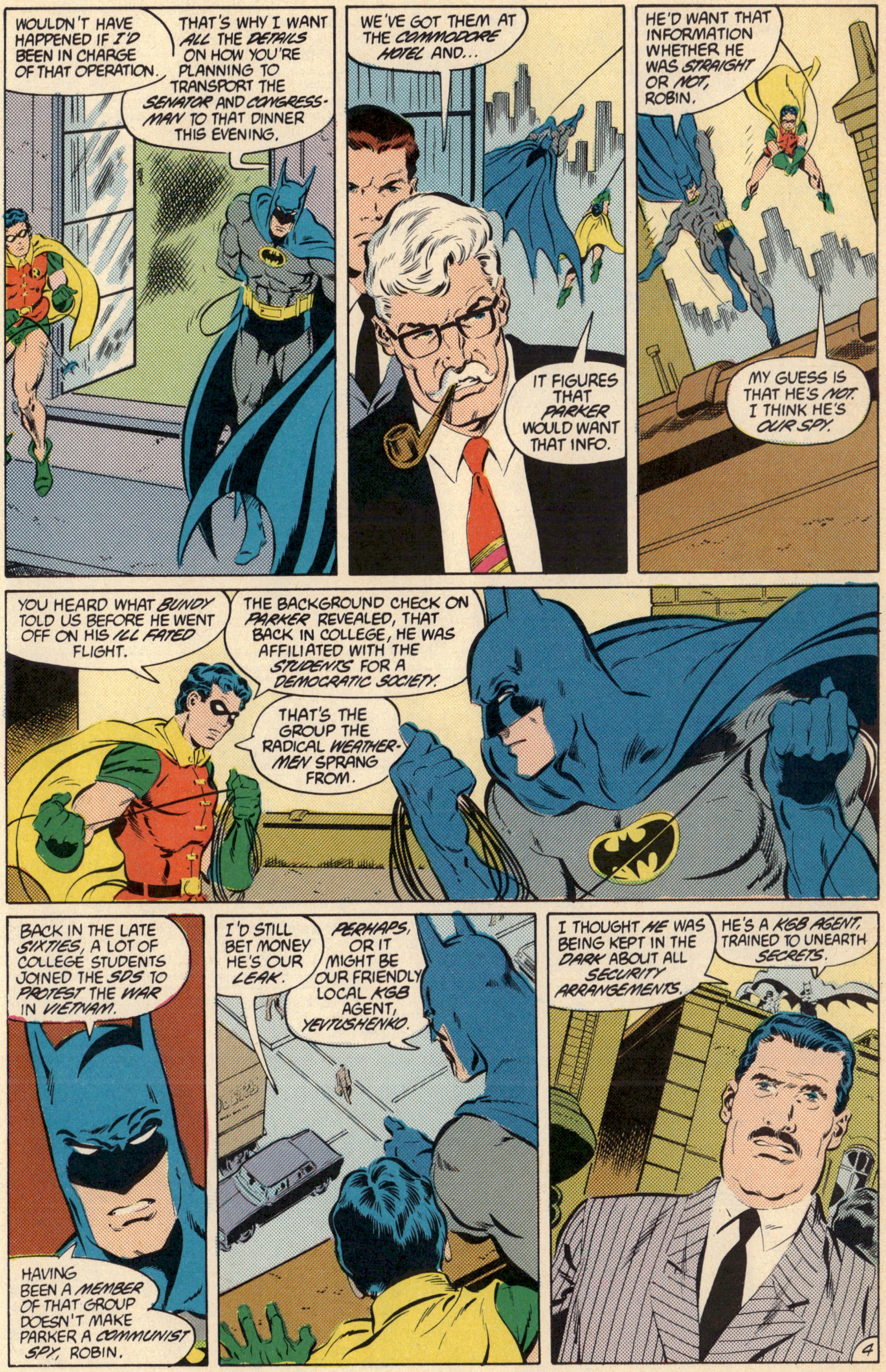
WOULDN'T HAVE HAPPENED IF I'D BEEN IN CHARGE OF THAT OPERATION.
THAT'S WHY I WANT ALL THE DETAILS ON HOW YOU'RE PLANNING TO TRANSPORT THE SENATOR AND CONGRESSMAN TO THAT DINNER THIS EVENING.
WE'VE GOT THEM AT THE COMMODORE HOTEL AND...
IT FIGURES THAT PARKER WOULD WANT THAT INFO.
HE'D WANT THAT INFORMATION WHETHER HE WAS STRAIGHT OR NOT, ROBIN.
MY GUESS IS THAT HE'S NOT. I THINK HE'S OUR SPY.
YOU HEARD WHAT BUNDY TOLD US BEFORE HE WENT OFF ON HIS ILL FATED FLIGHT.
THE BACKGROUND CHECK ON PARKER REVEALED, THAT BACK IN COLLEGE, HE WAS AFFILIATED WITH THE STUDENTS FOR A DEMOCRATIC SOCIETY.
THAT'S THE GROUP THE RADICAL WEATHERMEN SPRANG FROM.
BACK IN THE LATE SIXTIES, A LOT OF COLLEGE STUDENTS JOINED THE SDS TO PROTEST THE WAR IN VIETNAM.
HAVING BEEN A MEMBER OF THAT GROUP DOESN'T MAKE PARKER A COMMUNIST SPY, ROBIN.
I'D STILL BET MONEY HE'S OUR LEAK.
PERHAPS, OR IT MIGHT BE OUR FRIENDLY LOCAL KGB AGENT, YEVTUSHENKO.
I THOUGHT HE WAS BEING KEPT IN THE DARK ABOUT ALL SECURITY ARRANGEMENTS.
HE'S A KGB AGENT, TRAINED TO UNEARTH SECRETS.
4

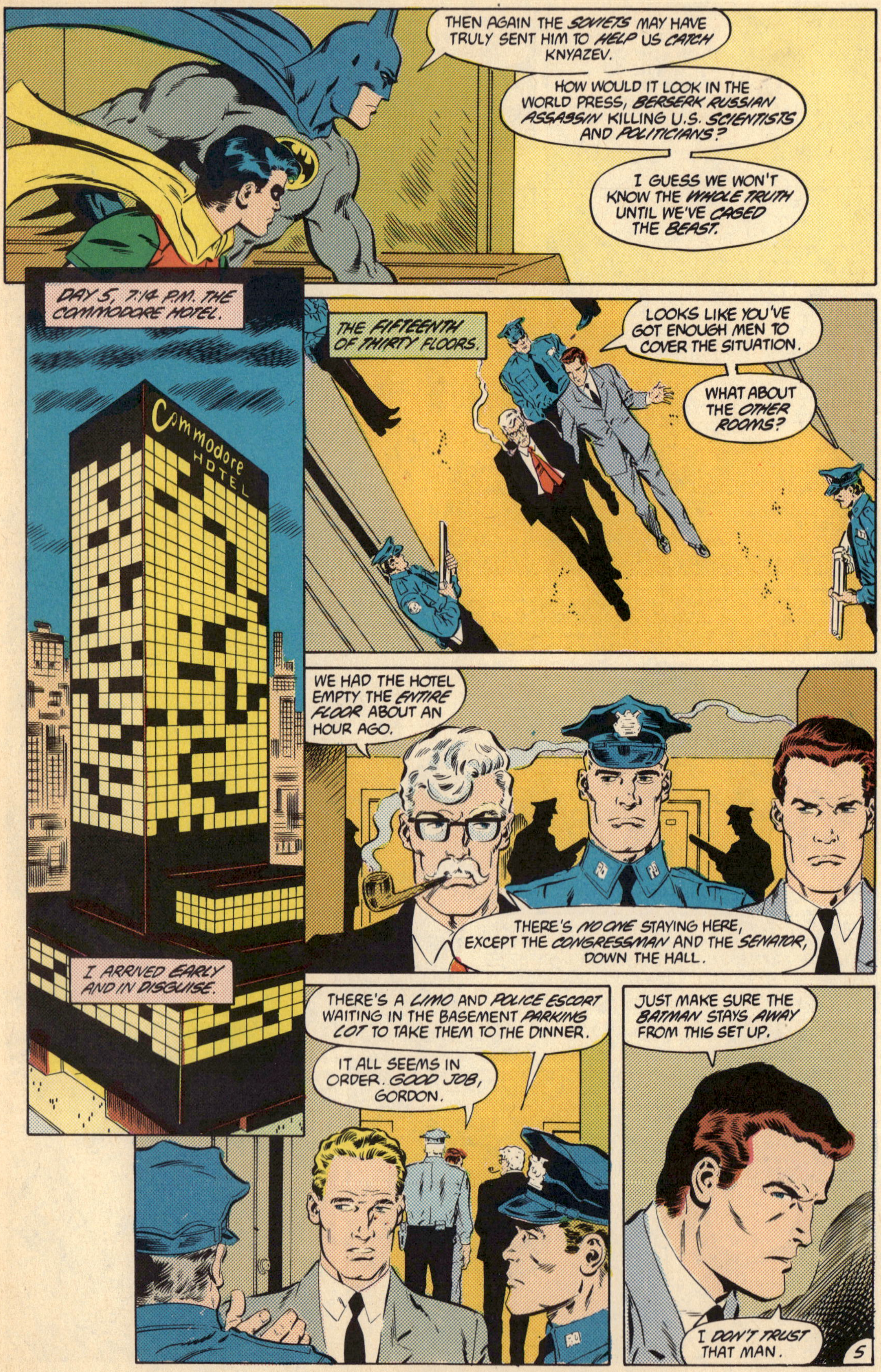
THEN AGAIN THE SOVIETS MAY HAVE TRULY SENT HIM TO HELP US CATCH KNYAZEV.
HOW WOULD IT LOOK IN THE WORLD PRESS, BERSERK RUSSIAN ASSASSIN KILLING U.S. SCIENTISTS AND POLITICIANS?
I GUESS WE WON'T KNOW THE WHOLE TRUTH UNTIL WE'VE CAGED THE BEAST.
DAY 5, 7:14 P.M. THE COMMODORE HOTEL.
Commodore HOTEL
I ARRIVED EARLY AND IN DISGUISE.
THE FIFTEENTH OF THIRTY FLOORS.
LOOKS LIKE YOU'VE GOT ENOUGH MEN TO COVER THE SITUATION.
WHAT ABOUT THE OTHER ROOMS?
WE HAD THE HOTEL EMPTY THE ENTIRE FLOOR ABOUT AN HOUR AGO.
THERE'S NO ONE STAYING HERE, EXCEPT THE CONGRESSMAN AND THE SENATOR, DOWN THE HALL.
THERE'S A LIMO AND POLICE ESCORT WAITING IN THE BASEMENT PARKING LOT TO TAKE THEM TO THE DINNER.
IT ALL SEEMS IN ORDER. GOOD JOB, GORDON.
JUST MAKE SURE THE BATMAN STAYS AWAY FROM THIS SET UP.
I DON'T TRUST THAT MAN.
5

"I WOULDN'T be at all SURPRISED to find out, it's that VIGILANTE who's leaking SECRET INFORMATION to the BEAST."

"WELL, IT'S TIME TO GET THIS SHOW ON THE ROAD."

I TOOK ONE LAST LOOK DOWN THE HALLWAY TO MAKE SURE EVERYTHING WAS IN ORDER.

THAT'S WHEN I SAW IT.

THE CONGRESSMAN'S DOOR KNOB WAS...

...DIFFERENT FROM ANY OF THE OTHERS ON THAT FLOOR.

I KNEW I WAS TOO LATE, BUT I HAD TO TRY.

"GET AWAY FROM THAT DOOR!"

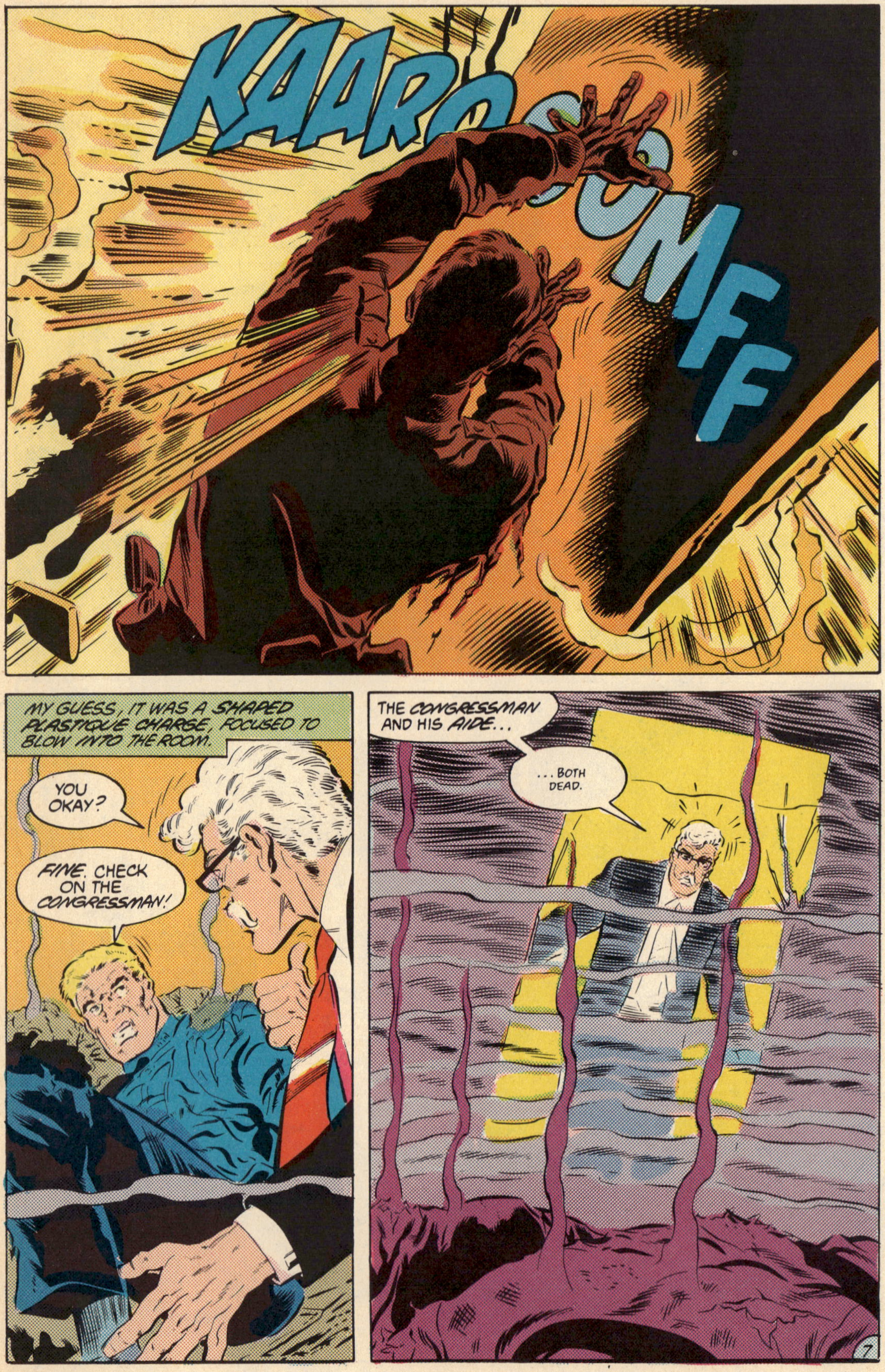
KAAROOOMFF
MY GUESS, IT WAS A SHAPED PLASTIQUE CHARGE, FOCUSED TO BLOW INTO THE ROOM.
YOU OKAY?
FINE. CHECK ON THE CONGRESSMAN!
THE CONGRESSMAN AND HIS AIDE...
...BOTH DEAD.
7

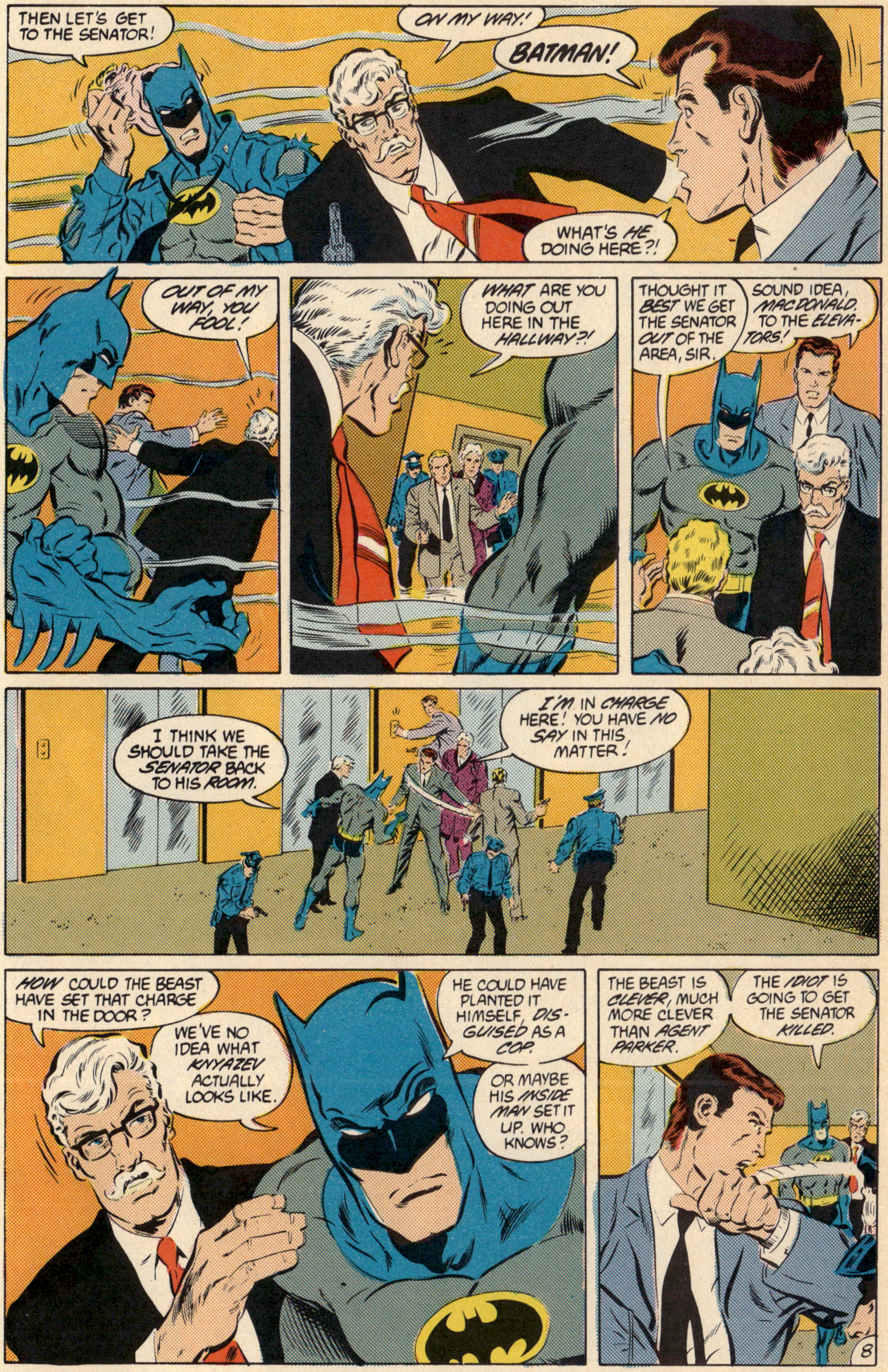
THEN LET'S GET TO THE SENATOR!
ON MY WAY!
BATMAN!
WHAT'S HE DOING HERE?!
OUT OF MY WAY, YOU FOOL!
WHAT ARE YOU DOING OUT HERE IN THE HALLWAY?!
THOUGHT IT BEST WE GET THE SENATOR OUT OF THE AREA, SIR.
SOUND IDEA, MACDONALD. TO THE ELEVATORS!
I THINK WE SHOULD TAKE THE SENATOR BACK TO HIS ROOM.
I'M IN CHARGE HERE! YOU HAVE NO SAY IN THIS MATTER!
HOW COULD THE BEAST HAVE SET THAT CHARGE IN THE DOOR?
WE'VE NO IDEA WHAT KNYAZEV ACTUALLY LOOKS LIKE.
HE COULD HAVE PLANTED IT HIMSELF, DISGUISED AS A COP.
OR MAYBE HIS INSIDE MAN SET IT UP. WHO KNOWS?
THE BEAST IS CLEVER, MUCH MORE CLEVER THAN AGENT PARKER.
THE IDIOT IS GOING TO GET THE SENATOR KILLED.
8

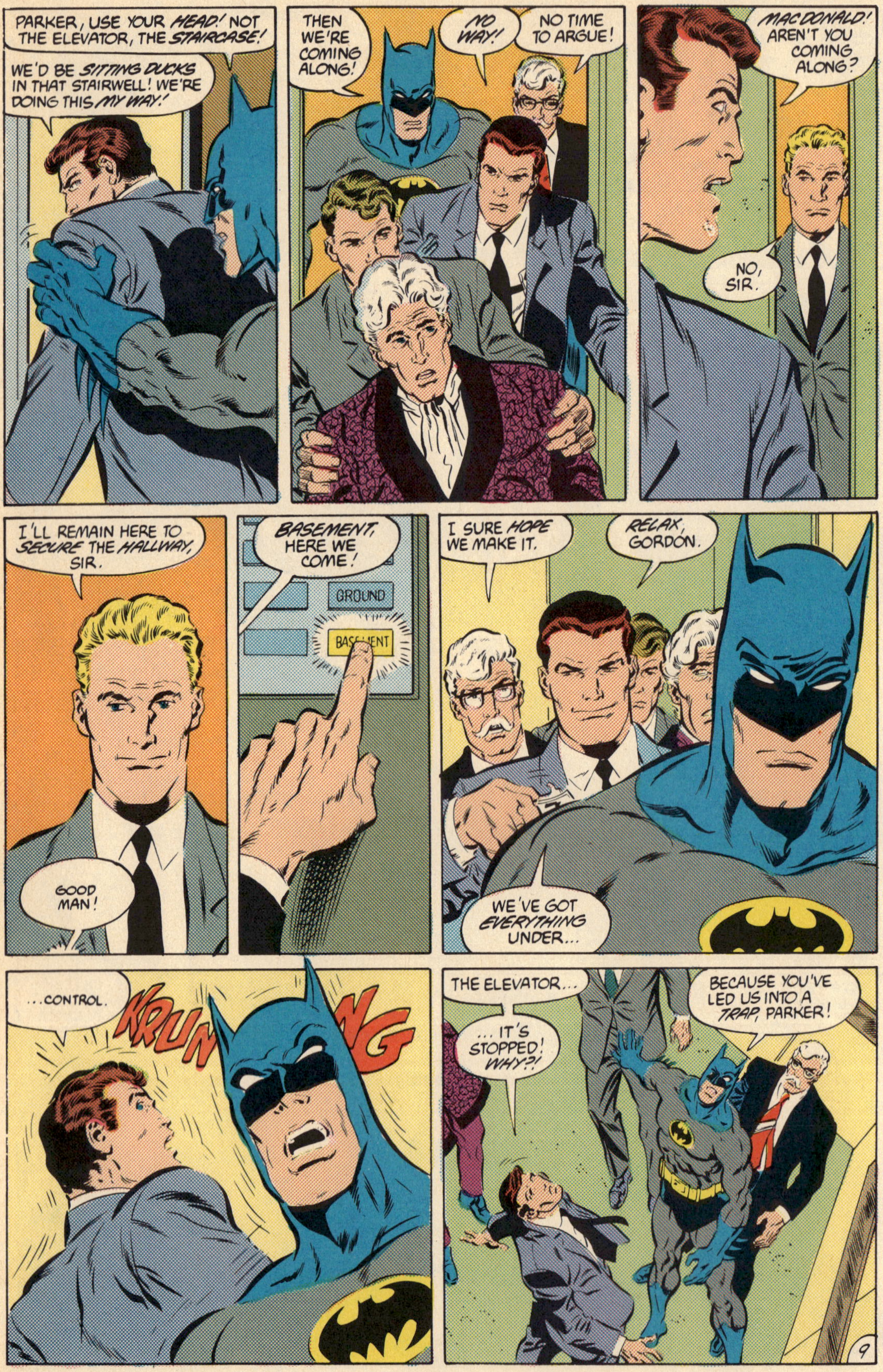
PARKER, USE YOUR HEAD! NOT THE ELEVATOR, THE STAIRCASE!
WE'D BE SITTING DUCKS IN THAT STAIRWELL! WE'RE DOING THIS MY WAY!
THEN WE'RE COMING ALONG!
NO WAY!
NO TIME TO ARGUE!
MACDONALD! AREN'T YOU COMING ALONG?
NO, SIR.
I'LL REMAIN HERE TO SECURE THE HALLWAY, SIR.
GOOD MAN!
BASEMENT, HERE WE COME!
GROUND
BASEMENT
I SURE HOPE WE MAKE IT.
RELAX, GORDON.
WE'VE GOT EVERYTHING UNDER...
...CONTROL.
KRUNNNG
THE ELEVATOR...
...IT'S STOPPED! WHY?!
BECAUSE YOU'VE LED US INTO A TRAP, PARKER!
9

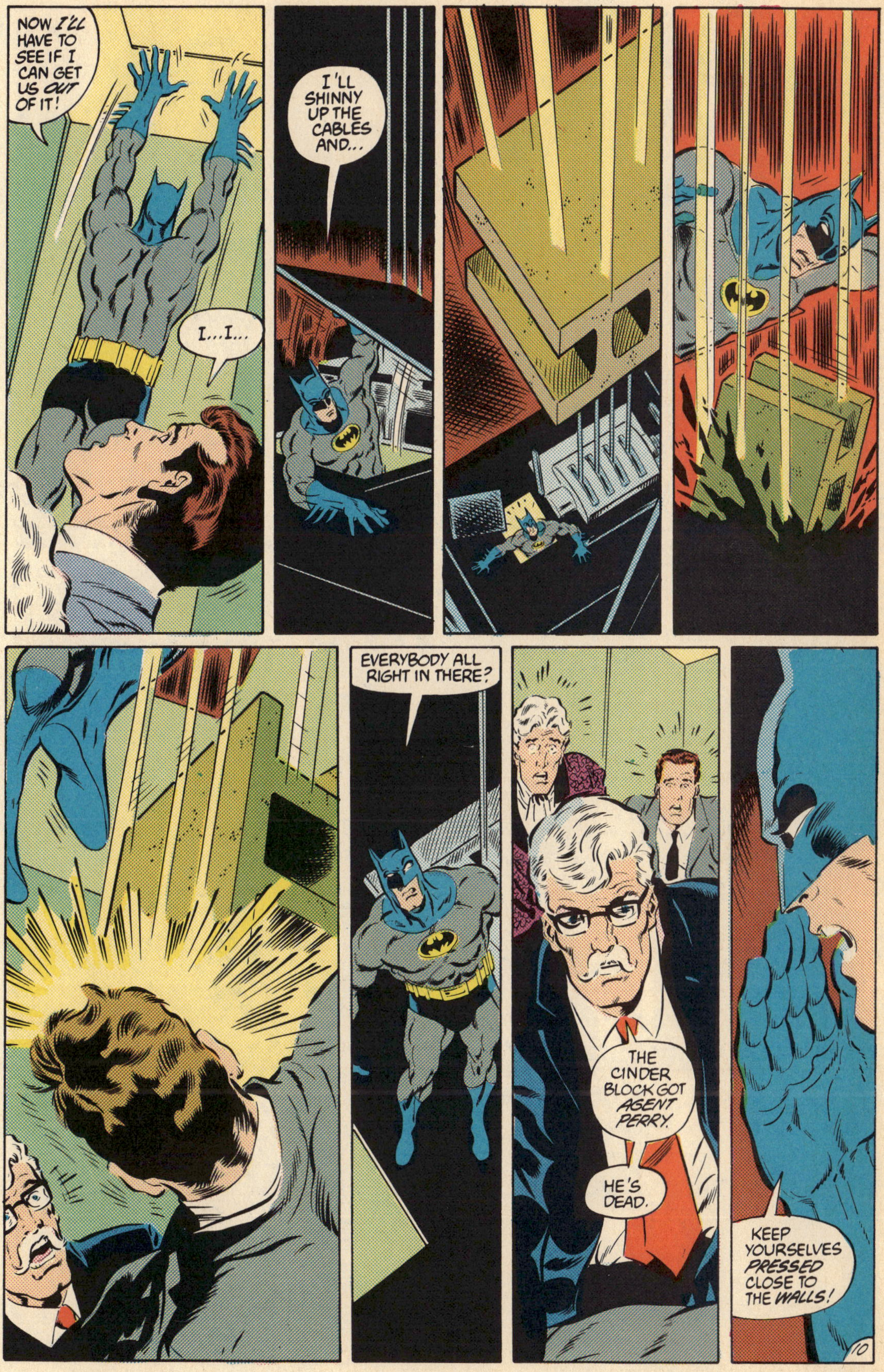

NOW I'LL HAVE TO SEE IF I CAN GET US OUT OF IT!
I...I...
I'LL SHINNY UP THE CABLES AND...
EVERYBODY ALL RIGHT IN THERE?
THE CINDER BLOCK GOT AGENT PERRY.
HE'S DEAD.
KEEP YOURSELVES PRESSED CLOSE TO THE WALLS!
10

CAN'T STAY HERE!

HAVE TO GO AFTER HIM.

Hotel must be having some construction taking place on the top floor, fifteen stories above me.

The management has provided all the concrete missiles the beast will ever need.

You can always tell a good hotel by the way the staff foresees and attends to the every need of their guests.

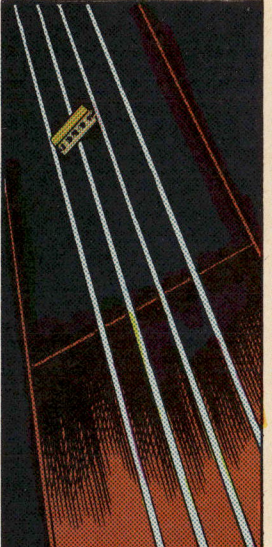

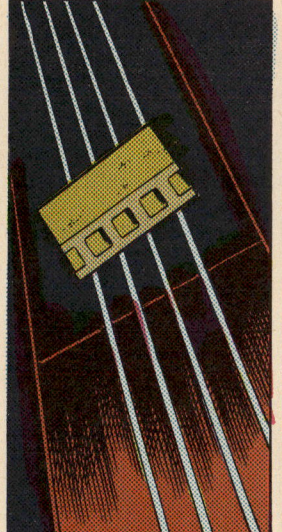

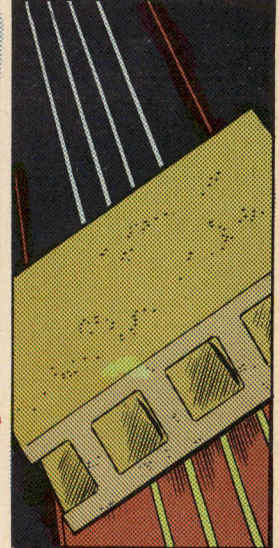

THOSE CEMENT BLOCKS BUILD UP A LOT OF MOMENTUM, FALLING FIFTEEN STORIES.

THEY HIT THE ELEVATOR COMPARTMENT WITH THE POWER OF AN ANTI-TANK ROCKET.

THAT'S RIGHT! I SAID THE BEAST IS ON THE TOP FLOOR!

GET A SQUAD OF MEN UP THERE ON THE DOUBLE! TAKE HIM OUT BEFORE HE KILLS US ALL!

WE'RE ON OUR WAY, COMMISSIONER! HOLD ON!

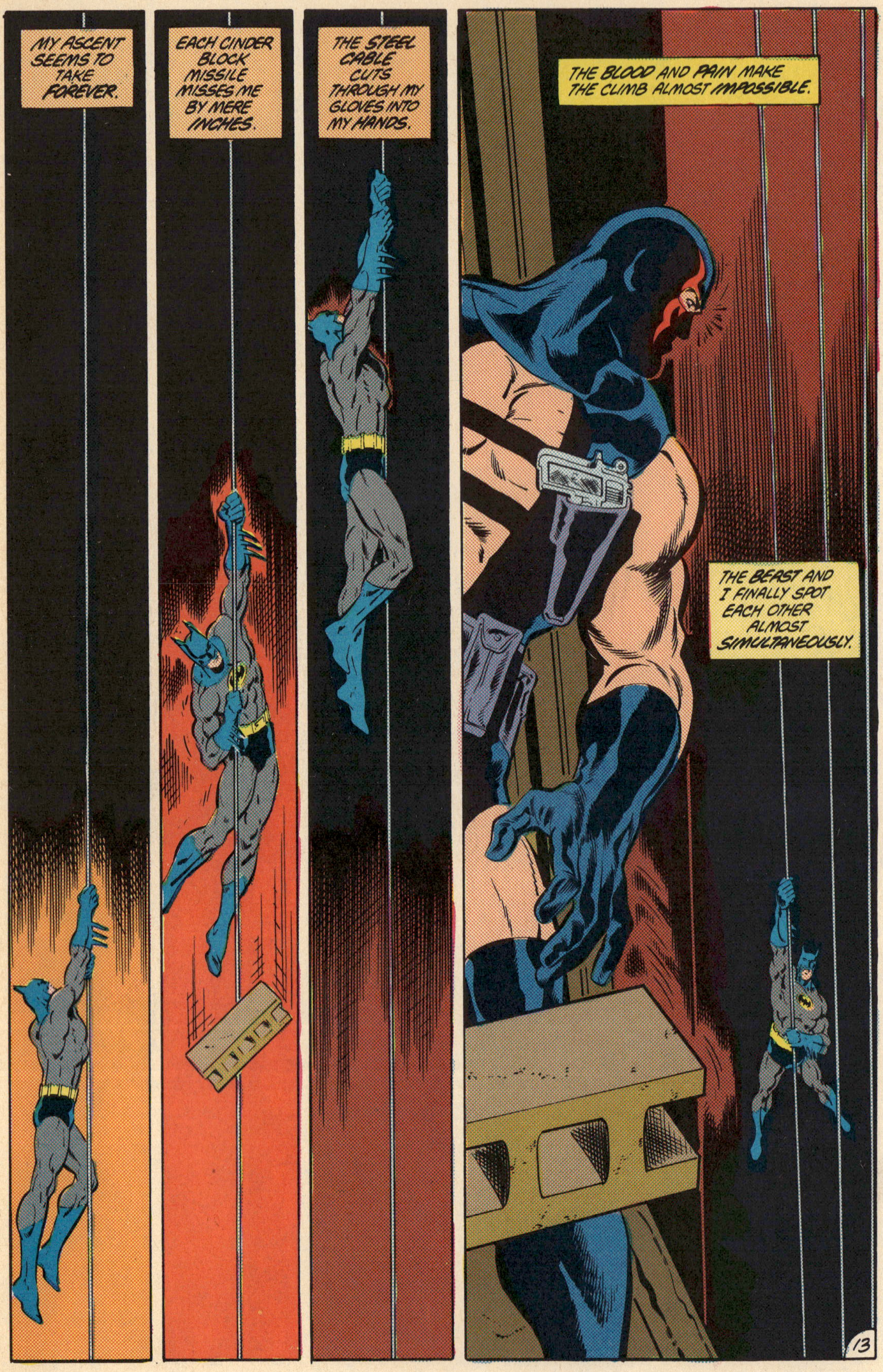
MY ASCENT SEEMS TO TAKE FOREVER.
EACH CINDER BLOCK MISSILE MISSES ME BY MERE INCHES.
THE STEEL CABLE CUTS THROUGH MY GLOVES INTO MY HANDS.
THE BLOOD AND PAIN MAKE THE CLIMB ALMOST IMPOSSIBLE.
THE BEAST AND I FINALLY SPOT EACH OTHER ALMOST SIMULTANEOUSLY.
13

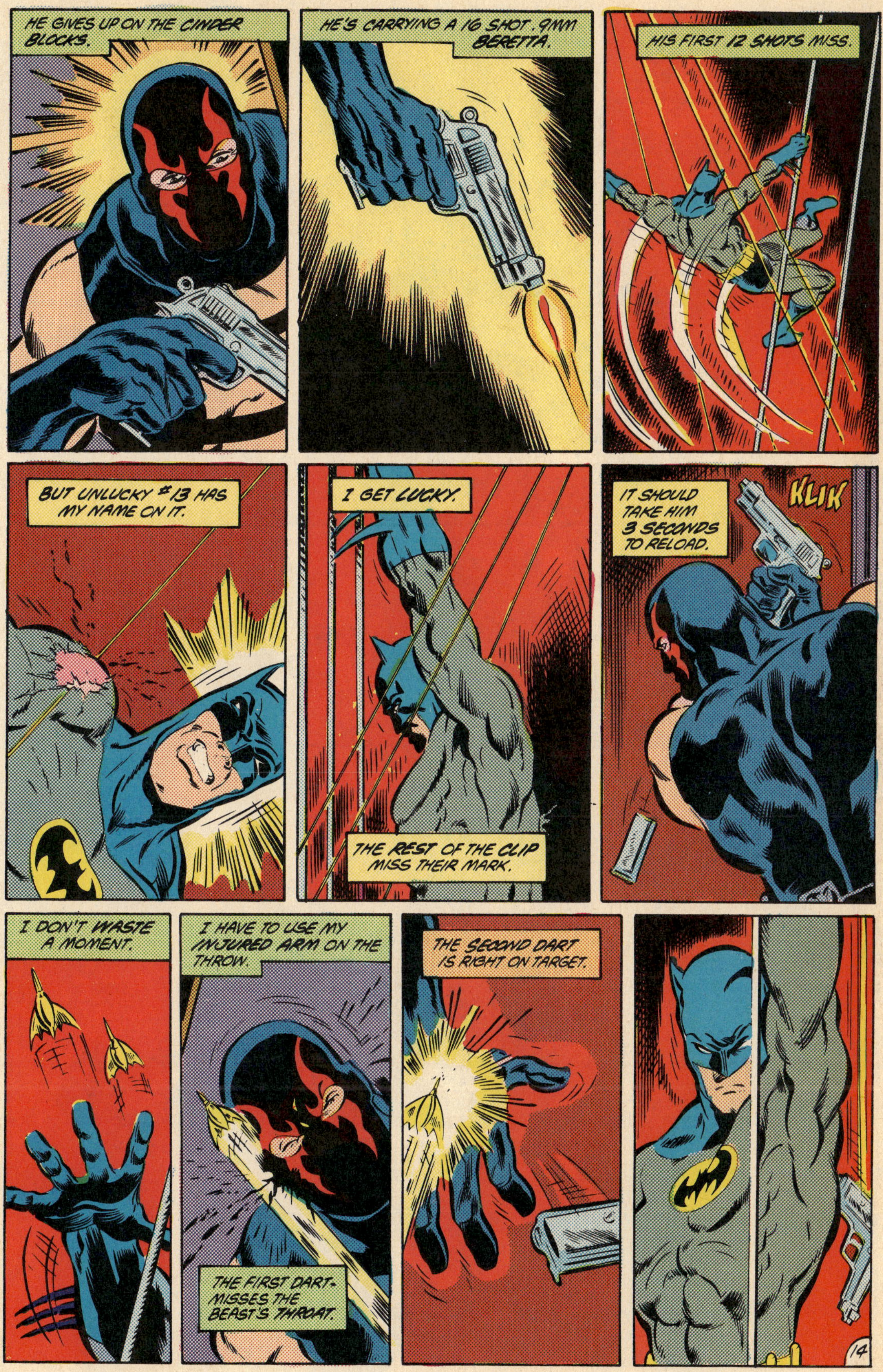
HE GIVES UP ON THE CINDER BLOCKS.
HE'S CARRYING A 16 SHOT 9MM BERETTA.
HIS FIRST 12 SHOTS MISS.
BUT UNLUCKY #13 HAS MY NAME ON IT.
I GET LUCKY.
THE REST OF THE CLIP MISS THEIR MARK.
IT SHOULD TAKE HIM 3 SECONDS TO RELOAD.
KLIK
I DON'T WASTE A MOMENT.
I HAVE TO USE MY INJURED ARM ON THE THROW.
THE FIRST DART MISSES THE BEAST'S THROAT.
THE SECOND DART IS RIGHT ON TARGET.
14

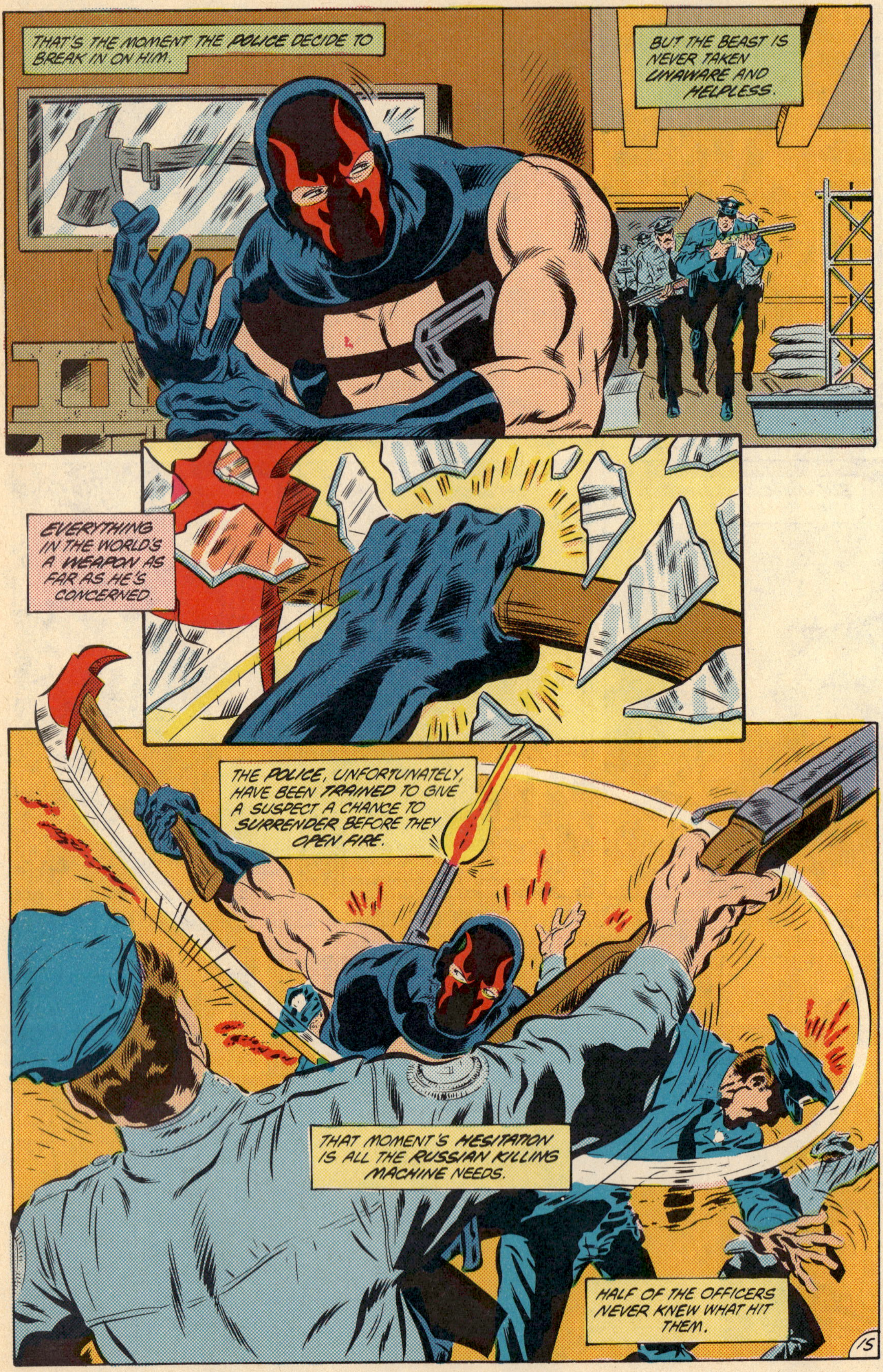
THAT'S THE MOMENT THE POLICE DECIDE TO BREAK IN ON HIM.
BUT THE BEAST IS NEVER TAKEN UNAWARE AND HELPLESS.
EVERYTHING IN THE WORLD'S A WEAPON AS FAR AS HE'S CONCERNED.
THE POLICE, UNFORTUNATELY, HAVE BEEN TRAINED TO GIVE A SUSPECT A CHANCE TO SURRENDER BEFORE THEY OPEN FIRE.
THAT MOMENT'S HESITATION IS ALL THE RUSSIAN KILLING MACHINE NEEDS.
HALF OF THE OFFICERS NEVER KNEW WHAT HIT THEM.
15

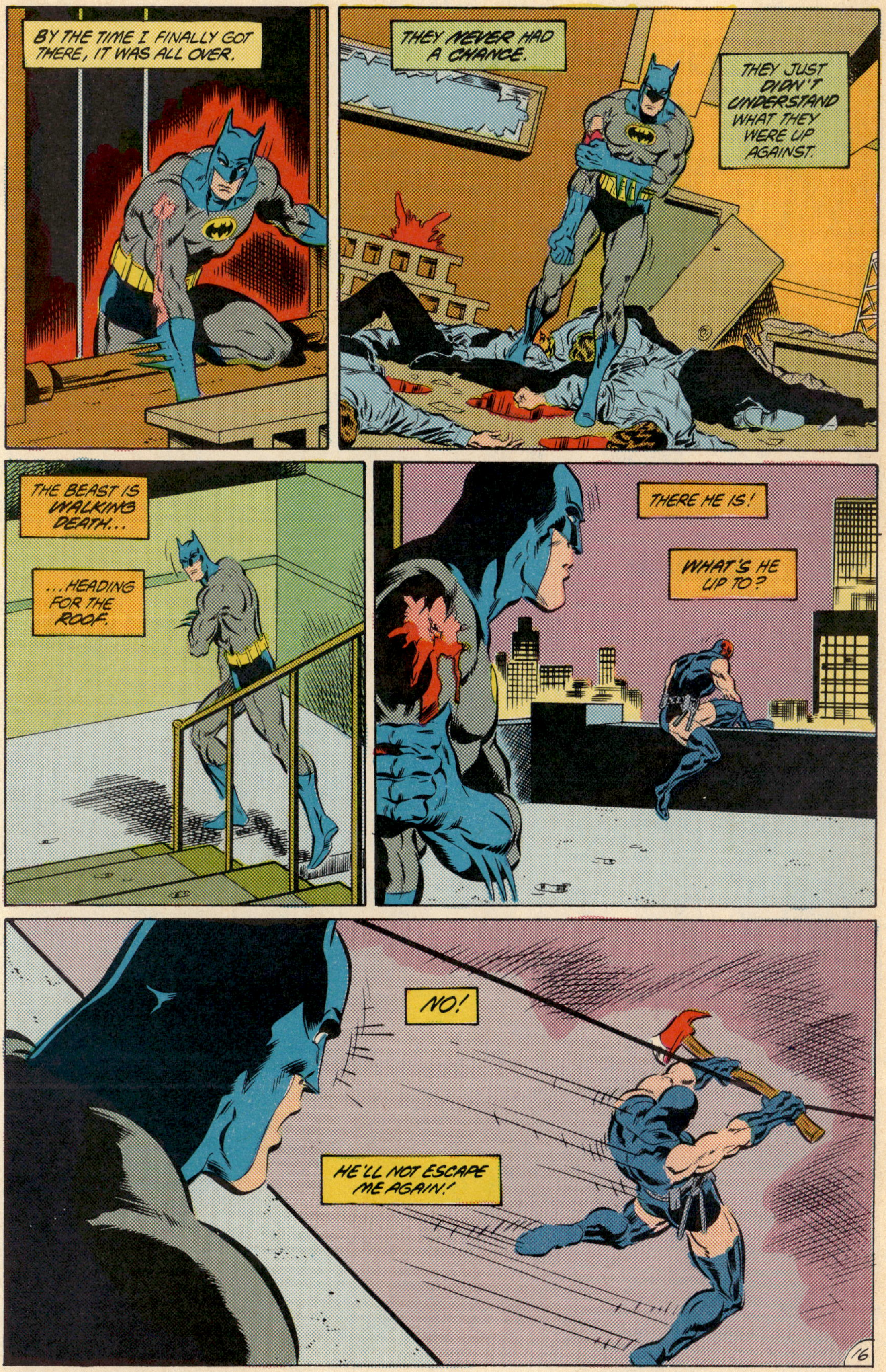
BY THE TIME I FINALLY GOT THERE, IT WAS ALL OVER.
THEY NEVER HAD A CHANCE.
THEY JUST DIDN'T UNDERSTAND WHAT THEY WERE UP AGAINST.
THE BEAST IS WALKING DEATH...
...HEADING FOR THE ROOF.
THERE HE IS!
WHAT'S HE UP TO?
NO!
HE'LL NOT ESCAPE ME AGAIN!
16

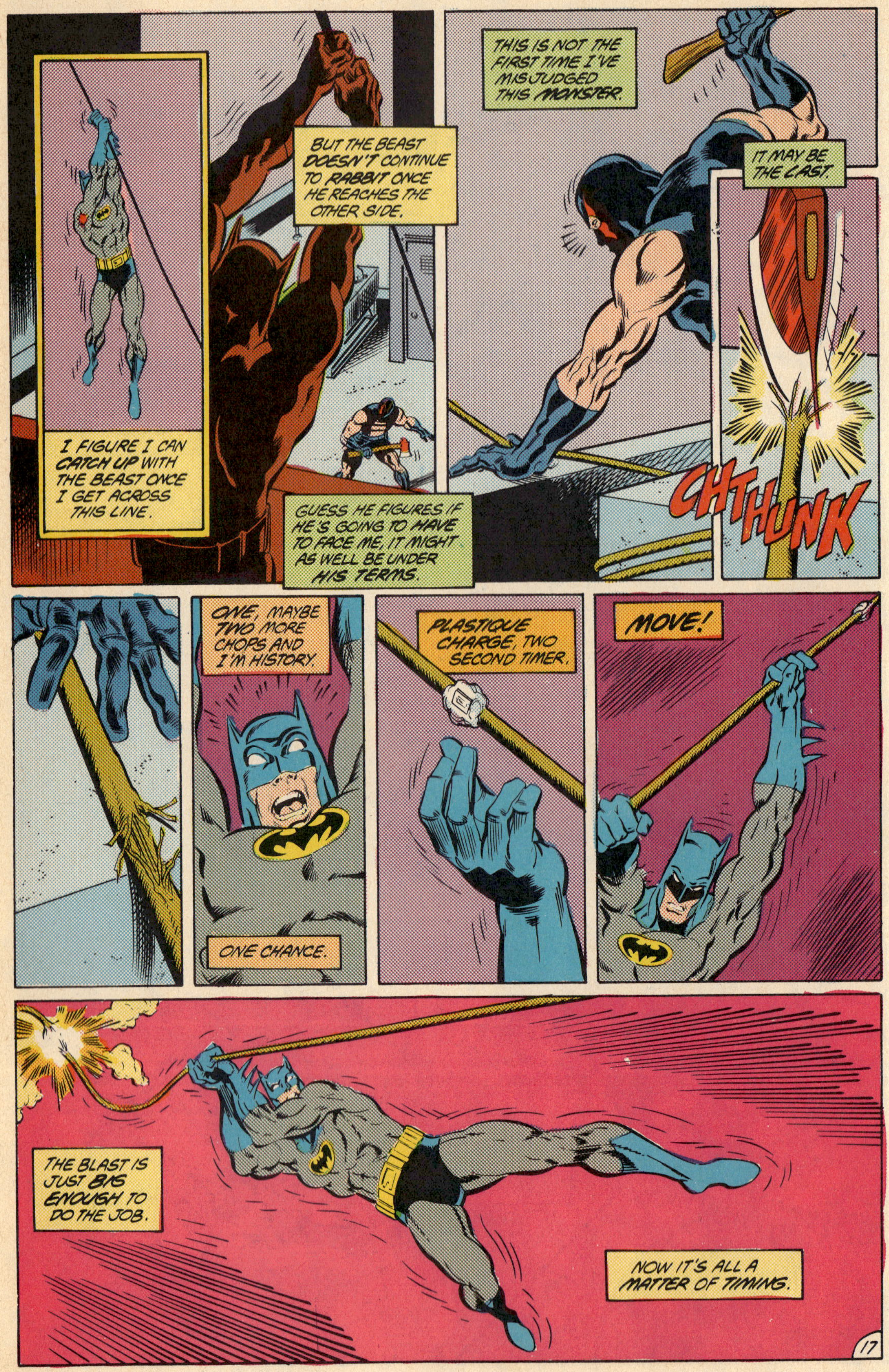
I FIGURE I CAN CATCH UP WITH THE BEAST ONCE I GET ACROSS THIS LINE.
BUT THE BEAST DOESN'T CONTINUE TO RABBIT ONCE HE REACHES THE OTHER SIDE.
GUESS HE FIGURES IF HE'S GOING TO HAVE TO FACE ME, IT MIGHT AS WELL BE UNDER HIS TERMS.
THIS IS NOT THE FIRST TIME I'VE MISJUDGED THIS MONSTER.
IT MAY BE THE LAST.
CHTHUNK
ONE, MAYBE TWO MORE CHOPS AND I'M HISTORY.
ONE CHANCE.
PLASTIQUE CHARGE, TWO SECOND TIMER.
MOVE!
THE BLAST IS JUST BIG ENOUGH TO DO THE JOB.
NOW IT'S ALL A MATTER OF TIMING.
17

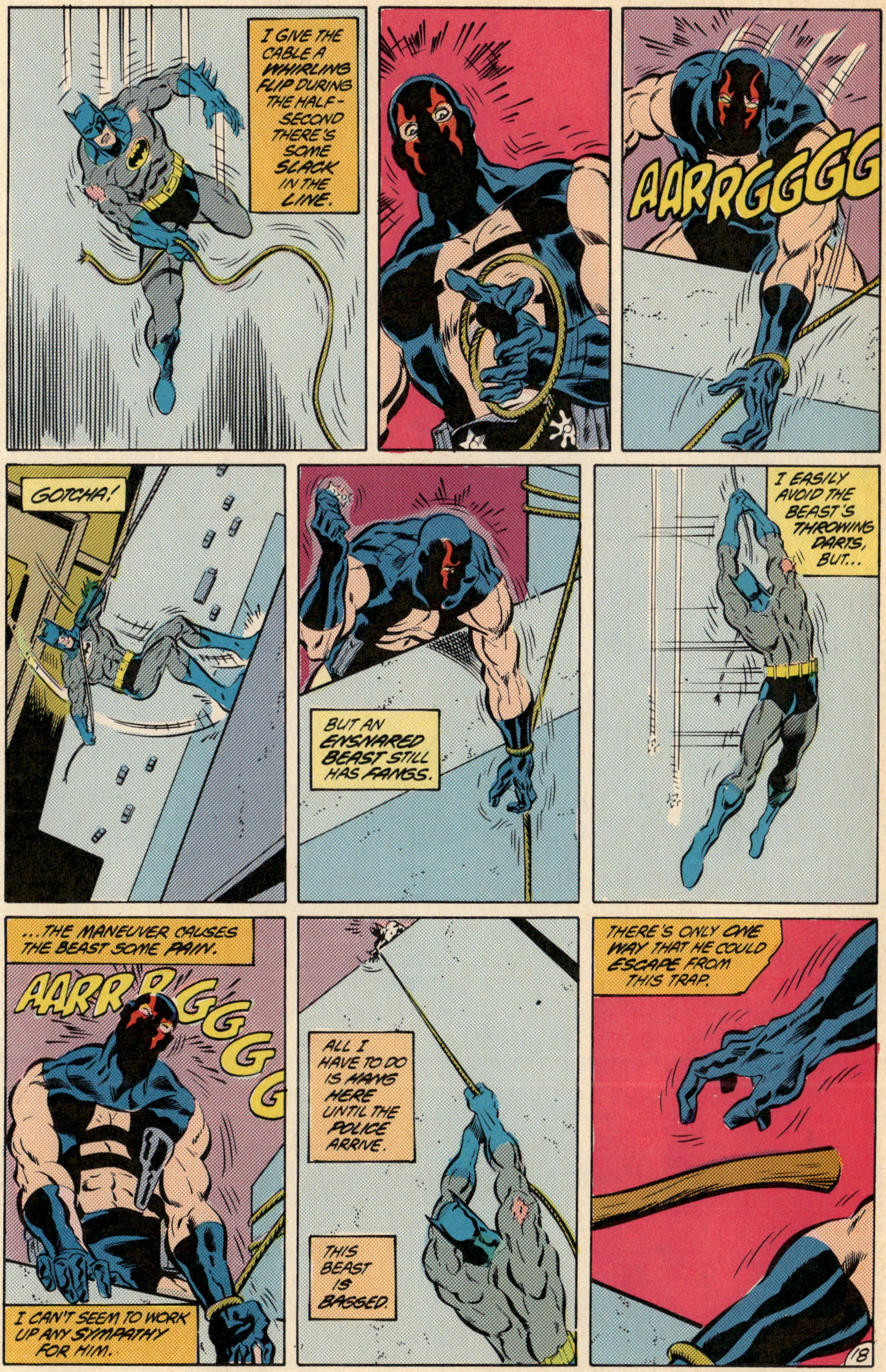

I GIVE THE CABLE A WHIRLING FLIP DURING THE HALF-SECOND THERE'S SOME SLACK IN THE LINE.
AARRGGGG
GOTCHA!
BUT AN ENSNARED BEAST STILL HAS FANGS.
I EASILY AVOID THE BEAST'S THROWING DARTS, BUT...
...THE MANEUVER CAUSES THE BEAST SOME PAIN.
AARRRGGGG
I CAN'T SEEM TO WORK UP ANY SYMPATHY FOR HIM.
ALL I HAVE TO DO IS HANG HERE UNTIL THE POLICE ARRIVE.
THIS BEAST IS BAGGED.
THERE'S ONLY ONE WAY THAT HE COULD ESCAPE FROM THIS TRAP.
18

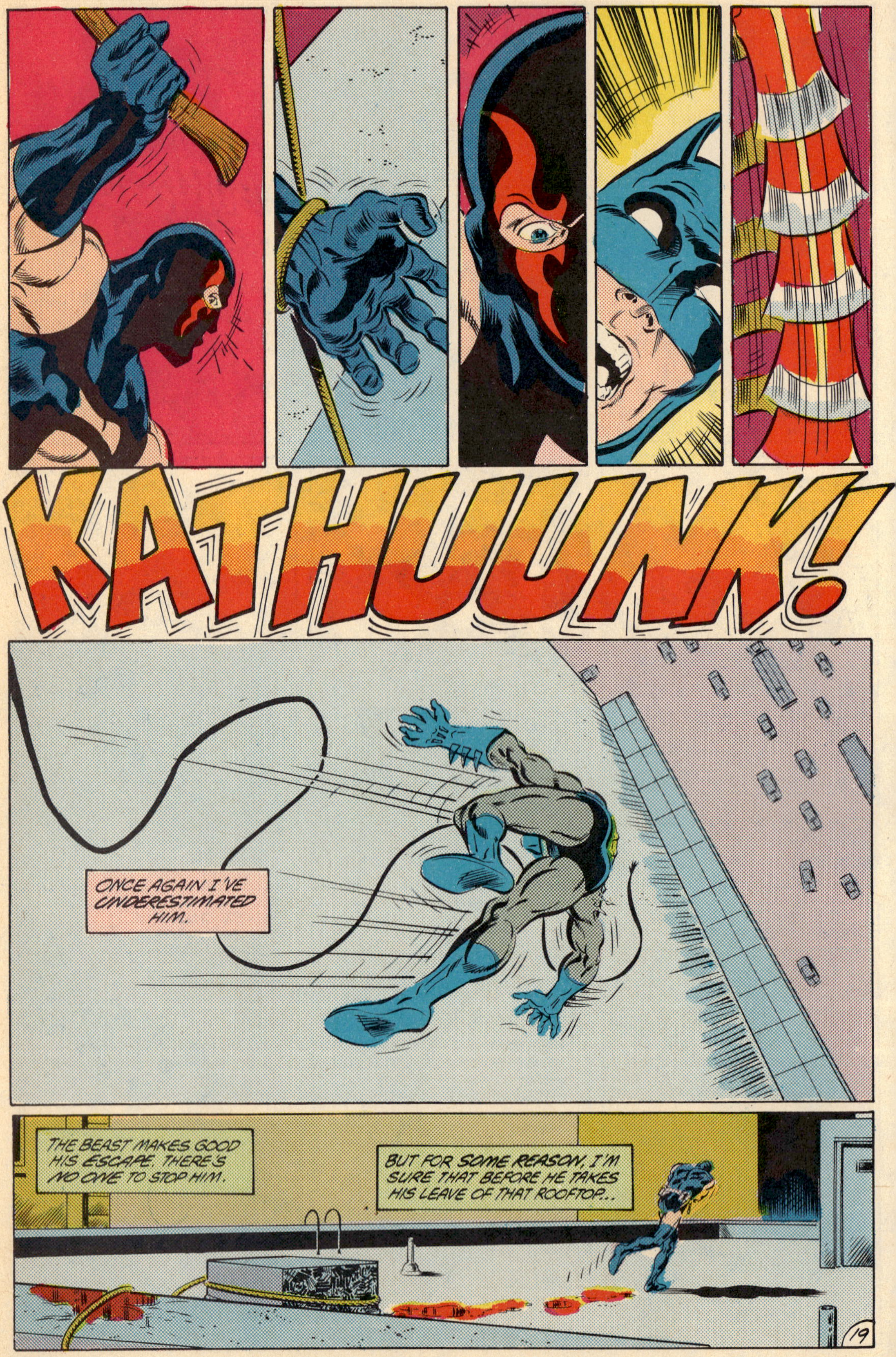
KATHUUNK!
ONCE AGAIN I'VE UNDERESTIMATED HIM.
THE BEAST MAKES GOOD HIS ESCAPE. THERE'S NO ONE TO STOP HIM.
BUT FOR SOME REASON, I'M SURE THAT BEFORE HE TAKES HIS LEAVE OF THAT ROOFTOP...
19

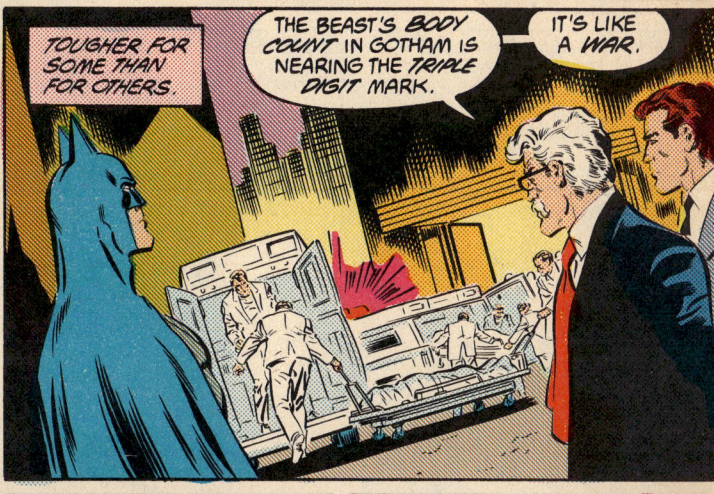

...THE BEAST TURNS AROUND AND SWEARS AN *OATH.*

IF ANYONE WERE AROUND TO HEAR IT, THEY *WOULDN'T* UNDERSTAND THE WORDS. THEY'RE IN RUSSIAN.

BUT ONE LOOK INTO THE *MAN'S* EYES WOULD CLARIFY HIS MEANING.

"*I WILL BE BACK!*"

SO WILL I, AS SOON AS I GET BANDAGED UP A BIT.

IT'S BEEN A *TOUGH* NIGHT.

TOUGHER FOR SOME THAN FOR OTHERS.

THE BEAST'S *BODY COUNT* IN GOTHAM IS NEARING THE *TRIPLE DIGIT* MARK.

IT'S LIKE A *WAR.*

WELL, AT LEAST WE SAVED *ONE* OF THE BEAST'S INTENDED VICTIMS, SENATOR *DAYLE.*

MAKE THAT *TWO.*

THREE IF YOU COUNT *ME.*

RALPH *BUNDY!* YOU'RE SUPPOSED TO BE *DEAD!*

KILLED IN THAT *PLANE CRASH* THIS MORNING!

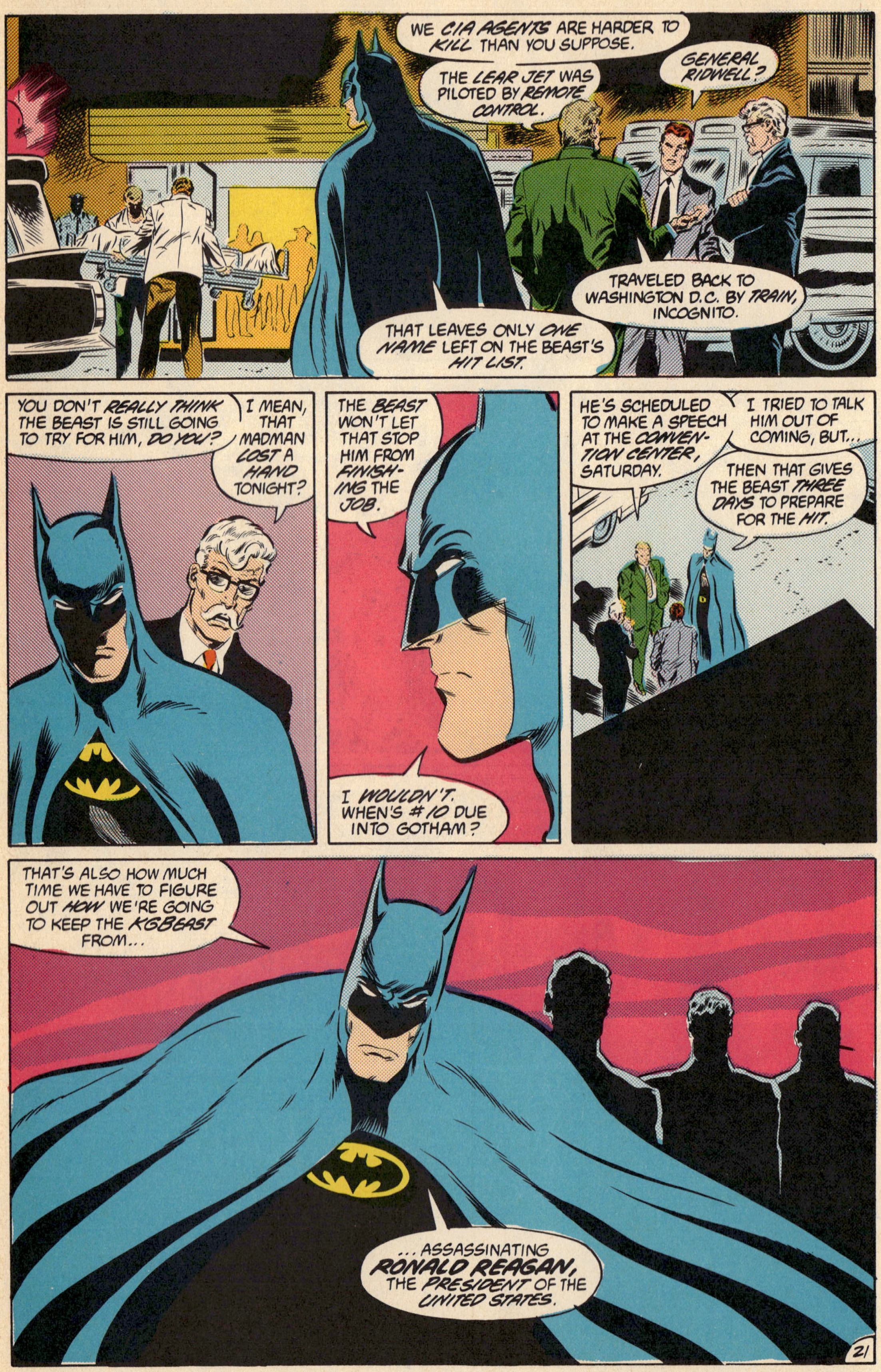
WE CIA AGENTS ARE HARDER TO KILL THAN YOU SUPPOSE.
THE LEAR JET WAS PILOTED BY REMOTE CONTROL.
GENERAL RIDWELL?
TRAVELED BACK TO WASHINGTON D.C. BY TRAIN, INCOGNITO.
THAT LEAVES ONLY ONE NAME LEFT ON THE BEAST'S HIT LIST.
YOU DON'T REALLY THINK THE BEAST IS STILL GOING TO TRY FOR HIM, DO YOU?
I MEAN, THAT MADMAN LOST A HAND TONIGHT?
THE BEAST WON'T LET THAT STOP HIM FROM FINISHING THE JOB.
I WOULDN'T. WHEN'S #10 DUE INTO GOTHAM?
HE'S SCHEDULED TO MAKE A SPEECH AT THE CONVENTION CENTER, SATURDAY.
I TRIED TO TALK HIM OUT OF COMING, BUT...
THEN THAT GIVES THE BEAST THREE DAYS TO PREPARE FOR THE HIT.
THAT'S ALSO HOW MUCH TIME WE HAVE TO FIGURE OUT HOW WE'RE GOING TO KEEP THE KGBEAST FROM...
...ASSASSINATING RONALD REAGAN, THE PRESIDENT OF THE UNITED STATES.
21

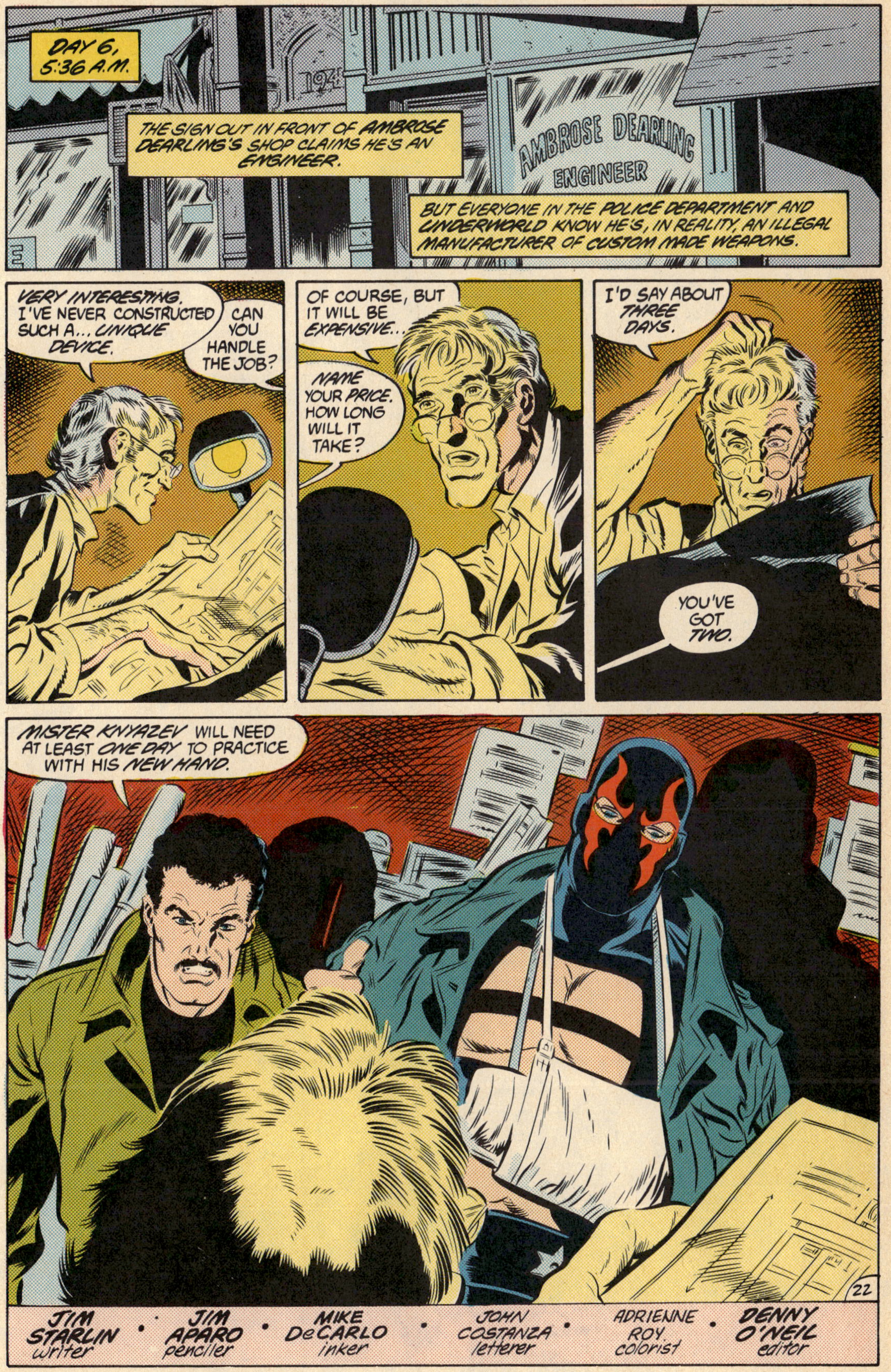
DAY 6, 5:36 A.M.
THE SIGN OUT IN FRONT OF AMBROSE DEARLING'S SHOP CLAIMS HE'S AN ENGINEER.
AMBROSE DEARLING ENGINEER
BUT EVERYONE IN THE POLICE DEPARTMENT AND UNDERWORLD KNOW HE'S, IN REALITY, AN ILLEGAL MANUFACTURER OF CUSTOM MADE WEAPONS.
VERY INTERESTING. I'VE NEVER CONSTRUCTED SUCH A... UNIQUE DEVICE.
CAN YOU HANDLE THE JOB?
OF COURSE, BUT IT WILL BE EXPENSIVE...
NAME YOUR PRICE. HOW LONG WILL IT TAKE?
I'D SAY ABOUT THREE DAYS.
YOU'VE GOT TWO.
MISTER KNYAZEV WILL NEED AT LEAST ONE DAY TO PRACTICE WITH HIS NEW HAND.
22
JIM STARLIN writer • JIM APARO penciller • MIKE DeCARLO inker • JOHN COSTANZA letterer • ADRIENNE ROY colorist • DENNY O'NEIL editor

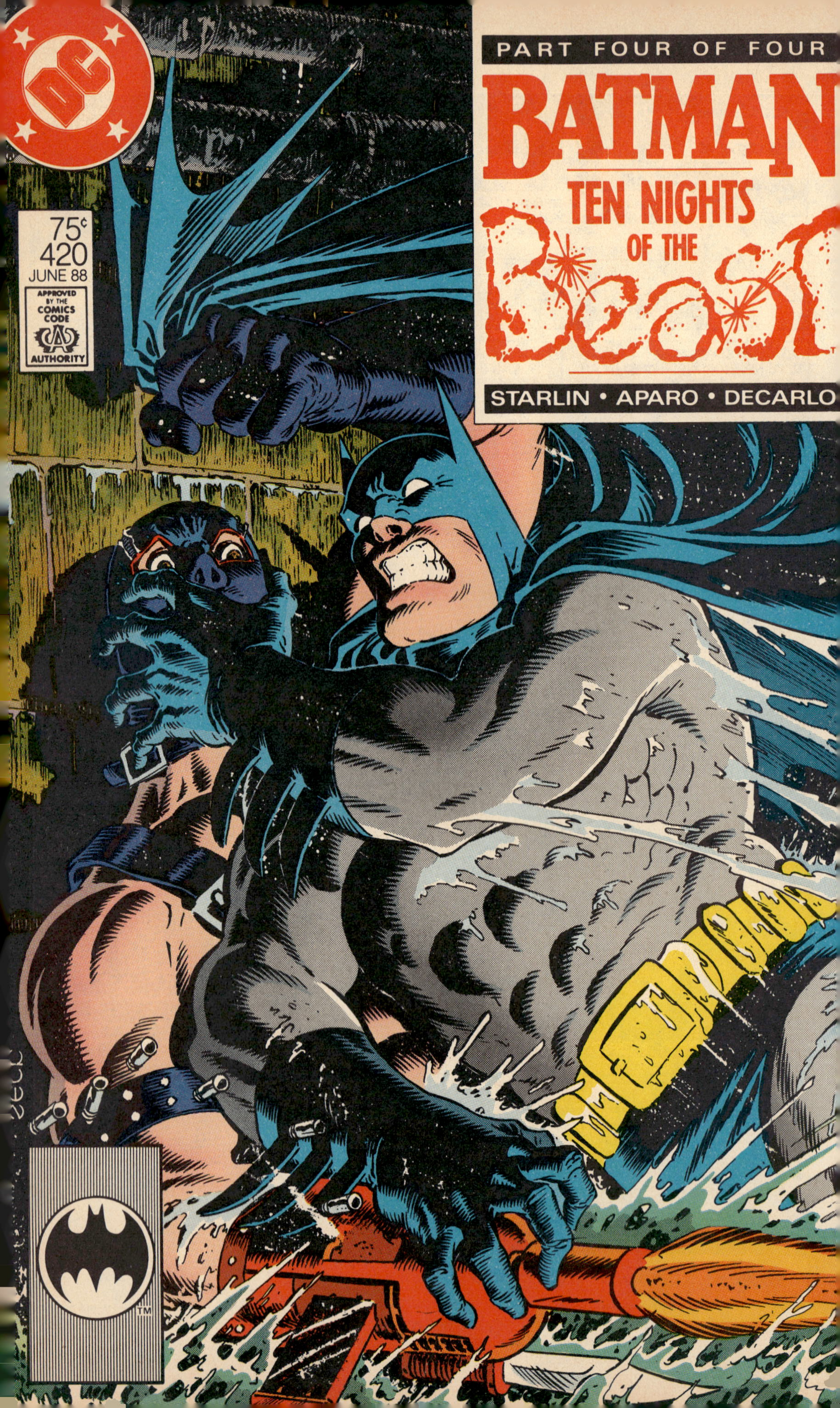
DC
PART FOUR OF FOUR
BATMAN
TEN NIGHTS OF THE BEAST
STARLIN • APARO • DECARLO
75¢
420
JUNE 88
APPROVED BY THE COMICS CODE AUTHORITY

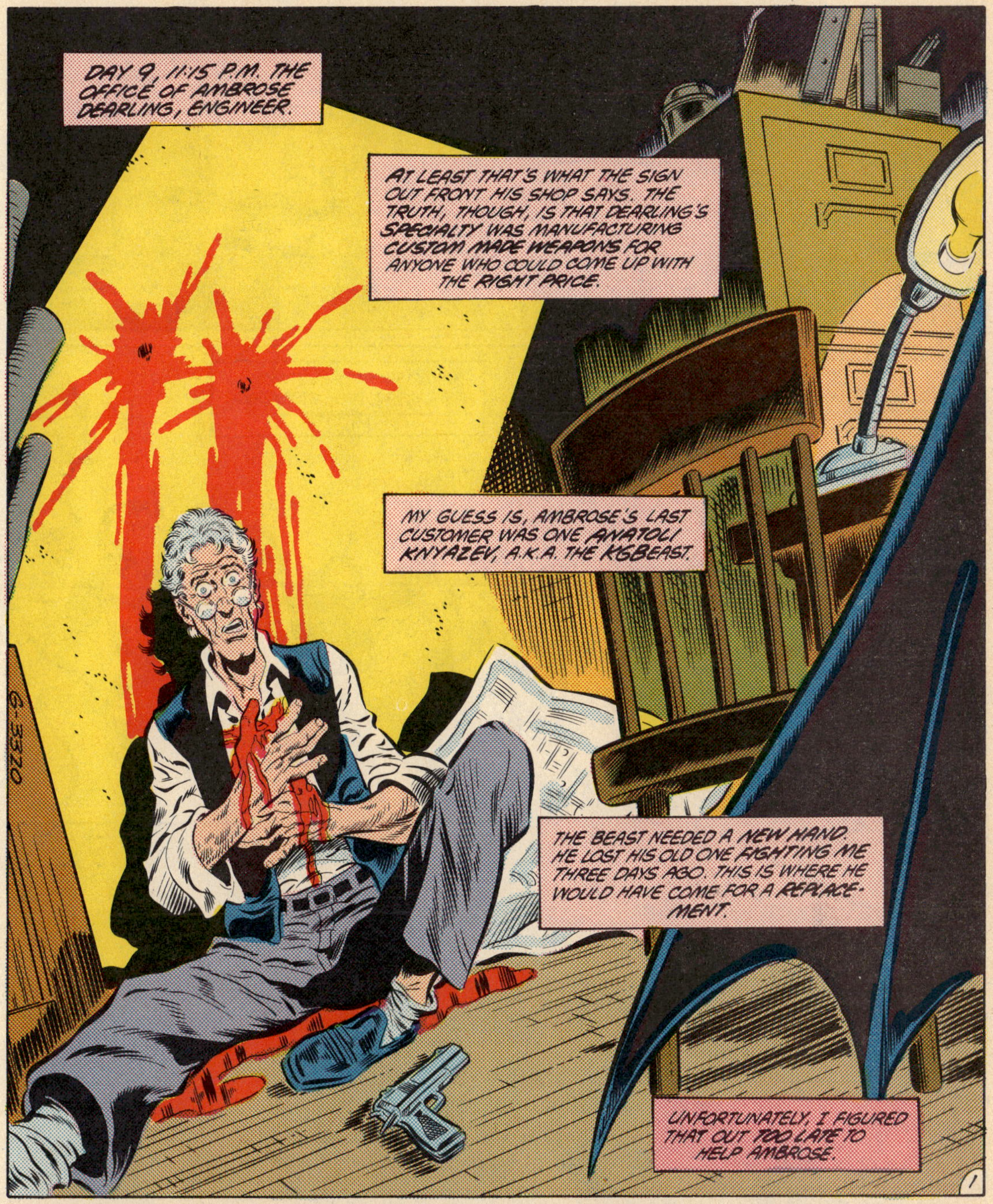
DAY 9, 11:15 P.M. THE OFFICE OF AMBROSE DEARLING, ENGINEER.
AT LEAST THAT'S WHAT THE SIGN OUT FRONT HIS SHOP SAYS. THE TRUTH, THOUGH, IS THAT DEARLING'S SPECIALTY WAS MANUFACTURING CUSTOM MADE WEAPONS FOR ANYONE WHO COULD COME UP WITH THE RIGHT PRICE.
MY GUESS IS, AMBROSE'S LAST CUSTOMER WAS ONE ANATOLI KNYAZEV, A.K.A. THE KGBEAST.
THE BEAST NEEDED A NEW HAND. HE LOST HIS OLD ONE FIGHTING ME THREE DAYS AGO. THIS IS WHERE HE WOULD HAVE COME FOR A REPLACE-MENT.
UNFORTUNATELY, I FIGURED THAT OUT TOO LATE TO HELP AMBROSE.

TEN NIGHTS OF THE BEAST PART 4

JIM STARLIN *writer* · JIM APARO *penciler* · MIKE DeCARLO *inker* · JOHN COSTANZA *letterer* · ADRIENNE ROY *colorist* · DENNY O'NEIL *editor*

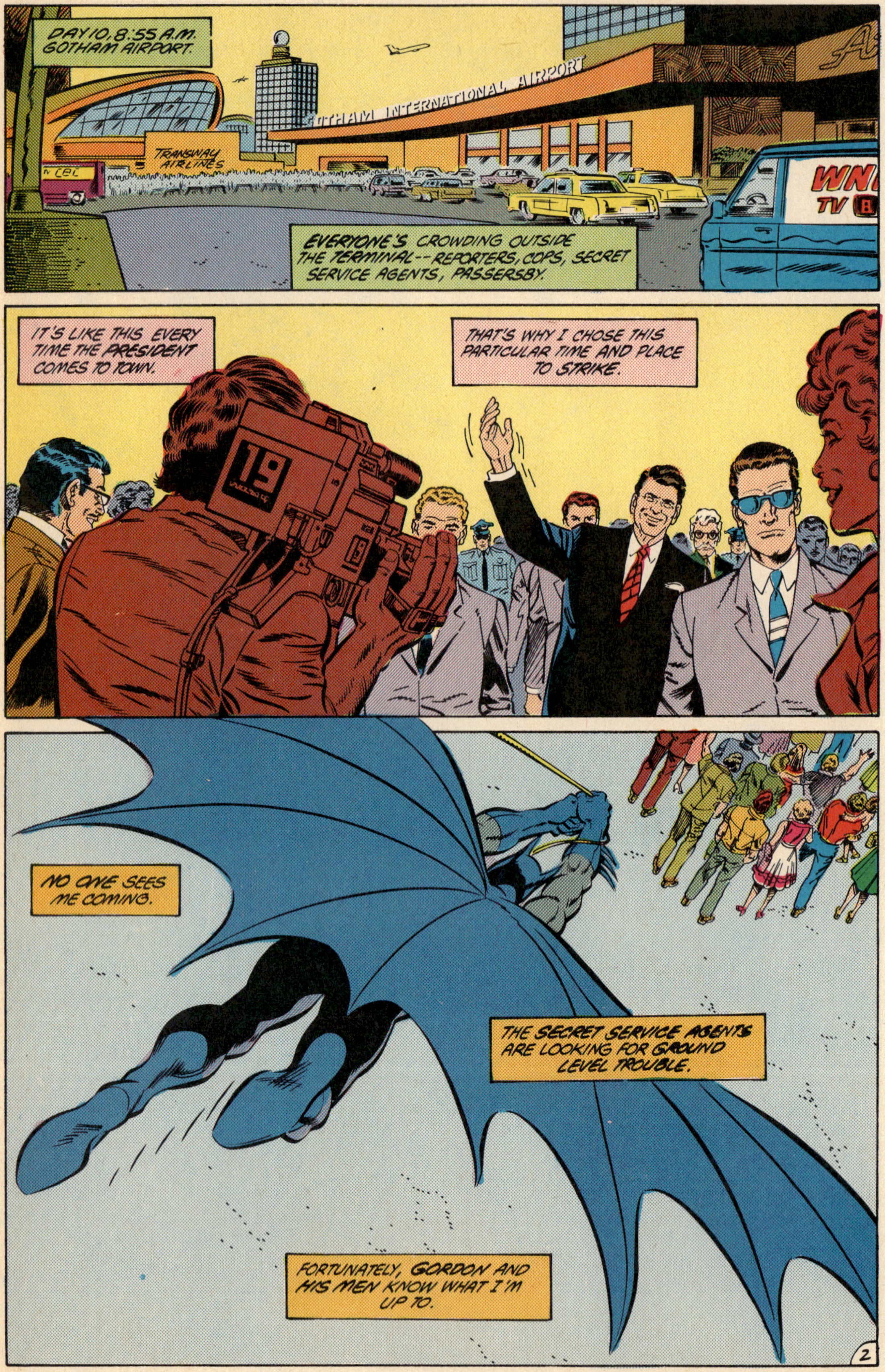
DAY 10, 8:55 A.M. GOTHAM AIRPORT.
GOTHAM INTERNATIONAL AIRPORT
TRANSWAY AIRLINES
EVERYONE'S CROWDING OUTSIDE THE TERMINAL--REPORTERS, COPS, SECRET SERVICE AGENTS, PASSERSBY.
IT'S LIKE THIS EVERY TIME THE PRESIDENT COMES TO TOWN.
THAT'S WHY I CHOSE THIS PARTICULAR TIME AND PLACE TO STRIKE.
NO ONE SEES ME COMING.
THE SECRET SERVICE AGENTS ARE LOOKING FOR GROUND LEVEL TROUBLE.
FORTUNATELY, GORDON AND HIS MEN KNOW WHAT I'M UP TO.
2

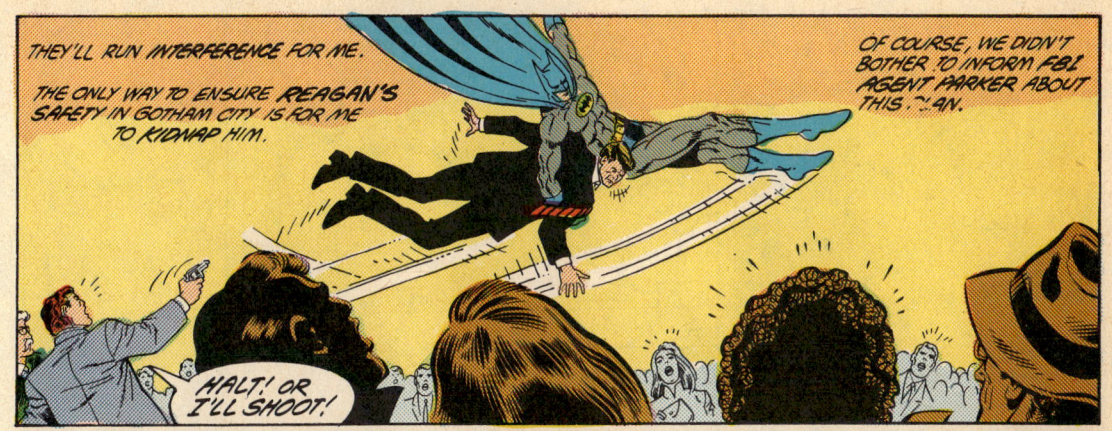

THEY'LL RUN INTERFERENCE FOR ME. THE ONLY WAY TO ENSURE *REAGAN'S* SAFETY IN GOTHAM CITY IS FOR ME TO *KIDNAP* HIM.

OF COURSE, WE DIDN'T BOTHER TO INFORM *F.B.I. AGENT PARKER* ABOUT THIS...

HALT! OR I'LL SHOOT!

I WARNED YOU...

KBLAM

SORRY, SLIPPED...

I APOLOGIZE FOR THIS *UNORTHODOX* PROCEDURE, MR. PRESIDENT.

I TAKE IT I'M BEING *KIDNAPPED?*

NO, SIR. YOU'RE BEING *ESCORTED* TO YOUR *HOTEL.*

I BELIEVE YOU KNOW *C.I.A.* AGENT *RALPH BUNDY.*

I HOPE YOU HAVE A *GOOD* REASON FOR THIS STUNT, SON.

JUST TRYING TO KEEP YOU *ALIVE*, SIR.

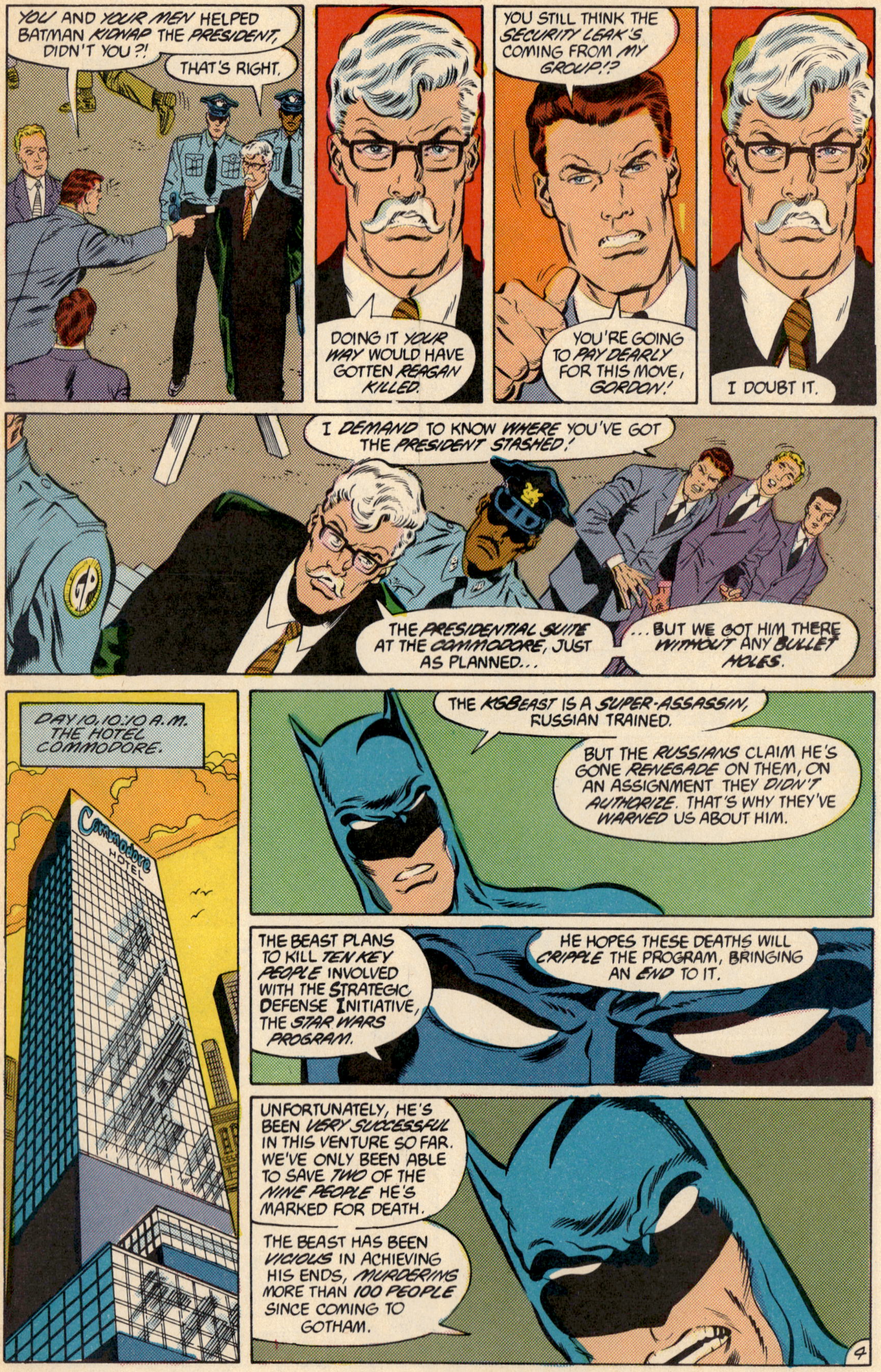

YOU AND YOUR MEN HELPED BATMAN KIDNAP THE PRESIDENT, DIDN'T YOU?!
THAT'S RIGHT.
DOING IT YOUR WAY WOULD HAVE GOTTEN REAGAN KILLED.
YOU STILL THINK THE SECURITY LEAK'S COMING FROM MY GROUP!?
YOU'RE GOING TO PAY DEARLY FOR THIS MOVE, GORDON!
I DOUBT IT.
I DEMAND TO KNOW WHERE YOU'VE GOT THE PRESIDENT STASHED!
THE PRESIDENTIAL SUITE AT THE COMMODORE, JUST AS PLANNED...
...BUT WE GOT HIM THERE WITHOUT ANY BULLET HOLES.
DAY 10, 10:10 A.M. THE HOTEL COMMODORE.
COMMODORE HOTEL
THE KGBEAST IS A SUPER-ASSASSIN, RUSSIAN TRAINED.
BUT THE RUSSIANS CLAIM HE'S GONE RENEGADE ON THEM, ON AN ASSIGNMENT THEY DIDN'T AUTHORIZE. THAT'S WHY THEY'VE WARNED US ABOUT HIM.
THE BEAST PLANS TO KILL TEN KEY PEOPLE INVOLVED WITH THE STRATEGIC DEFENSE INITIATIVE, THE STAR WARS PROGRAM.
HE HOPES THESE DEATHS WILL CRIPPLE THE PROGRAM, BRINGING AN END TO IT.
UNFORTUNATELY, HE'S BEEN VERY SUCCESSFUL IN THIS VENTURE SO FAR. WE'VE ONLY BEEN ABLE TO SAVE TWO OF THE NINE PEOPLE HE'S MARKED FOR DEATH.
THE BEAST HAS BEEN VICIOUS IN ACHIEVING HIS ENDS, MURDERING MORE THAN 100 PEOPLE SINCE COMING TO GOTHAM.
4

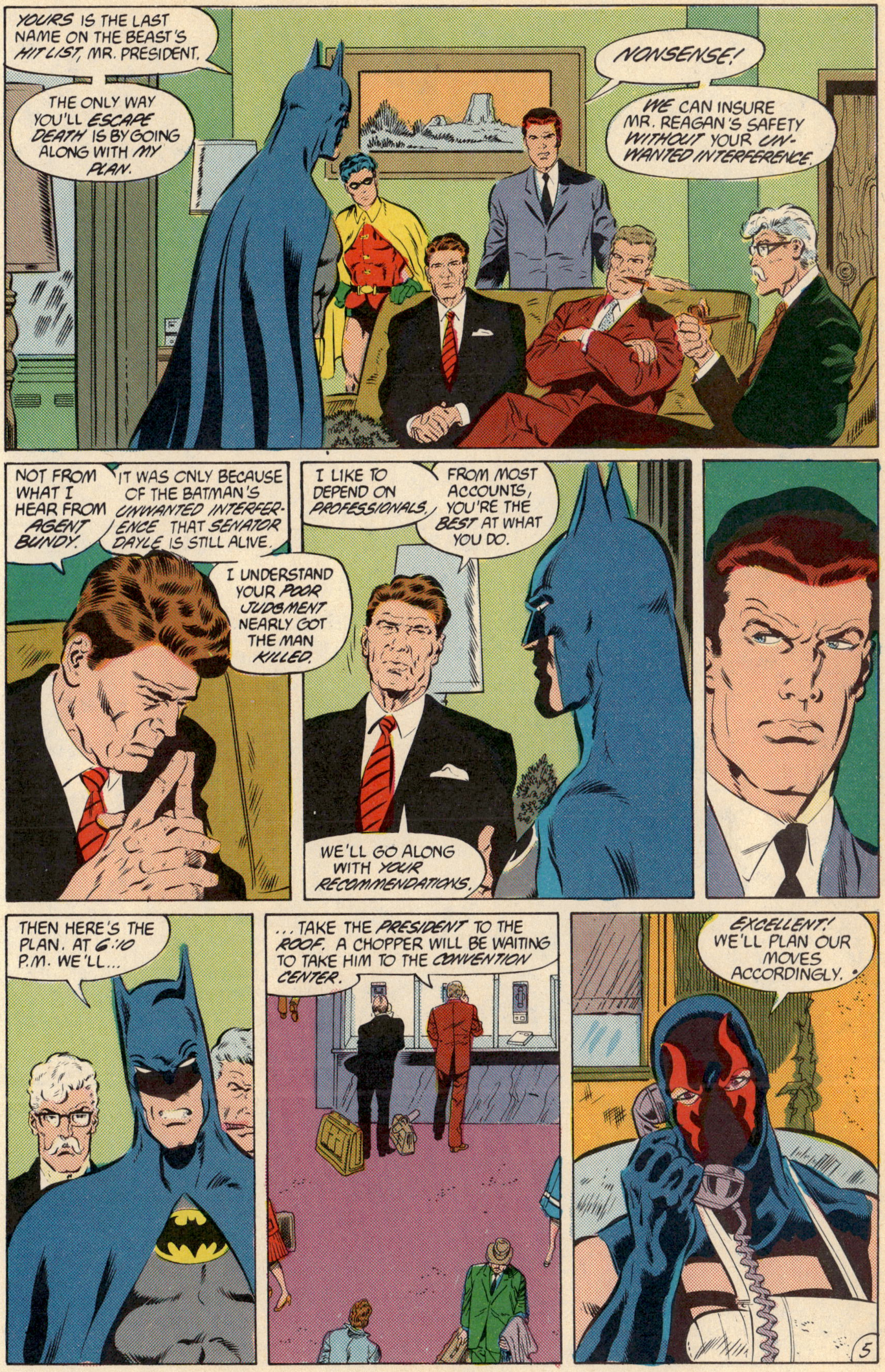
YOURS IS THE LAST NAME ON THE BEAST'S HIT LIST, MR. PRESIDENT.
THE ONLY WAY YOU'LL ESCAPE DEATH IS BY GOING ALONG WITH MY PLAN.
NONSENSE!
WE CAN INSURE MR. REAGAN'S SAFETY WITHOUT YOUR UNWANTED INTERFERENCE.
NOT FROM WHAT I HEAR FROM AGENT BUNDY.
IT WAS ONLY BECAUSE OF THE BATMAN'S UNWANTED INTERFERENCE THAT SENATOR DAYLE IS STILL ALIVE.
I UNDERSTAND YOUR POOR JUDGMENT NEARLY GOT THE MAN KILLED.
I LIKE TO DEPEND ON PROFESSIONALS.
FROM MOST ACCOUNTS, YOU'RE THE BEST AT WHAT YOU DO.
WE'LL GO ALONG WITH YOUR RECOMMENDATIONS.
THEN HERE'S THE PLAN. AT 6:10 P.M. WE'LL...
...TAKE THE PRESIDENT TO THE ROOF. A CHOPPER WILL BE WAITING TO TAKE HIM TO THE CONVENTION CENTER.
EXCELLENT! WE'LL PLAN OUR MOVES ACCORDINGLY.
5

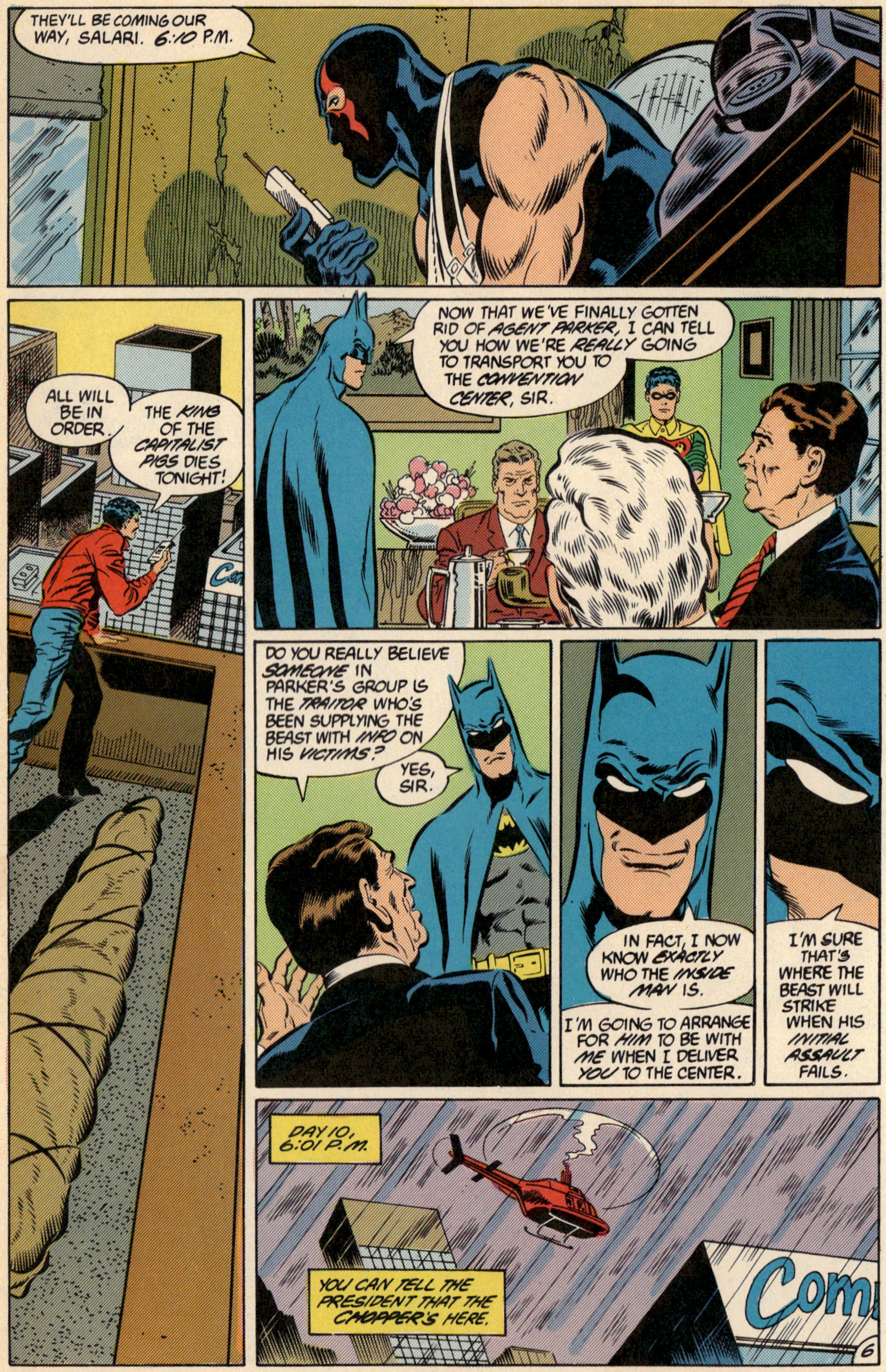
THEY'LL BE COMING OUR WAY, SALARI. 6:10 P.M.
ALL WILL BE IN ORDER.
THE KING OF THE CAPITALIST PIGS DIES TONIGHT!
NOW THAT WE'VE FINALLY GOTTEN RID OF AGENT PARKER, I CAN TELL YOU HOW WE'RE REALLY GOING TO TRANSPORT YOU TO THE CONVENTION CENTER, SIR.
DO YOU REALLY BELIEVE SOMEONE IN PARKER'S GROUP IS THE TRAITOR WHO'S BEEN SUPPLYING THE BEAST WITH INFO ON HIS VICTIMS?
YES, SIR.
IN FACT, I NOW KNOW EXACTLY WHO THE INSIDE MAN IS.
I'M GOING TO ARRANGE FOR HIM TO BE WITH ME WHEN I DELIVER YOU TO THE CENTER.
I'M SURE THAT'S WHERE THE BEAST WILL STRIKE WHEN HIS INITIAL ASSAULT FAILS.
DAY 10, 6:01 P.M.
YOU CAN TELL THE PRESIDENT THAT THE CHOPPER'S HERE.
6

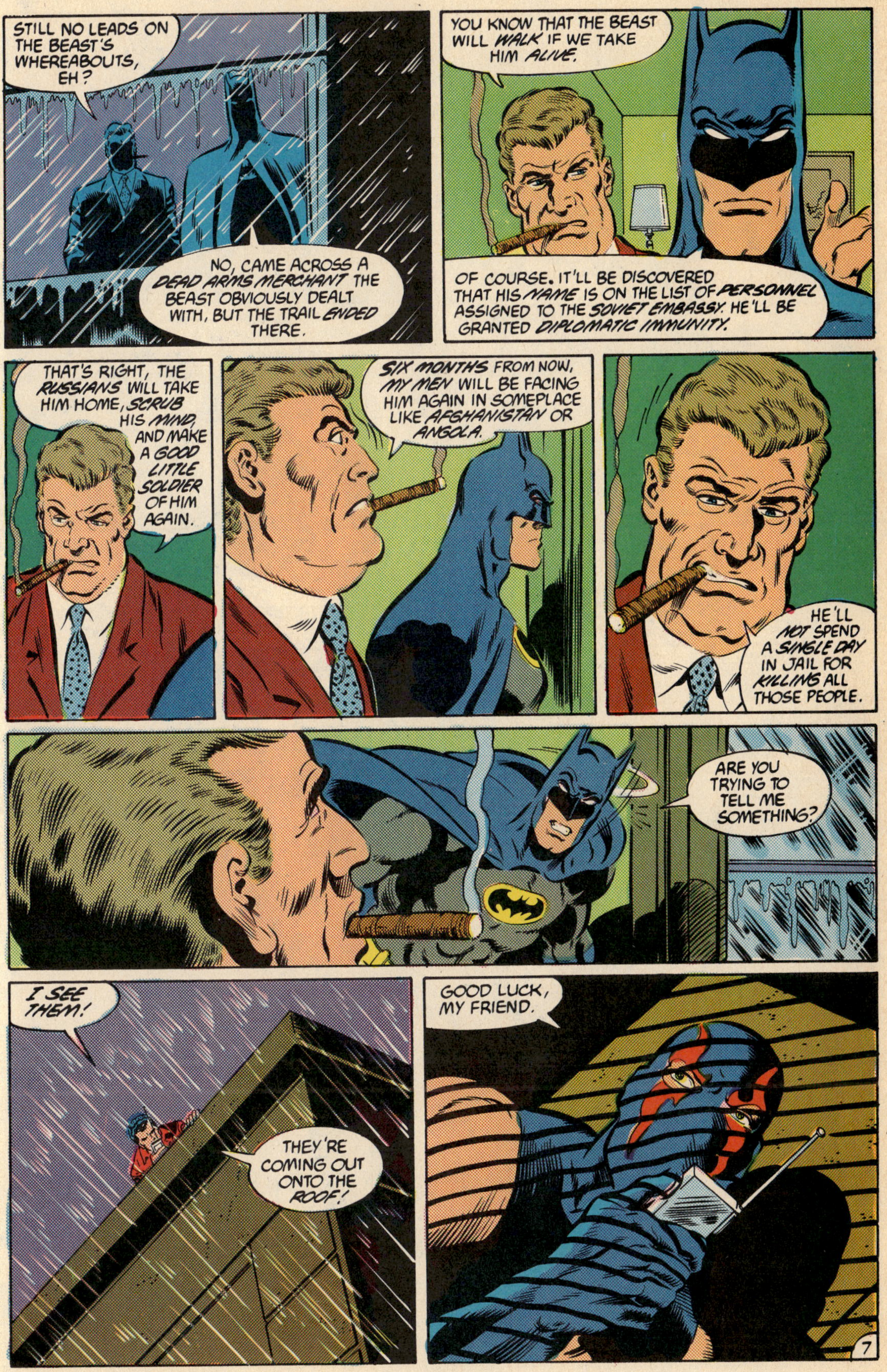

STILL NO LEADS ON THE BEAST'S WHEREABOUTS, EH?
NO, CAME ACROSS A DEAD ARMS MERCHANT THE BEAST OBVIOUSLY DEALT WITH, BUT THE TRAIL ENDED THERE.
YOU KNOW THAT THE BEAST WILL WALK IF WE TAKE HIM ALIVE.
OF COURSE. IT'LL BE DISCOVERED THAT HIS NAME IS ON THE LIST OF PERSONNEL ASSIGNED TO THE SOVIET EMBASSY. HE'LL BE GRANTED DIPLOMATIC IMMUNITY.
THAT'S RIGHT, THE RUSSIANS WILL TAKE HIM HOME, SCRUB HIS MIND, AND MAKE A GOOD LITTLE SOLDIER OF HIM AGAIN.
SIX MONTHS FROM NOW, MY MEN WILL BE FACING HIM AGAIN IN SOMEPLACE LIKE AFGHANISTAN OR ANGOLA.
HE'LL NOT SPEND A SINGLE DAY IN JAIL FOR KILLING ALL THOSE PEOPLE.
ARE YOU TRYING TO TELL ME SOMETHING?
I SEE THEM!
THEY'RE COMING OUT ONTO THE ROOF!
GOOD LUCK, MY FRIEND.
7

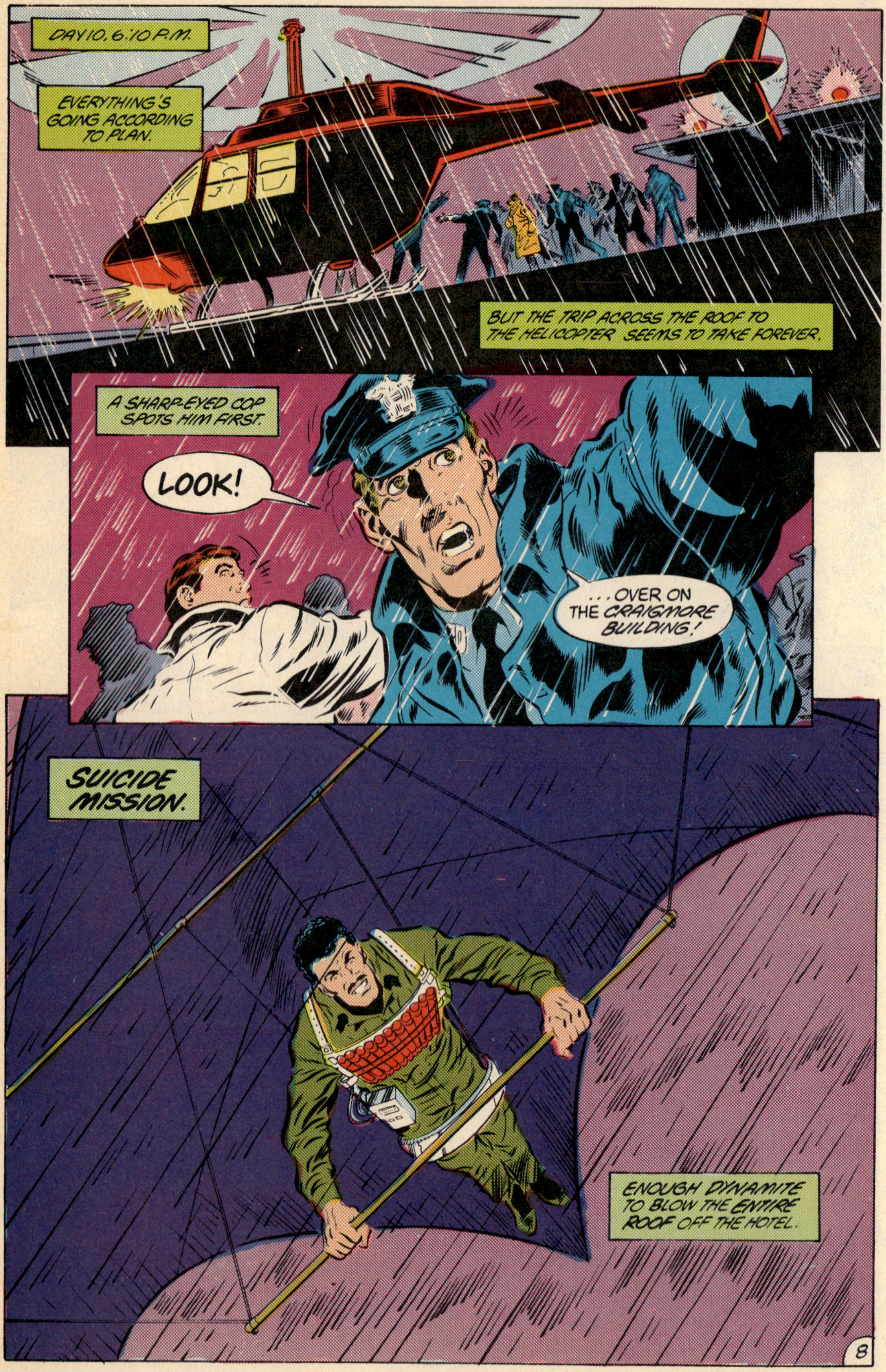
DAY 10, 6:10 P.M.
EVERYTHING'S GOING ACCORDING TO PLAN.
BUT THE TRIP ACROSS THE ROOF TO THE HELICOPTER SEEMS TO TAKE FOREVER.
A SHARP-EYED COP SPOTS HIM FIRST.
LOOK!
...OVER ON THE CRAIGMORE BUILDING!
SUICIDE MISSION.
ENOUGH DYNAMITE TO BLOW THE ENTIRE ROOF OFF THE HOTEL.
8

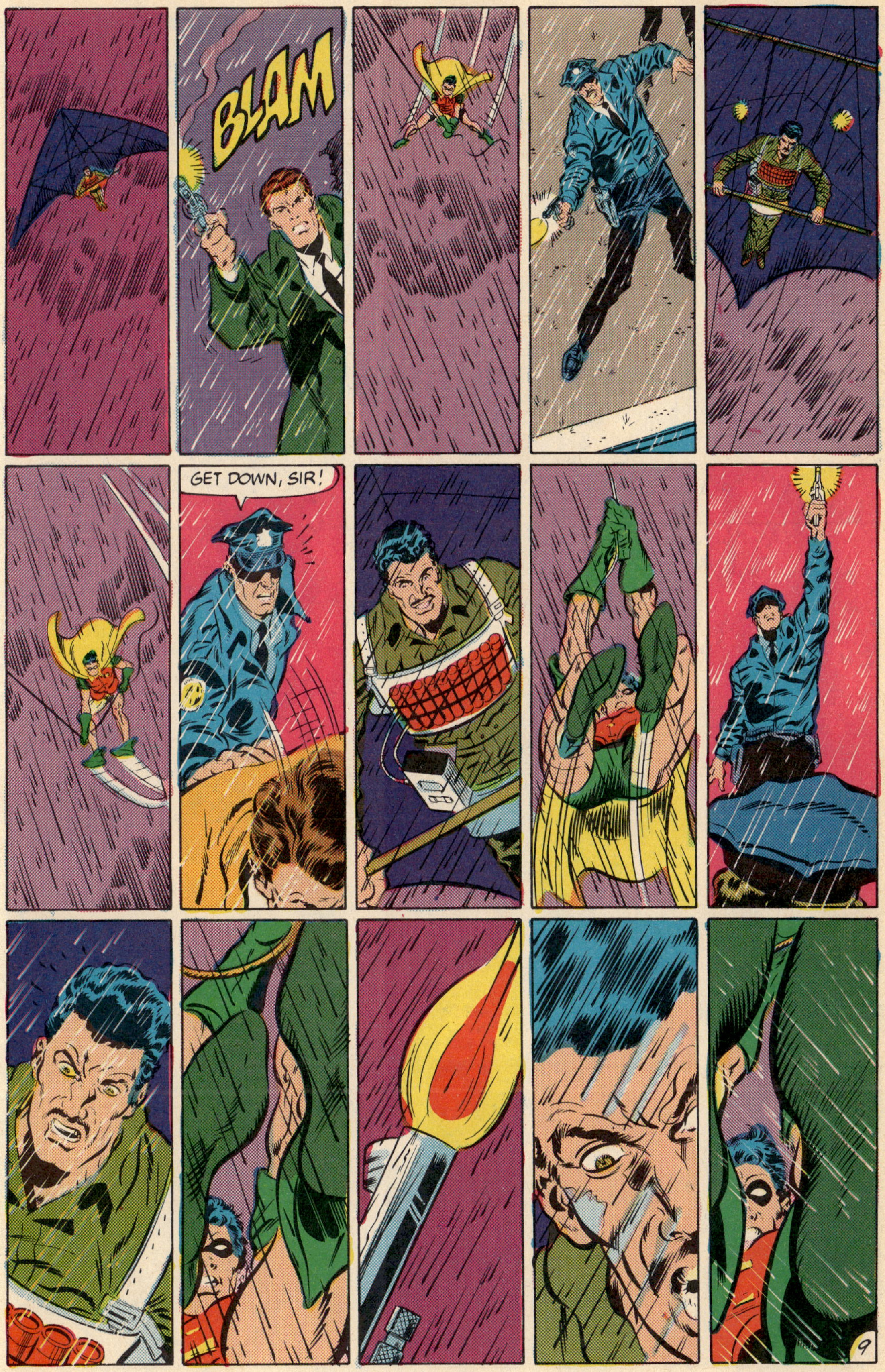
BLAM
GET DOWN, SIR!
9

WHUD

ROBIN ONLY GETS *ONE* CHANCE TO KNOCK THE ASSASSIN OFF COURSE.

HE DOESN'T WASTE THE OPPORTUNITY.

SALAR! AND SOME WINDOWS ARE THE ONLY FATALITIES.

A FINE JOB, LAD.

THANK YOU, MR. PRESIDENT.

MR. PRESIDENT! ARE YOU ALL RIGHT!

I'M FIT AS A FIDDLE, PARKER. HOW ARE YOU?

GORDON!! WHERE'S THE PRESIDENT?!

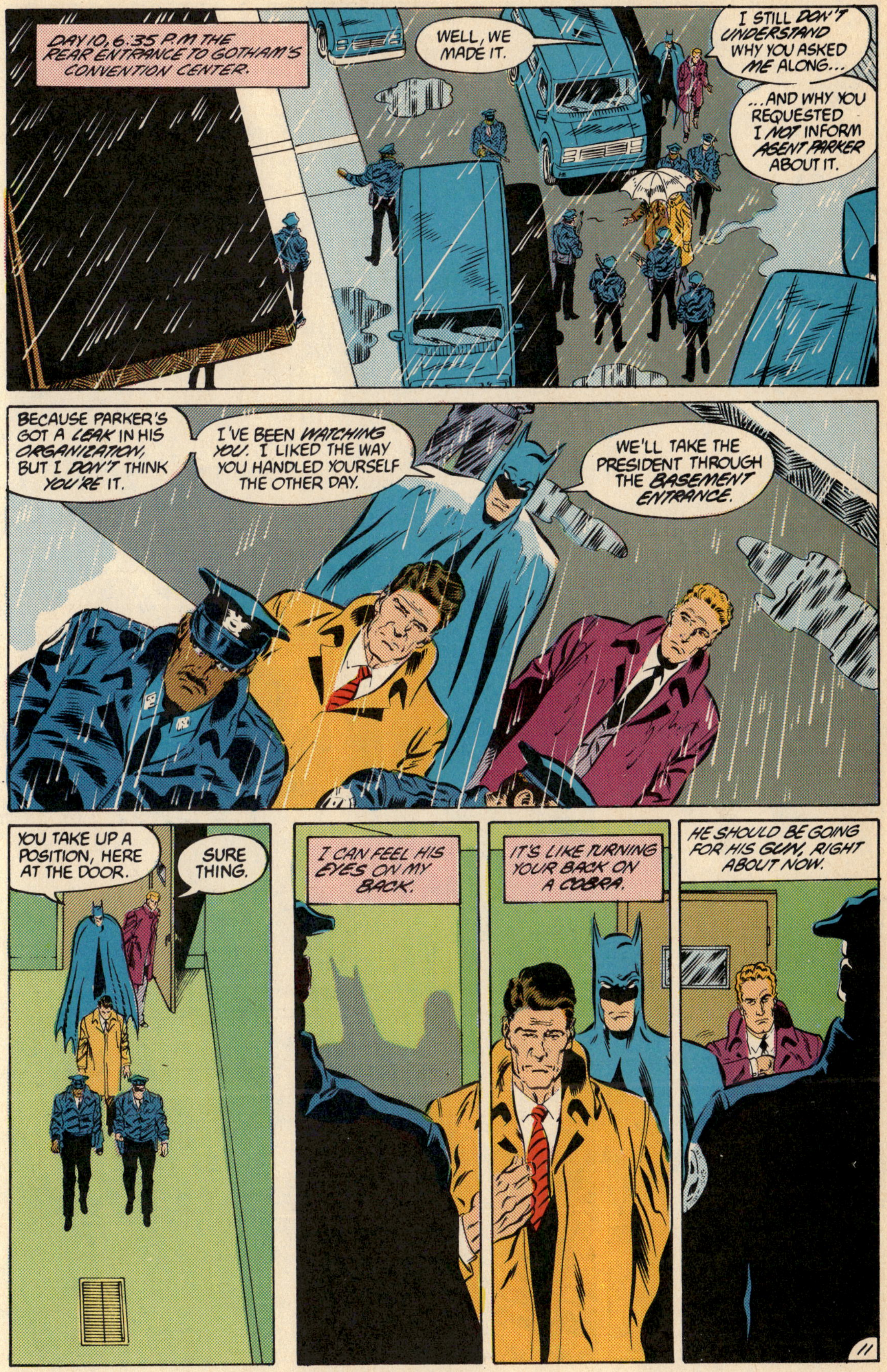
DAY 10, 6:35 P.M. THE REAR ENTRANCE TO GOTHAM'S CONVENTION CENTER.
WELL, WE MADE IT.
I STILL DON'T UNDERSTAND WHY YOU ASKED ME ALONG...
...AND WHY YOU REQUESTED I NOT INFORM AGENT PARKER ABOUT IT.
BECAUSE PARKER'S GOT A LEAK IN HIS ORGANIZATION. BUT I DON'T THINK YOU'RE IT.
I'VE BEEN WATCHING YOU. I LIKED THE WAY YOU HANDLED YOURSELF THE OTHER DAY.
WE'LL TAKE THE PRESIDENT THROUGH THE BASEMENT ENTRANCE.
YOU TAKE UP A POSITION, HERE AT THE DOOR.
SURE THING.
I CAN FEEL HIS EYES ON MY BACK.
IT'S LIKE TURNING YOUR BACK ON A COBRA.
HE SHOULD BE GOING FOR HIS GUN, RIGHT ABOUT NOW.
11

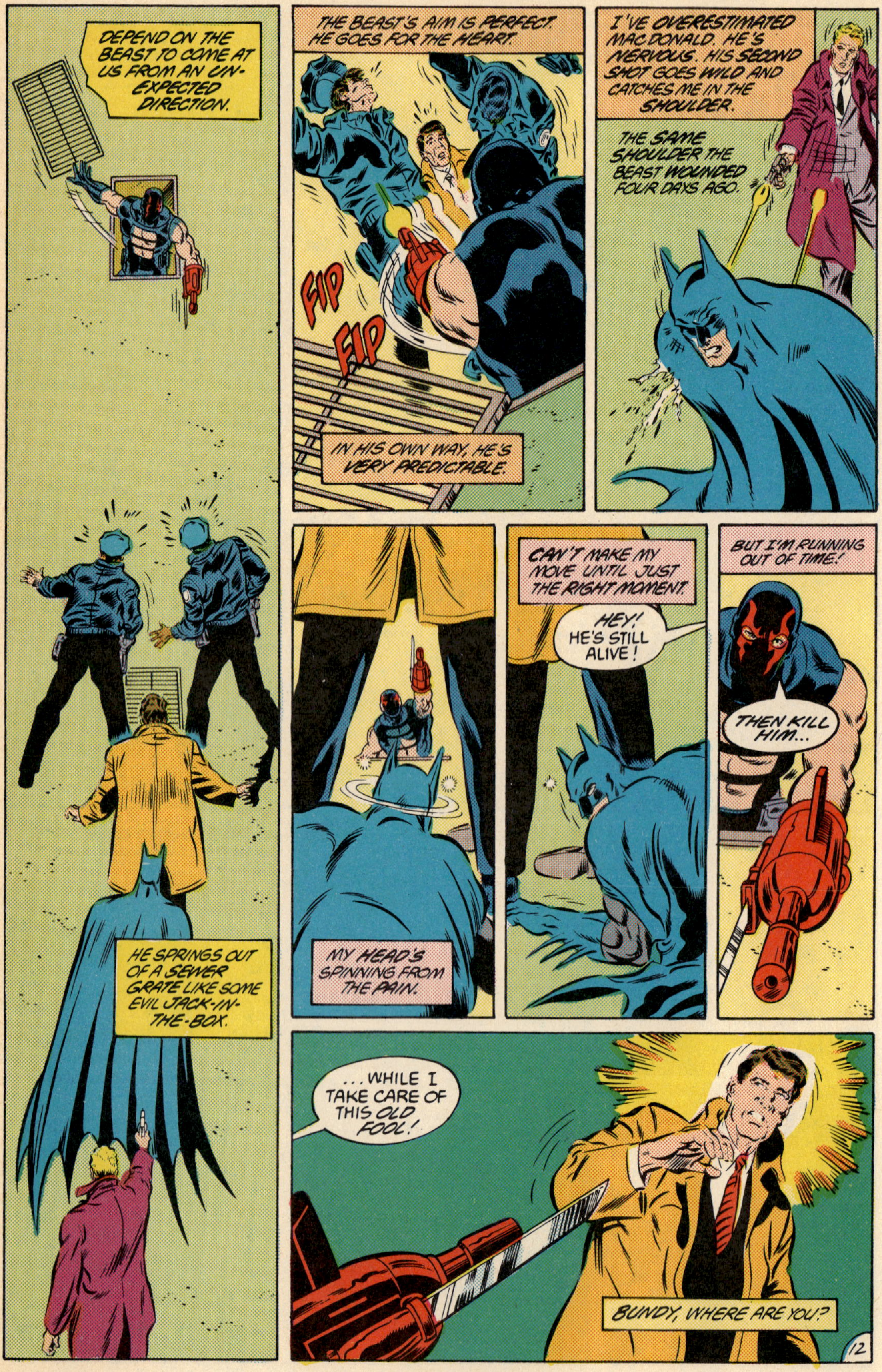

DEPEND ON THE BEAST TO COME AT US FROM AN UN-EXPECTED DIRECTION.
HE SPRINGS OUT OF A SEWER GRATE LIKE SOME EVIL JACK-IN-THE-BOX.
THE BEAST'S AIM IS PERFECT. HE GOES FOR THE HEART.
FIP
FIP
IN HIS OWN WAY, HE'S VERY PREDICTABLE.
I'VE OVERESTIMATED MACDONALD. HE'S NERVOUS. HIS SECOND SHOT GOES WILD AND CATCHES ME IN THE SHOULDER.
THE SAME SHOULDER THE BEAST WOUNDED FOUR DAYS AGO.
MY HEAD'S SPINNING FROM THE PAIN.
CAN'T MAKE MY MOVE UNTIL JUST THE RIGHT MOMENT.
HEY! HE'S STILL ALIVE!
BUT I'M RUNNING OUT OF TIME!
THEN KILL HIM...
...WHILE I TAKE CARE OF THIS OLD FOOL!
BUNDY, WHERE ARE YOU?
12

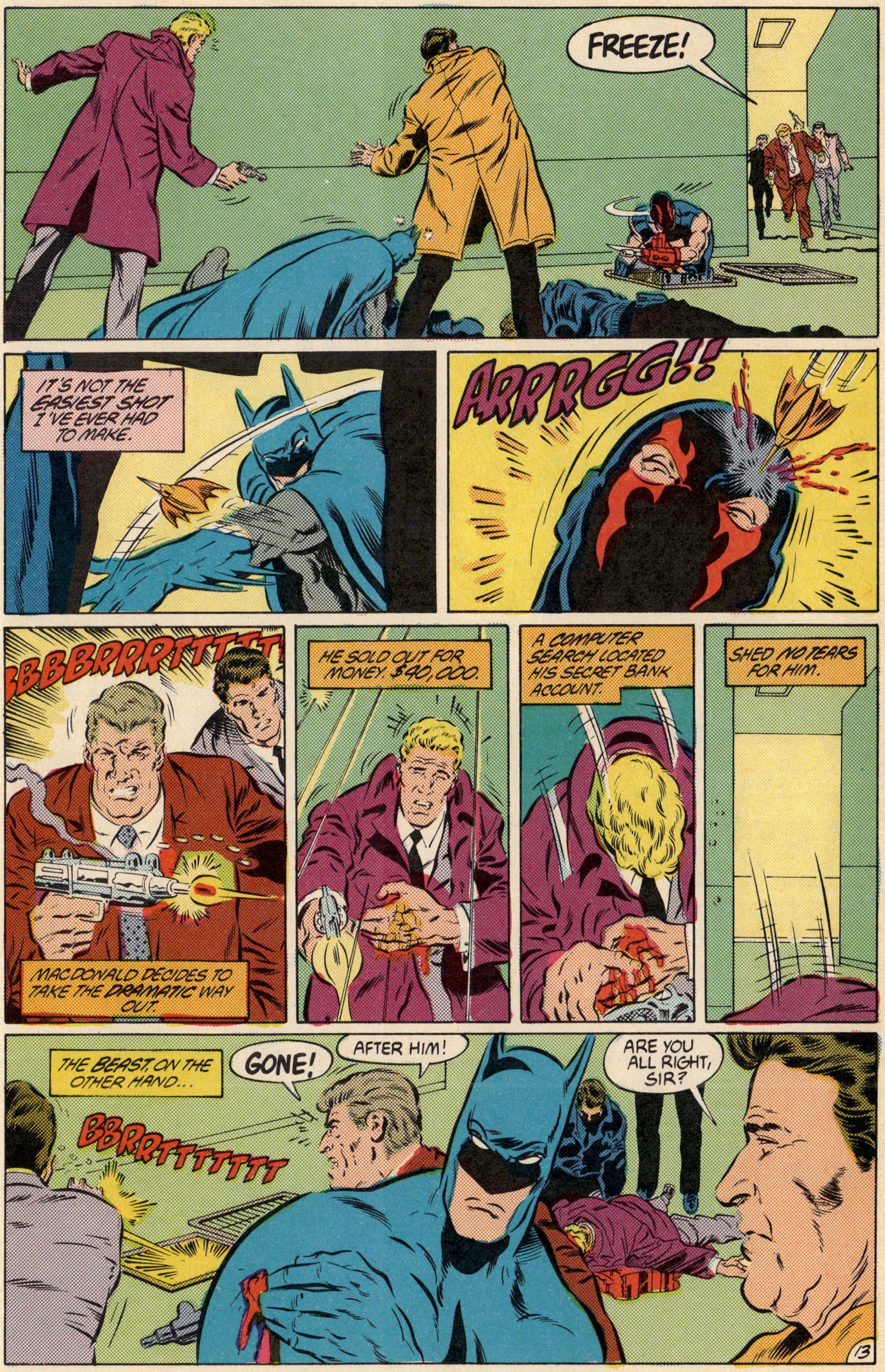

FREEZE!
IT'S NOT THE EASIEST SHOT I'VE EVER HAD TO MAKE.
ARRRGG!!
BBBBRRRRTTTTTT
MACDONALD DECIDES TO TAKE THE DRAMATIC WAY OUT.
HE SOLD OUT FOR MONEY. $40,000.
A COMPUTER SEARCH LOCATED HIS SECRET BANK ACCOUNT.
SHED NO TEARS FOR HIM.
THE BEAST, ON THE OTHER HAND...
BBRRRTTTTTTTT
GONE!
AFTER HIM!
ARE YOU ALL RIGHT, SIR?
13

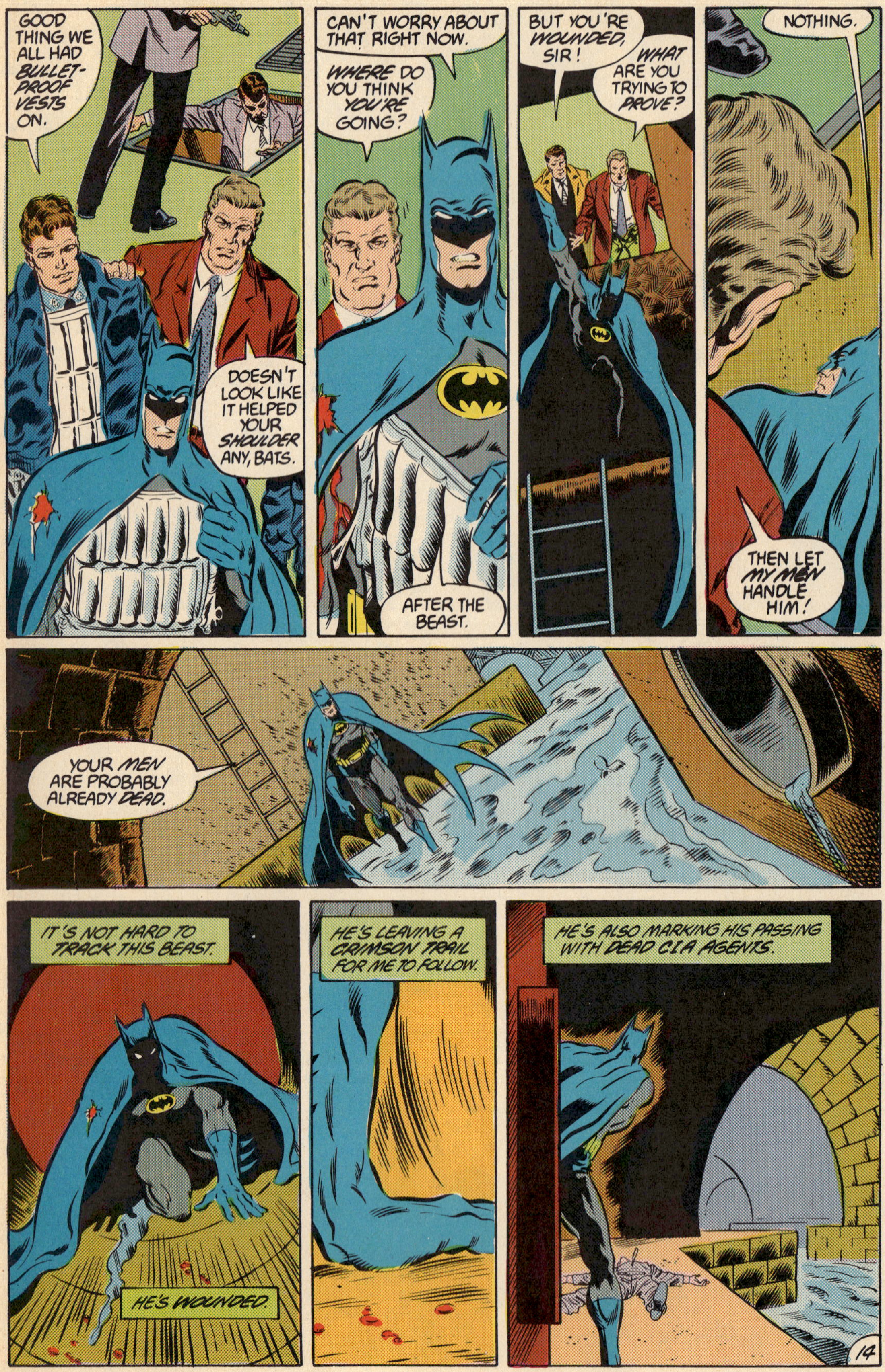
GOOD THING WE ALL HAD BULLET-PROOF VESTS ON.
DOESN'T LOOK LIKE IT HELPED YOUR SHOULDER ANY, BATS.
CAN'T WORRY ABOUT THAT RIGHT NOW.
WHERE DO YOU THINK YOU'RE GOING?
AFTER THE BEAST.
BUT YOU'RE WOUNDED, SIR!
WHAT ARE YOU TRYING TO PROVE?
NOTHING.
THEN LET MY MEN HANDLE HIM!
YOUR MEN ARE PROBABLY ALREADY DEAD.
IT'S NOT HARD TO TRACK THIS BEAST.
HE'S WOUNDED.
HE'S LEAVING A CRIMSON TRAIL FOR ME TO FOLLOW.
HE'S ALSO MARKING HIS PASSING WITH DEAD C.I.A. AGENTS.
14

THE TRAIL KEEPS LEADING *DEEPER* INTO THE BOWELS OF THE CITY.

HAVE TO TAKE IT *EXTREMELY* EASY FROM HERE ON.

I'M NOT ALONE DOWN HERE.

DEATH'S WAITING FOR ME.

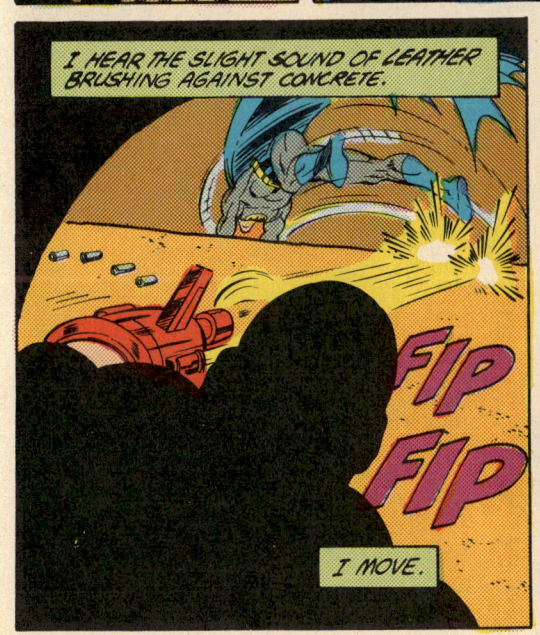

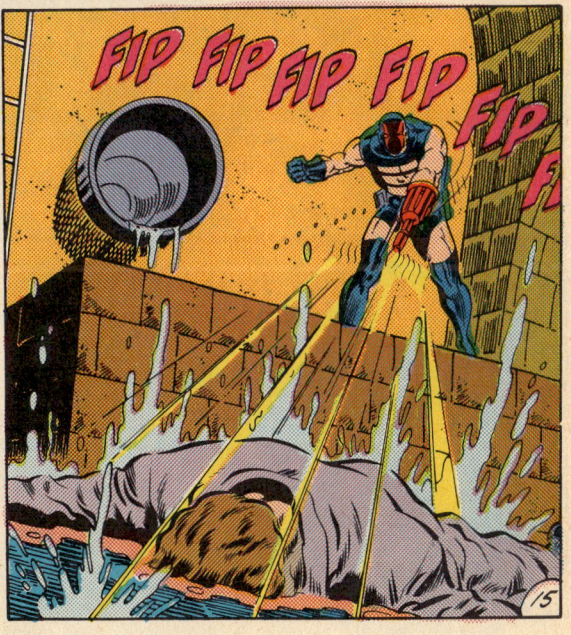

THE BEAST KNOWS I'LL BE COMING FOR HIM.

IF I WERE HIM, I'D SET UP AN *AMBUSH*.

I HEAR THE SLIGHT SOUND OF LEATHER BRUSHING AGAINST CONCRETE.

FIP FIP

I MOVE.

FIP FIP FIP FIP FIP

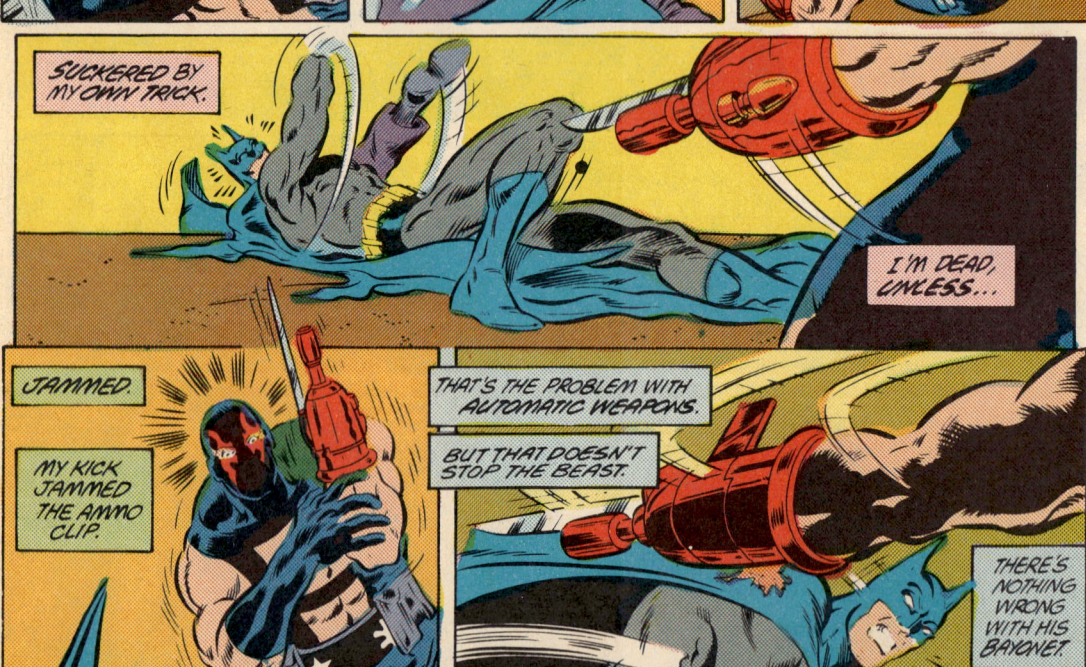

WHUMP

The flying dead man maneuver buys me a half second.

Have to put that gun out of action.

FIIP

Then the beast turns the tables on me.

Suckered by my own trick.

I'm dead, unless...

Jammed. My kick jammed the ammo clip.

That's the problem with automatic weapons.

But that doesn't stop the beast.

There's nothing wrong with his bayonet.

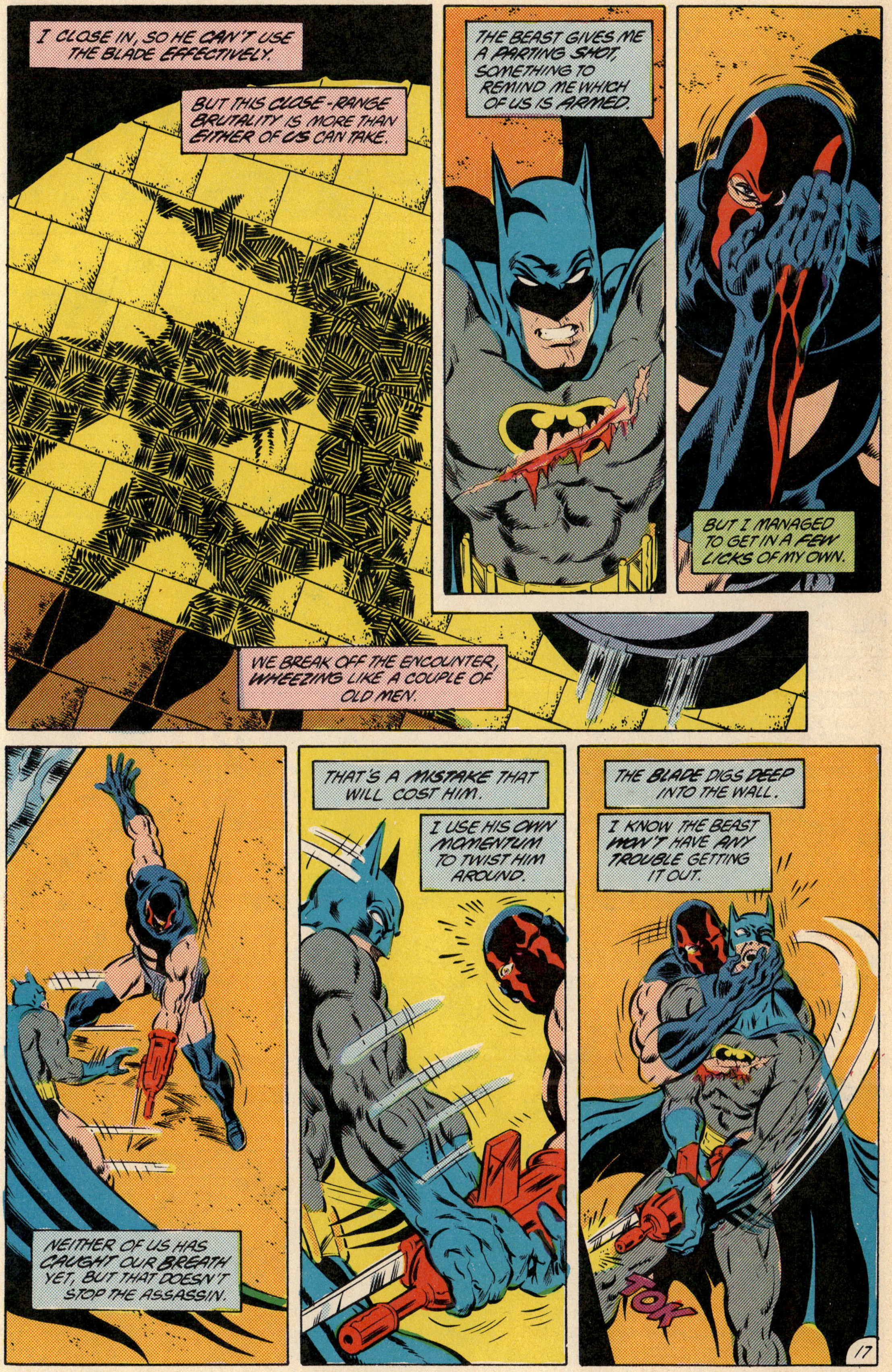
I CLOSE IN, SO HE CAN'T USE THE BLADE EFFECTIVELY.
BUT THIS CLOSE-RANGE BRUTALITY IS MORE THAN EITHER OF US CAN TAKE.
THE BEAST GIVES ME A PARTING SHOT, SOMETHING TO REMIND ME WHICH OF US IS ARMED.
BUT I MANAGED TO GET IN A FEW LICKS OF MY OWN.
WE BREAK OFF THE ENCOUNTER, WHEEZING LIKE A COUPLE OF OLD MEN.
NEITHER OF US HAS CAUGHT OUR BREATH YET, BUT THAT DOESN'T STOP THE ASSASSIN.
THAT'S A MISTAKE THAT WILL COST HIM.
I USE HIS OWN MOMENTUM TO TWIST HIM AROUND.
THE BLADE DIGS DEEP INTO THE WALL.
I KNOW THE BEAST WON'T HAVE ANY TROUBLE GETTING IT OUT.
TOK
17

SO I SHATTER IT BEFORE HE GETS THE CHANCE.

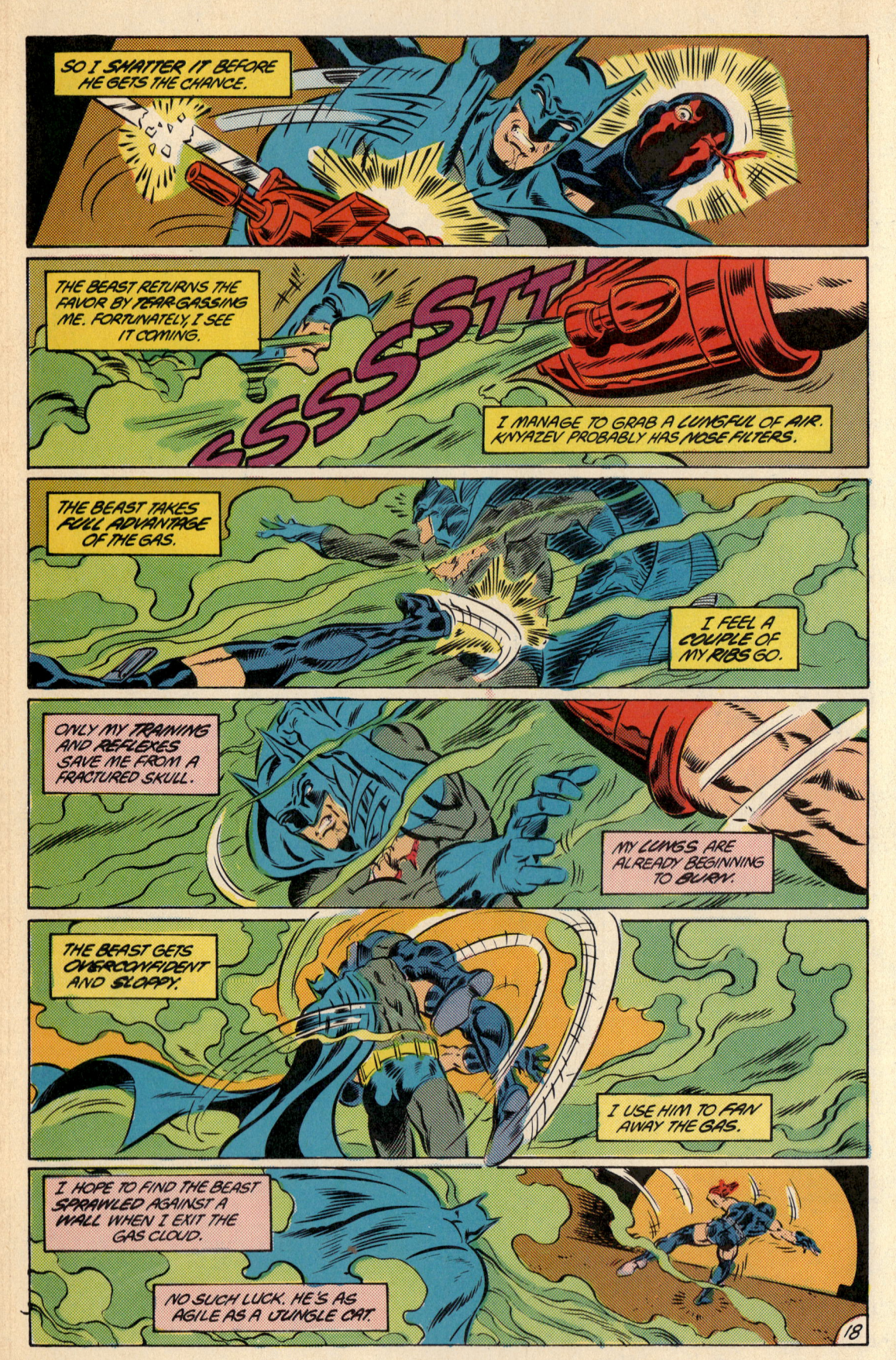

THE BEAST RETURNS THE FAVOR BY TEAR-GASSING ME. FORTUNATELY, I SEE IT COMING.

I MANAGE TO GRAB A LUNGFUL OF AIR. KNYAZEV PROBABLY HAS NOSE FILTERS.

THE BEAST TAKES FULL ADVANTAGE OF THE GAS.

I FEEL A COUPLE OF MY RIBS GO.

ONLY MY TRAINING AND REFLEXES SAVE ME FROM A FRACTURED SKULL.

MY LUNGS ARE ALREADY BEGINNING TO BURN.

THE BEAST GETS OVERCONFIDENT AND SLOPPY.

I USE HIM TO FAN AWAY THE GAS.

I HOPE TO FIND THE BEAST SPRAWLED AGAINST A WALL WHEN I EXIT THE GAS CLOUD.

NO SUCH LUCK. HE'S AS AGILE AS A JUNGLE CAT.

KNYAZEV DECIDES TO RABBIT.

HE OBVIOUSLY HOPES TO SET UP ANOTHER AMBUSH.

HE TEARS DOWN TO THE LOWEST AND OLDEST SECTION OF THE SYSTEM.

FORTUNATELY, I HAD A CASE THAT BROUGHT ME DOWN HERE BEFORE.

I HAVE THIS SECTION OF PIPES AND PASSAGES MEMORIZED.

THAT'S HOW I KNOW ABOUT THE BACK DOOR.

HE HEARS ME LAND AND REACTS INSTANTLY.

LUCKILY, I'VE FAIRLY QUICK REFLEXES MYSELF.

IT'S ALMOST OVER.

THE BEAST IS RUNNING OUT OF PLACES TO ESCAPE TO.

HE SPOTS THE DOOR, JUST AS I EXPECTED.

I DON'T RUSH IN AFTER HIM.

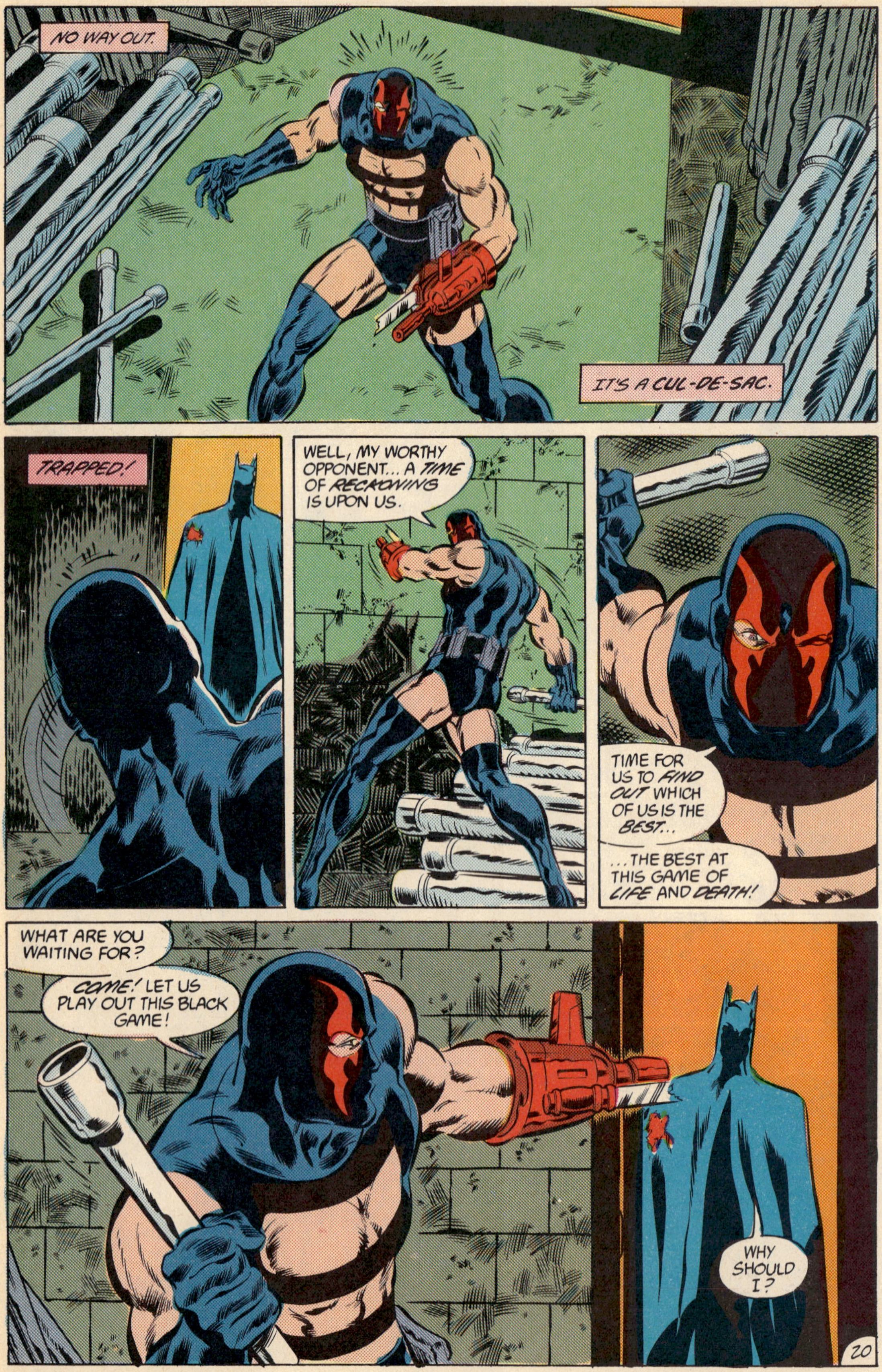
NO WAY OUT.
IT'S A CUL-DE-SAC.
TRAPPED!
WELL, MY WORTHY OPPONENT... A TIME OF RECKONING IS UPON US.
TIME FOR US TO FIND OUT WHICH OF US IS THE BEST...
...THE BEST AT THIS GAME OF LIFE AND DEATH!
WHAT ARE YOU WAITING FOR?
COME! LET US PLAY OUT THIS BLACK GAME!
WHY SHOULD I?
20

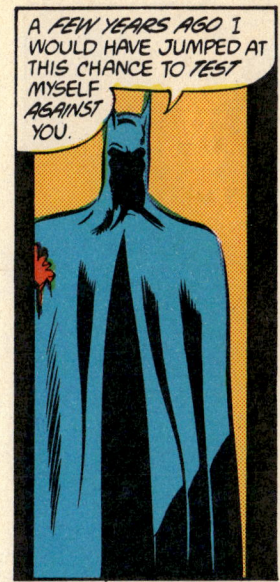

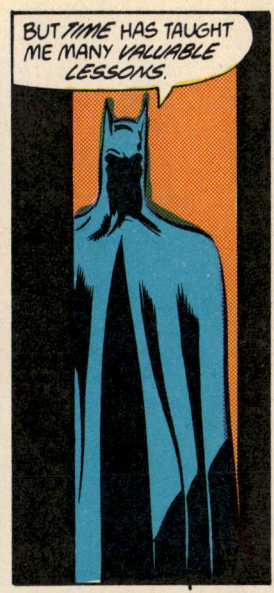

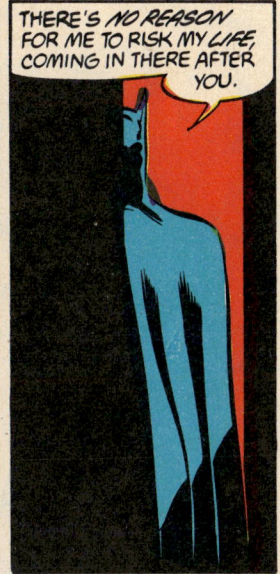

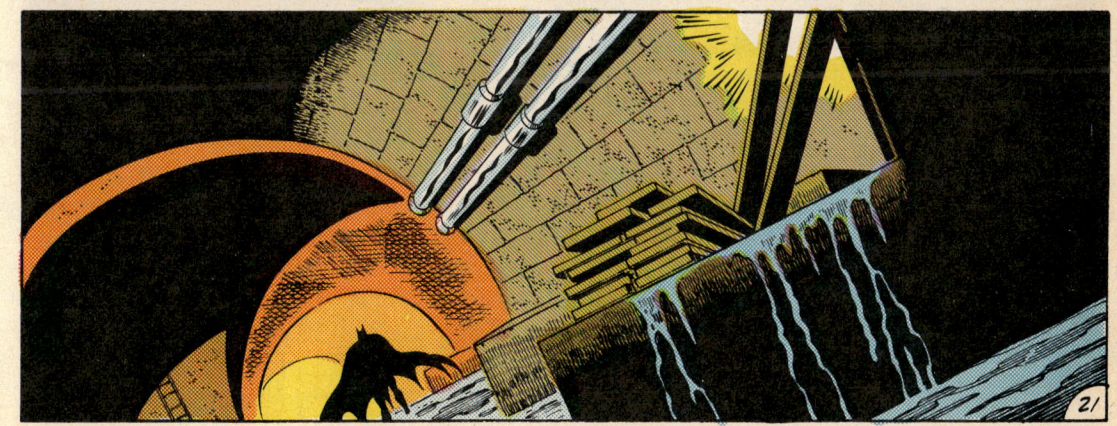

A FEW YEARS AGO I WOULD HAVE JUMPED AT THIS CHANCE TO *TEST* MYSELF AGAINST YOU.

BUT *TIME* HAS TAUGHT ME MANY *VALUABLE* LESSONS.

THERE'S *NO REASON* FOR ME TO RISK MY *LIFE*, COMING IN THERE AFTER YOU.

IT WOULD NEITHER *ACCOMPLISH* NOR *PROVE* ANYTHING WORTHWHILE.

SOMETIMES YOU HAVE TO *IGNORE* THE RULES.

SOMETIMES CIRCUMSTANCES ARE SUCH THAT THE RULES *PERVERT* JUSTICE.

I'M NOT IN THIS BUSINESS TO *PROTECT* THE RULES. I SERVE *JUSTICE*.

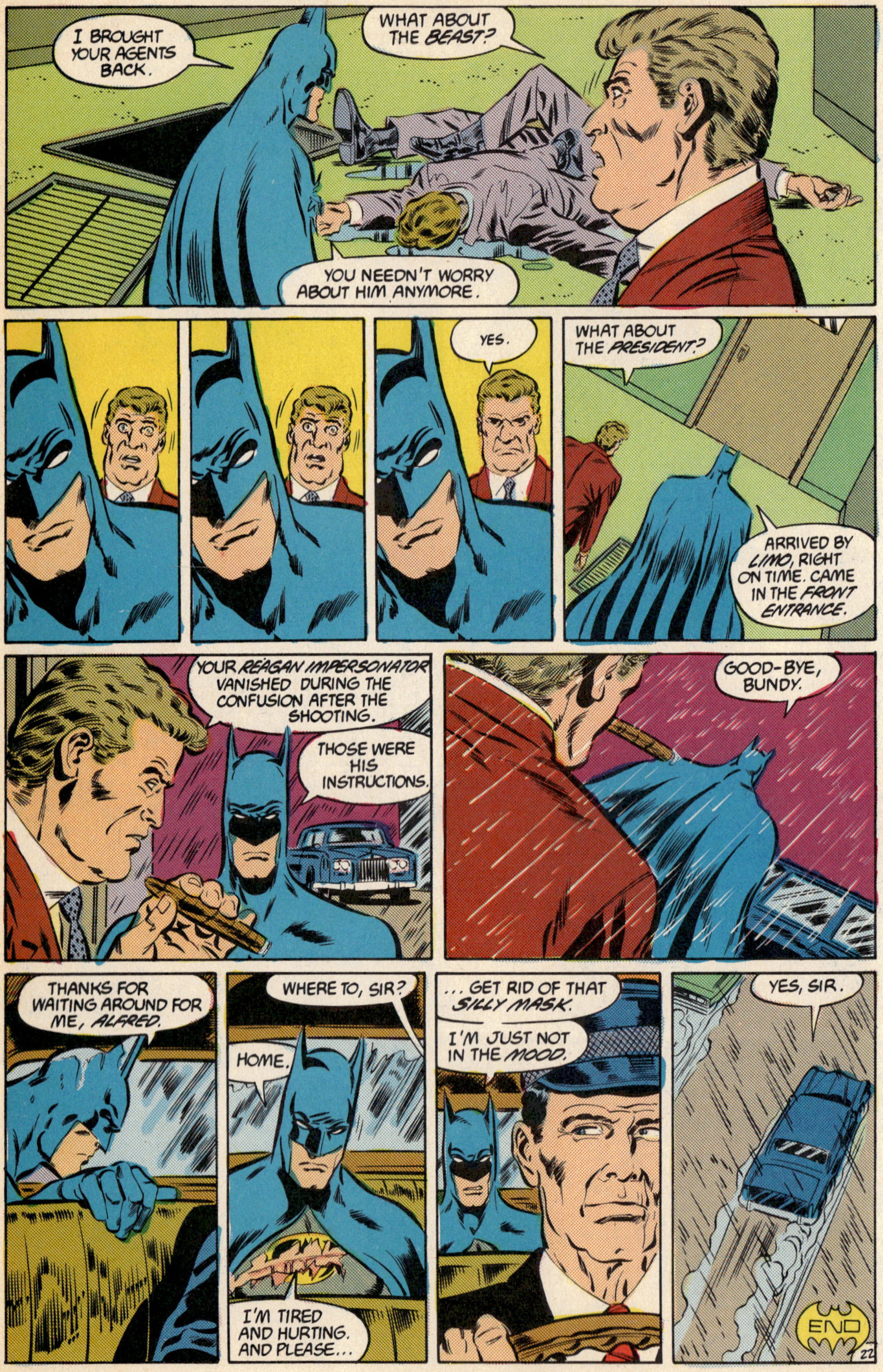
I BROUGHT YOUR AGENTS BACK.
WHAT ABOUT THE BEAST?
YOU NEEDN'T WORRY ABOUT HIM ANYMORE.
YES.
WHAT ABOUT THE PRESIDENT?
ARRIVED BY LIMO, RIGHT ON TIME. CAME IN THE FRONT ENTRANCE.
YOUR REAGAN IMPERSONATOR VANISHED DURING THE CONFUSION AFTER THE SHOOTING.
THOSE WERE HIS INSTRUCTIONS.
GOOD-BYE, BUNDY.
THANKS FOR WAITING AROUND FOR ME, ALFRED.
WHERE TO, SIR?
HOME.
I'M TIRED AND HURTING. AND PLEASE...
... GET RID OF THAT SILLY MASK.
I'M JUST NOT IN THE MOOD.
YES, SIR.
END
22